Natasha Carthew is a [...]
Cornwall, where sh[...]

Natasha writes and presents extensively on socioeconomic
issues and how authentic rural working-class voices are
represented for press and broadcast, including for *Writers' &
Artists' Yearbook*, the *Guardian*, the Dark Mountain Project,
The Bookseller, *Book Brunch*, *The Big Issue*, *Mslexia*, *The
Economist*, the Booker Foundation and BBC Radio 3, BBC
Radio 4 and ITV. *Undercurrent* is her first work of memoir.

Praise for *Undercurrent*

'A powerful story of social inequality told
with the depth of voice that only comes from
a writer passionately rooted in place'
Raynor Winn

'This important and beautifully lyrical book
asks questions about identity, belonging and
the ability of words to transform a life'
The Times

'Haunting and powerful, a book about the
sea and the power of belonging, about secrets
and words . . . I read it in one sitting'
Kate Mosse

'A fierce, urgent memoir by one of
our most important writers'
Amy-Jane Beer

'Ferocious . . . A story of humour, resilience
and doing things "with Kernewek pride"'
TLS

'Carthew shines the light on another side of Cornwall,
one far from the world of bright Instagram pictures and
celebrity travel shows . . . Her humanity and sense of
humour shine through on every page, ensuring that the
often dark subject matter fuels a rich, rewarding read'
Petroc Trelawney

'A proud, defiant account . . . Carthew
is walking fire, fury and sinew'
Caught by the River

'A simmering dissection of rural poverty'
Luke Turner

'Tough and lovely prose . . . [Carthew] tells
her story with poetry and power'
BBC Countryfile magazine

Undercurrent

Also by Natasha Carthew:

Undercurrent

A Cornish Memoir of Poverty, Nature and Resilience

NATASHA CARTHEW

CORONET

First published in Great Britain in 2023 by Coronet
An imprint of Hodder & Stoughton Limited
An Hachette UK company

This paperback edition published in 2024

1

Paperback ISBN 9781399706513
ebook ISBN 9781399706490

Typeset in Bembo MT by Hewer Text UK Ltd, Edinburgh
Printed and bound in Great Britain by Clays Ltd, Elcograf S.p.A.

Hodder & Stoughton policy is to use papers that are natural, renewable
and recyclable products and made from wood grown in sustainable
forests. The logging and manufacturing processes are expected to
conform to the environmental regulations of the country of origin.

Hodder & Stoughton Limited
Carmelite House
50 Victoria Embankment
London EC4Y 0DZ

www.hodder.co.uk

Author's Note

The story of *Undercurrent* is mine, told to the best of my recollection. I have changed names and distinguishing details where necessary, but have presented everything with honesty and integrity, based on my own memory.

Memoir, like any account based on recall, is subject to human error and I acknowledge that this is my account of childhood, but this is my story, told the only way I know how, with heart.

Natasha Carthew

Contents

Fire

Air

Prologue: Ebb

The overwhelming ocean is in constant motion when you are a child, the stink of seaweed and salt, and the way wet grit and earth smell at the end of a full tide storm. The crash of waves as you sleep and the sound of a soft intake of breath as it retreats.

There's a Cornish saying that nothing is left behind in an autumnal tide: the powerful tug between the sun and the equator makes the water surface stronger, and it pulls and builds until we are left with what are known as great tides. As I stand here on my childhood beach in my forties, all I can see is the stretch of grey rocks and the serpent-scarred sand where the ebb has come and gone, and the over-shadowing feel of the village behind me, that sense of being looked upon. Downderry stretches all along the butt-edge of this part of the bay: a juxtaposition of old and new, rich and poor, of pretty fishermen's cottages that line the coastal street, and the bullying millionaire houses that dominate the high north and easterly hills with their balconies, glass walls and swimming-pools. It is the village I grew up in.

The slow sift and drift of the tide of my childhood seemed always to be at that outgoing phase: no matter how I stood and reached for the water it always stretched and stopped just out

of grasp, its draw slow, painful, retreating towards other continents and versions of me that I thought I would never get to see.
I would never be a traveller, moving beyond the confines of
my small world to the expanses beyond. And I would never be
that writer, never be one of those names I traced on the covers
of the books borrowed from the mobile library, the lifeline
books. My destiny was sunk so deep in poverty that I would
never have the opportunity to explore – this is what they told
me, what the teachers said with their tuts and whispers, and
what the parents of the posh kids who lived in those big houses
up on the hill said with their titters: that their kids didn't play
with poor kids no matter how rich those kids were in heritage,
how wealthy they were in the colour and depth of nature, the
pleasure of simple, wild knowledge.

I stand here now with the sea spray on my face and the
rhythm of the receding waves in my ears, and I wonder what
it was about that quiet, abiding girl that snapped and kicked
until, over time, she became this, not a slim shadow of her
former self but a big punchy radiant light. What was it about
the small world around me that made me want to reach out
and tear a hole in its fabric, not content to accept my place at
the poverty table? When was the moment that I decided to
stretch my thinking further than what I could see, beyond
what was expected of me?

There is still a part of me that hates this village, how each
house and path and landmark holds some catch-breath memory
as I walk the two-mile-long coastal road that connects Seaton
to Downderry end to end. Memories that are embedded in
every foundation, every step, the places I grew up and the
places my father, his parents and their families were born, lived

and died, our initials still scratched in concrete in each and every footing, but built over now with extensions, double driveways, patios. The road is the same but the buildings are higher, and the pockets of green between each house have been paved, the trees where we used to play in front of our flat replaced by too-big houses. The fields that surround the upper reaches of the village are no longer a sea of green and umber, but glimpsed tufts of what used to be: the swathe of gold that was our daffodil field a dead memory, nothing left of it but two neat borders of yellow in the front garden of a solitary over-sized house, sitting heavy upon sacred land and my breaking heart as I walk to keep myself on track. Past the shop on the left and the butcher's that's now a house on the right, the Working Men's Club that has been renamed and rebranded for the blow-ins as a soulless village hall, then finally down the dog-shit-covered path that passes the pub and the wall where we working-class kids used to sit and drink and think about the purpose of all of this, us. All those lonely hours that I walked this same stretch of hoary sand, a notebook in my hand trying to write the things I didn't yet understand, the anger that was around me, in me. The glimmer of who I could be forever catching at the corner of my eye, that light of hope magnificent, then snuffed out with the crash down to the sea that was this cold grey peninsula place: reality. Scraping by, penury, scarcity of food, fuel and the freedom of simply being yourself without the dusting off, the oh-well, the getting on with things simply to survive, get by.

As a young girl I knew that I didn't want to spend the rest of my life cleaning holiday homes, and I certainly didn't want to marry a farmer – if anything, I wanted to *be* a farmer – but in

Cornwall in the eighties that dream was strictly reserved for boys, sons of landowners. I was gay, a tomboy, different from all the other girls. I was ambitious, headstrong and, although as a young kid I didn't know exactly what I wanted, I knew there was something out there worth fighting for, if I could just find it. My saving grace was the natural world, and every day the nature that surrounded and imprinted on me was dissected and copied down into my notebook, words to keep me safe, keep me hidden in the tangle of hedgerows and rock-pools.

I have returned to Downderry to write this. The same way a hand returns to a scar and a finger traces the outline of thin, damaged skin: curiosity is that kid wondering, and before you know it the thing you don't understand starts bleeding.

It is September, early autumn, but already the bay has endured at least one high tide. I can tell by the trail of weed and driftwood banked against the muddy clay cliffs, and the way the tiny stream that passes our old primary school has settled into its usual winter shape in the sand, shrugging on the imprint of a serpent, like a snakeskin shirt, everything finding its place effortlessly, without thought, the obedience of nature breath-taking in its simplicity, but not me. I lift my collar to the sou'-westerly wind and walk towards the trim of rocks until my boots sink in, a little glue to hold me down, keep me home-stuck, if only for a moment. A minute too long, too much, too many memories resurface and I close my eyes, lose myself to the lift of warm wind and the sound of gulls circling, shouting, storm warning.

Like a flotsam-strewn shore, my youth is still a mess of vast, broken bits of unrecognisable rock and silt. Beneath the fine film of water that is the ocean there is another world hidden away from every other element, and it is still where I go in mind when I find myself overwhelmed by wonder. I've got good at shrinking myself down to childhood during times of great intensity. I still carry seashells in the pockets of all my jackets, like good-luck charms, have a way of running my nail over the spires, whorls, sutures and lips, a way to remember, a way to forget.

My memory is razor-sharp for the things that hurt, the inflicted and the self-inflicted and the drift of tide that washes between the lines of youth and all the landmarks and milestones you carry and pass until finally you are stamped an adult. The times I ran down onto the beach, punching my fists bloody against the slate rocks, or the night I climbed the cliffs and dared myself to jump off, the infliction of damage done by others, harm to the head and heart.

Bad memories are big, but they are mostly two-dimensional, like scenes in a movie watched over and over again. Good memories are always small, like trinket gifts of blue sea-glass, heart-shaped stones and exotic shells. They are beautiful precious things hidden in the lining of a forgotten childhood pocket. I am here to confront the bad, to press play all over again so that I might rediscover the good and pause the moments that somehow got lost in the sand.

The village of my childhood is the keeper of secrets: not only does it hold the key to my past, but to the lives of all those who grew up in rural poverty. Perhaps this filter of recollection through which I walk the streets of my childhood will unlock something of the truth of why we have arrived where we are now. Poverty and inequality in Cornwall are worse than ever, with twenty neighbourhoods in the county currently among the 10 per cent most deprived in England. My hope is that in some way the things I am prepared to learn about my past will ultimately inform the future.

The short-lived moments that pass through this place will be the things that, for visitors, will forever come to mind – the beautiful far-reaching vistas after the fog lifts, the smell of an early catch as the bellyful trawlers return to harbour, the taste of cream teas and mass-produced pasties lingering on the lips – but the truth of this place, the reality of it, is that Cornwall, my home, is a place of deep, long-lasting deprivation, a place of forever summers and even longer winters, filled with despair and hardship and fear.

These two things, the beauty of the Cornish landscape and the brutality of growing up nose pushed against it, have without doubt informed the greatest part of my life.

This, then, is that story, a story of what ebbs and flows just below the surface of a beautiful ocean day, the unseen, the undercurrent.

When the sea spray starts to thicken and become drizzle, I close my eyes and return to what I believe to be one of my earliest memories. My hands are plump, small, my eyes tightly closed. I can see my hands fixed firm against the ledge of the large, square window frame. Like today, and often in the Cornwall that holiday-makers rarely get to see, it is raining. Me and my sister are watching the oily raindrops as they smack up against the glass, and we are deciding which bead to bet on, fastest to the bottom. I remember the window shaking with the wind, the draught against my fingers – that loose-framed sash-window always vibrated, especially when the gusts blew in from the south-west, the sea less than a hundred metres from our second-floor flat. Certain winds brought different weather, but those sou'-westers always had us believe we were afloat, the window in the front room, which doubled as our parents' bedroom, becoming the wheelhouse on our pretend fishing trawler, the reflection of the lamp in the corner suddenly a navigational star out there in the pitch-black night.

Imagination was our thing, making stuff up and making do with the little we had not just out of necessity but a need to shut out certain things: the raised voices, slammed doors, fists punched into walls.

I open my eyes and narrow them to the darkening horizon to see a lone seagull come into the bay, glide towards the shore and land on the cool damp sand. I watch as she calls her two babies out of hiding. When she leads them towards the gully where the lugworms are at their fattest I'm suddenly reminded of my own mother, how she worked every available cleaning job in the village so she could provide for me and my sister. My father's money was his own and went on fags, women and drink, my mother's meagre wage on food, rent, and the clothes on our backs.

Some folk call seagulls opportunists, scavengers, thieves, but in truth they are intelligent, resourceful and loyal. They have found a way to succeed despite being thought of as the under-class of the bird world, adept at foraging on land, in the air and the sea. When their habitat is taken over by tourists they refuse to retreat, and I love that – it reminds me of Mum, a woman who argued that a council house in this village, the village that my forefathers built from the shore-side up, was the only place good enough for her girls.

This story is about opportunity and the lack of it, the story of poverty and of undercurrents, the hidden limitations that crash upon your own particular shore without you knowing it and wash into your dreams to drown you at night. It is a book of inequity, written with my experience as an activist and campaigner for equal rights firm in its foundation, but with my passion for nature writing at its heart, a modern telling of disadvantage and a county in peril. It is a lone seagull following the undertow, searching for scraps in order to survive.

My childhood homeland bequeathed me two things: the beauty and breadth of nature and all the things that a country upbringing provides, and the disadvantage of rural isolation, a contradiction that is hard to explain, hard to define, except it is all animal, a beast, part sheep, part wolf.

Standing in the wind and the rain, that ocean sound is as loud as a fist making contact; it is the smell of memory once decayed and the ebb of decline resurfacing, the beginnings of a storm gathering on the horizon, my own undercurrent resurfacing, an ocean of memories, rising.

WATER

Blue Windows

That first memory. Storm. The rain that lifted from the ocean and hit out at our tiny flat, and the flashes of lightning that lit the front room with every shade and depth of blue.

'Sheet, fork, cloud to sea.' I had a way of knowing nature before I could read one word in a book or write my name, wildlife words that slipped into my consciousness like verse, perfect poetry that was written for me alone, pre-birth. It was what ocean fog tasted like on my tongue, the sound of the sea whispering in my ears, the sensation of cuddling, damp salty towels, and the warm silver sand sinking until soggy beneath my feet.

Our earliest memories are made up of all the senses waking and yawning for the first time: the smell of bland food or the look on your parent's face, proud smile. Then there's that first moment of senses joining together, the memory made clear, the sight of what I now know is the colour of dark, cavernous blue. First recollections are the sound of nature's impact smashing against itself, and the feel of the huge loose window shaking against the palms of my hands, the smell of the salt sea rising and the taste of hot-milk chocolate silken on my tongue. It is lights out, power cut, the brief flash of the lighthouse,

3

candles in corners and the safety of my older sister and mother pulling up closer. In that dimly lit room, my infant mind emptied of thought until the creak of timber stairs, floorboards brought a sixth-sense feeling that, at the age of five, was nameless, shapeless, but recognisable now as fear.

Storm is fire-flashes and unpredictable light; it is noise and that blue punching up against the window, a colour no daylight can replicate. It is other senses too, the pleasure in a child's mug and three faces pressed together in love; it is the sound that angry boots make on the landing and the key turning, fumbling quick in the lock. It is a question softly spoken but full of noise: 'Why are you all still up?'

Storm is the dream that starts with the suck-sharp intake of breath that is the ocean pulling from the sand and the lowering of tone as it draws back around. It is the breath of every childhood moment, all teeth and tarred fur. It is an incredible stillness trapped in motion. Storm is the ocean of infancy at night, an animal's bite.

***

I grew up in the seventies and eighties in the sprawling village of Downderry, a small fishing and agricultural village settled neatly in the south-east corner of Cornwall, considered relatively new by Cornwall's standards. The village's origins date back to the early nineteenth century and it had been home to the Carthew family and my paternal grandmother's Moore family right from the start.

It is a village of three building histories, that of the early days when fishing and farming families built their terraced cottages along the cliff edge, the second stage when the Carthews started to build affordable homes in the 1950s, and finally the giant contemporary homes that started to be built in the eighties and haven't stopped.

Looking inland from the sea, the first layer of housing is the few remaining coastal cottages that peer out over the cliff edge in a thin line, their eyes on the ocean and the memory of a once robust fishing trade given way to tourism. If you squint you can imagine the crab and lobster pots stacked up on the neatly mown lawns, picture the large trawler nets hitched high against the wall-plugged hooks, the women stopping between chores to stand and look at the horizon, wondering, praying.

The second layer remains unseen, the council houses and the prefab holiday-park bungalows that act as temporary emergency accommodation, and the caravans that have been snuck into fields and hidden below the canopy of low-hanging trees, the homes that exist in the shadows of the bully buildings.

The third mark of residence is as fat and wide as the hills that hold it: the intimidating houses that jut up and out towards the beach, their glass walls and balconies imposing, bug-eyed, staring at each other like giant steel-and-hardwood-framed carcasses, soulless, glancing at the ocean only in passing.

A village has more to it than can be seen with a pure, peeled eye. The secrets of a place have other dimensions than bricks and mortar, buried deep in the depths of it. They are the things that catch on the breeze, the tall tales and confessions of love and hate, blather words, discretions given to the ether. The moments that take confidences by the hand and throw them to the wind, the waves, towards the wild ways of our ancestors, their wayward souls waiting like gossip-gatherers in the wings, reaching down to us, the next generation to carry the burden of stewardship.

As a small child, growing up on the south coast of Cornwall only ever meant one of three things to me: going to the beach, the beach, and returning home from the beach. As a small girl, yet to start school, it was my entire life.

If the sound of the ocean filled the nights with fear, the sight of it in the turn-a-new-page daylight meant it was not a monster but a kitten, a plaything, and every morning I couldn't wait to get down there to look into its eyes and reassure myself that it was just soft sand, rock-face, slip-and-slide cliff clay, water.

The quickest route to the beach from our flat was across the road and a short walk beside the fences and hedges until you reached a gate that said 'No Trespassing' and opened into an incredible enchanted garden. The large ornate stretch of green had a sticky lily-pad pond at its core and neat labyrinth hedges that led to places we weren't supposed to go, and statues that spat and peed and watched as you passed, making sure you didn't dally but cut straight through to the gap in the hedge. The ornate gate that had lost its hinges and the wait for Mum to lift it so we could pass and the which-way rope and crooked steps that dangled you down the side of the cliff until you landed either flat on your face or firm-footed in the sand.

Mum always said it was 'just us' who were allowed to 'trespass', and although this was one house she didn't clean, she told us that the lady in the big house liked us because me and my sister were well-mannered, respectful, good girls. We didn't put our hands in the pool to feel for frogs and fish, didn't climb the trees or pick the flowers: we kept to the path, the straight and narrow.

We didn't speak unless we were spoken to, always said hello, yes, please, thank you. Our mum took pride in our obedience, took any compliment as her own, homemade badges to crimp and sew and wear to prove to the world that although she was a young mother she was a good one: she knew what it took to fit in, prove to the world that she could do this.

That 'just us' has stayed with me over the years. There were so many occasions in those early days when I thought we were treated as special, different, but I now know it was just pity, pity for the poor, pretty, polite girls. We were the only girls living on that lesser-populated westerly side of the village: there was an expectation that we would be good, quiet, abiding, so we were.

So silent, so mindful not to make a noise, we'd slip on our wellies in the hall outside the flat and make our way down the stairs towards the enchanted garden, down the cliff to the wide, beautiful expanse that called to us.

★★★

The beach at that age meant freedom. It meant my body could run and climb and hide in the bits of fallen roadside wall, and my mind could shrink down to the smallest secret find, fill my hands with sweet-sized pebbles and shells and sand-softened sea-glass, everything perfect, pocket-sized. The beach was season-less, timeless, a thin stretch of uneven sand-land and an ocean that extended as far as I could comprehend, a silver stretch of forever where I could run and jump and dig just for the sake of being in it. It was a world of my own where I could seaweed-sit and reach for the everyday jewels and riches that hid beneath the weed and banked-up at the edges of the first rock pools, Mum always beside me, smiling, encouraging me to look, always.

The enchanting sea-glass came in four colours and in order of value: the route from bottom to top went green, brown, white and blue. Green was everyday, like the big houses that were all over the village, while brown and white were like the old cottages you sometimes chanced across, and blue was the rarest find of all, tiny beads of glass that were like our flat and the caravans and council houses, secretive, dark, hiding out of sight.

The tourists always collected the boring green glass, along with the yellow periwinkles, gathered up in buckets to glue onto bottles and ashtrays later, but we locals, my sister and the older kids, cared more for the rarer colours, the early-bird morning catch: toffee brown, fizzy-pop white and the bubble-gum blue treasure. Nobody ever mentioned where the glass came from, but anything plastic, or rubber, arrived from across the Channel, the broken bits of crate and ugly jelly flip-flops were always from 'nasty France', and even the bust-away buoys with 'Fowey' inked on the side we marked as 'foreign', French, from the country that was 'over there', the one that stole our cod and scallops and made the trawlermen bang the shiny splashy tables in the pub.

But the beautiful blue glass that lifted from the bottom of the ocean and washed up towards the cliffs, that first glimpse of colour in the belly of a rock-pool and the way the early-morning sun caught in its cerulean tint and winked, was in my mind an eye that belonged to a mermaid, a story to make up for later, a fresh legend to tell, like my ancestors used to, a new world to create.

The pleasure that is sunshine seen through the blue of ocean-smooth crystal, the ripple of all that is Heaven and earth spied

8

through the childhood prism of innocence, one small window but still as blue and brilliant as the one at home.

Perhaps looking through a bead of blue sea-glass was the moment when I first discovered what it was like to get lost, a minute of immersion into which I could fall, forget what I couldn't understand and slip into some other world, no thinking words, not yet, but my recollection of blue windows has never left me. No matter how strong the sun or how great the storm, that tiny world in my hand was a newly discovered planet that perhaps one day I would visit, another world completely where I could stand shore-side and look towards my childhood, see the girl I once was looking back.

***

From the two large windows at the front of our flat, I was the one looking out, but I wasn't yet aware of the world I existed in. I hadn't worked out the differences between people – locals and tourists, rich and poor, friends and enemies – but I was conscious of some semblance of other, not us.

Other people were a leap away. They were the ones in the other flats, the old farmer who never left his two rooms and the young couples with babies who never seemed to stay longer than a few months, and the girl from the upstairs flat, held in my dad's arms as they walked down our lane to the pub. Other villagers were the ones who walked past on their way to work, the woman who worked behind the fat metal counter in the butcher's and the men I sometimes saw down on the beach, tinkering with their boats and laughing with butt-ends stuck to their lips.

The biggest leap were the tourists, the faces in cars that smirked and blurred as they drove too fast, the folk we Cornish call emmets, the incomers who every summer crowded into the lane below, shouted, laughed and beeped their car-horns to let me know before I knew anything at all that they were not like me and that I would never in a million years be like them.

A child who knows nothing but watches everything soon learns the difference between light and shade. I was that child. Always the most curious, I sometimes got mistaken for shy but in truth my hunger for knowledge and how things went meant that, like a camera, my eyes were forever taking snapshots, my ears pinned back like mini-microphones, recording everything.

The things I wanted to learn couldn't be taught: they were not made of words but sense and feeling. From the youngest age people fascinated me, the nature of them, like the rock-pool animals that visited us daily: I learnt, by watching simple salt-water life, that some people were always stuck, like the immovable sea anemones, while others got to walk, like crabs.

When I went to the shop I noticed some people, the city tourists and the teens from the big houses, wore colourful clothes and danced around like they were on *Top of the Pops*, while I wore hand-me-downs from my sister, which were often handed down to her by our auntie, only a couple of years older than her.

Perhaps before I knew the detail of disadvantage I was preparing myself for the question, *Why?*

With the heavy-hearted hit of grown-up hindsight I know there is no particular answer, except just because. The beginnings of my life, like many children born into or unexpectedly thrown into poverty, there was no reason behind it. We were just poor and that was that.

Deprivation is not fair or unfair: it is the scarcity that exists by the skin of its teeth, alone and completely outside itself. The dictionary definition is 'a damaging lack of material benefits considered to be basic necessities in a society'. Just is, just because: circumstance, misfortune, bad fucking luck.

Nick Carthew and Barbara Stephens met when they were teenagers. My mum was eighteen and my dad was seventeen. They first met in a youth club in Southway, Plymouth, where the city's largest council-housing estate had been built in the wake of the Blitz, when demand for accommodation was acute. Southway was where my mum spent her teenage years with her parents, and where on one particular sunny afternoon, while sitting up in her bedroom window with her best friend, she watched my father, who had come to Plymouth from Cornwall to visit a mate, pass her house. She turned to her buddy and told her that she was going to marry him.

Love at first sight, for my mother anyway, or intuition perhaps, but when both of them were eighteen they got engaged and by nineteen Mum was pregnant with my sister. They married in a register office in Plymouth in 1967 and my sister was born six months later. During that time my mum was doing an art course in the city, studying painting, photography, window dressing and graphics. Off the back of that she had managed to do a short internship at Clarks Shoes in Somerset and had wanted to be a shoe designer. One of the highlights of her short career, short because she became pregnant so young, was being interviewed by Angela Rippon for West Country TV about the 'end of course' clothes she designed.

My dad worked for his father's building firm, Carthew and Son, as a painter-decorator. The business had started with my great-grandfather Sam, and passed down to my grandfather Eric. I never knew these men, but they were the stuff of legend in our village, known for being dangerous. They were gamblers, freemasons, Cornish Mafia, and notorious for being tight with money, making their apprentices spend hours straightening nails instead of buying new ones and reclaiming floorboards from house fires to pass off as new.

My parents, like everyone's, were people I sometimes knew well, but when I think of them as teenagers, falling in love, I feel like, in retrospect, I didn't really know them at all, or why they did the things they did.

My chances of success were scuppered early on because my parents were young, they had no money, and their parents either had no money or no heart to help. In any case it meant when my mum gave birth aged nineteen to my sister, the three of them moved into a two-roomed corrugated-tin hut in the garden of my great-uncle, a hut that backed onto his pigeon coop, known simply as the Sugar Shack.

Family members lived in flats and cottages all around Downderry but the shack was where my parents set up their first home, with my new-born sister, smack-bang in the middle of December, winter. The shack never existed in my lifetime, but I remember the black and white photo of my mum snuggling my sister as a baby in a scramble of trees and briar outside it, smiling, content, in love. But nothing stays stable for long.

Blue windows; my first memory of home was the deep blue bead of sea-glass held between my finger and thumb, and the ocean looming large in the window, one small room, one wardrobe and our bunk-beds pushed tightly into the corner. Home to me was a draughty south-facing one-bedroom flat on the second floor of a low-rise block, five rows of three flats each, grubby façade, no garden, not much of anything except it was our home.

Less of a calm-water initiation and more like a baptism of fire, wind, cut knees and earth pushed deep into the wound. Before you know how to walk or run, you learn to exist on the back foot.

Disadvantage is a lonely word. It exits the limited realms of childhood knowledge and understanding. As a little girl I didn't notice the size of our home, the cold as it came through the gaps around the windows. It didn't bother me that my parents slept in the front room, yet the cut of poverty slipped beneath my skin without me noticing, carving deep into my flesh as I watched the world pass by outside the window every day.

Before the pandemic, more than one in five people in the UK lived in poverty, according to the Joseph Rowntree Foundation UK poverty report for 2020-21. That's 14 million people, a fifth of the population living in poverty in this country. Four million of those people are more than 50 per cent below the poverty line, and 1.5 million are destitute, unable to afford basic essentials like food, housing, clothes, fuel, the things we need to survive.

It's not just the statistical facts and figures of hunger and cold, it's the emotional impact on a life that is so disadvantaged at its foundation. The experience of poverty significantly affects the way we think, the way we feel and act. It crushes our confidence, our hopes and dreams for something better and suppresses our ability to participate in society. Before the coronavirus pandemic, more than one in five people in the UK lived in poverty; today it is one in four.

Disadvantage is a lonely word, and when I was growing up my mother never uttered it once. Looking back, I know that the blot of that word must have stuck to us like skin-sodden fog. There wasn't a day that went by that she didn't tell us how lucky we were to have the sea at the end of the road, or that the mountainous fields behind our flat were meant for my sister and me alone. We collected dog whelks and tiny ribbed cowries for the sake of prettiness, picked yellow cranesbill and red campion for the sake of jam-jar love, and I also had my sea-glass jewels to look at when the things I was yet to understand got too loud.

In Cornwall disadvantage is still something that is easily argued away with the exclamation of 'Look where you live!' But you can't keep warm and dry with a fascinating heritage, can't kick hunger into touch with a beautiful view.

I had the sea and the fields to look at and immerse myself in, but during the economic crisis of the late seventies the country was besieged with power cuts, high inflation, an oil crisis and years of national strikes. Folk learnt what it was to have to struggle, and all the ways to avoid the constant brawl of poverty.

As an infant I wasn't directly aware of these things, but I was aware of the tension, the words 'Not enough cash' on everyone's lips, the men who got angry while we played out in the pub beer garden on a Sunday afternoon, the women who stood in line behind Mum in the post office every other week to collect their miserly family allowance, the whispers between them wondering how to stretch it, hide it, make it last.

I never knew half of the things Mum had to endure until that first memory: the blue window storm and the first taste of hot chocolate on my lips, the recognition of happiness, laughter, a cocoon of safety, Mum's nest mixed with the sudden thump of boots on steps. When I close my eyes I find it easy to drop back down there, the rattling window and my podgy hands against the cold single-glaze, the rain falling against the glass like tears and that heart-stop thump feeling, fear.

'Come on, girls, back to bed.'

There were many nights when me and my sister would sit on the bottom bunk in our bedroom and talk about Dad, but it was mostly what we didn't say. Some nights the silences in the other room were worse than the shouts. Sometimes we fell asleep with the blankets pulled up over our heads until morning, false alarm, but I have one particular memory when we woke to the noise of shouting and smashing, the fear driving through us in waves.

'You awake?' asked my sister.

I pushed the blankets from me and sat up. 'Yes.' I rubbed my eyes. 'Is it Dad?'

'I think he's drunk.'

I waited for her to slide off the bed and down onto mine, feeling the cord that connected us to Mum pull tight with dread.

'What should we do?' I asked.

'Listen.'

I got out of bed and stood, five years old and helpless. I knew this.

'Mum's crying,' said my sister.

I opened the curtain for a peek of moonlight. 'Is she all right?' In the golden half-light I could see my sister was scared. 'What if she's not all right?'

'Dad wouldn't hurt her.'

'How do you know?'

My sister had good memories of him. I didn't.

I wondered if I should put on my plimsolls, go outside and run to the village phone box, 999, Police, please.

'We should go in,' I said.

'Don't. It might make him more . . .' I could see she was thinking of all the ways to say the thing, and then she just said it '. . . angry.'

I didn't care. I was afraid but I was angry too, and I quickly pushed past her and opened the door, knowing she had followed because I could feel her hands holding on to the back of my pyjamas.

We stood in the doorway that separated our bedroom from theirs and looked down at the floor.

'Tasha, mind your feet, sweetheart.' Mum came towards the open door and bent down to us briefly, then turned back to Dad, who was standing looking out of the window at the side of the room.

'Sit down, Nick, please. Calm down, for the girls.'

Mum's tin of pretty things and useful things that usually sat central to the small pine table lay sideways on the floor, its contents strewn everywhere, making a big mess when Mum didn't like mess, not even a small one. We got down onto our knees.

'You've been drinking again, too much.'

'Fucking bitch.'

'Nick, the kids.'

We upended the tin and my sister was quick to fill it, while I occasionally stopped to play, like perhaps this was normal everyday okay, clutching the slippery silver magnets that when held together the wrong way made your hands shake, opposites, and the foreign coins that made me look up at the window, past Dad and out at the ocean, the out there, the world beyond Mum's favourite pink vases and the statues of the man and the woman that he had placed on the outside windowsill, waiting for the wind to come and catch them, knock them down to the ground floor, smash.

As clear as the moon that reached fully into the window that night, I remember me and my sister, aged five and nine, standing in front of our mum while Dad charged the room and stood and punched and screamed so close that I will never be able to smell the stench of fags and drink on someone's breath without thinking of him.

All the while we shouted, 'Don't touch her,' and luckily for all of us he didn't.

After every violent memory I find myself returned to our bedroom, bottom bunk, dreams washing in and out with the tide and the memory of Dad's shouts, the muffled pop of everyday family things falling as he lashed out, another wall or a door gone into, and in the morning my small feet walking across shards of plaster, Mum up smiling, cup of tea, nothing to worry about my sweetheart. Quiet now, Dad asleep.

I never knew what disadvantage was. It's said that kids only start to know about it at seven or eight, but even then it isn't something you sit and think about. It's just the simple nature of 'us and them'. The origin of identity has its roots in a sense of self, perception, and I often think about that little girl who grew up drifting completely out of her depth. My father was a violent drunk; he gave up work as a painter-decorator and pushed us into poverty before I'd even started school. Suddenly we had less than we ever had, which led to arguments about money, something we kids never thought about until that moment.

Without knowing it my identity had suddenly become cemented in the hand-me-down clothes and the cold 'heat-off blankets-on nights' and the meals that were, more times than not, just simple hearty homemade soup.

The things I've naturally had to fight for go blade deep, all the wounds I've had to endure to ensure that I'm better today than I was yesterday, but I will always bear the scars.

When I think about disadvantage I think about my hardworking mother and all the early-morning late-night jobs she had to do. I think about the make-something-out-of-nothing food and the sink in the kitchen where we had strip-washes because she couldn't afford the electricity for hot water. My mother is what the fair share of my early childhood memory is made of: an undercurrent of calm, beautiful, familiar tidal water.

2

Underwater Love

Tide in, tide out, constant heartbeat.

If my father was the incoming storm, my mother's love was a deep, comforting wheel of warm water where a wave had washed over the rock-pools and stayed. In Cornwall we know that no matter what time of year you swim in the sea there are always secret sacred currents to drift towards. We don't always know how to find them, but somehow we recognise, through collective memory, that if we give ourselves over to the incoming tide, the drive of seawater generated by natural forces will find us. That, then, was my mum. Gulf Stream, with the tepid water circling and the sun pulled down: that was her unconditional love, a cosy duvet, or the warm sheets that draped over the ironing-board while a cold wind blew around.

'You under there, sweetheart?'

Of course I was. 'Yes, Mummy.'

'What are you doing?'

'Playing.' Always, imagining other worlds.

If you scrunched down small enough between the legs of the ironing-board you could imagine you were in a secret cave, easy, and if you closed your eyes tight, the warm salty air made you feel like you were on the beach at night.

Beneath the swathe of bedsheets the best kind of cave existed. It was warm, sparkly clean, not like the real caves that furrowed the cliffs, the ones with the slimy trickling walls that went drip-drip-drip. I loved the sound of the iron as it glided overhead, creaking and scraping as Mum smoothed out the creases in the sheets after a day of furious flapping on the washing line, the one that was rigged forty foot up into the rock-face behind our small block of flats, the line that she could only access by hanging out of the bathroom window on one leg, two storeys in the air.

'Mind you don't pull the sheet. Don't want the iron falling down on your head.'

I laughed. 'No, Mummy.'

I heard her laugh too, somewhere up there beyond my cave, her voice in the clouds.

'Where are you today?' she asked, the iron going swoosh above me.

'The beach.'

'Again?'

'The caves.'

'Over by Claydon?'

I nodded to myself.

'And what are you doing in the caves?' She rearranged the sheet and suddenly my cave let in a golden shaft of light.

'Winkle-picking.'

Mum laughed again. 'You're a clever girl, Natasha. Gonna be a writer some day, remembering all the stories that get told to you.'

'The winkle-pickers came from Ireland.' I lay flat on the carpet and pretended it was our grey sand, not khaki green. 'They used to come to Downderry every summer to pick winkles.' I squinted up and through the window at the clear sky that peeked beneath the sheet, rolled onto my back and turned it into the ocean, new blue.

'And what did they do with the winkles once they'd picked them all?'

'Easy. They walked the coast path to Plymouth to sell them in the market.'

'Good girl. You're my clever girl, you are.'

I smiled, because I was. I closed my eyes and imagined living in the caves, living off drips of field water and the tiny dark grey shellfish, the winkles. It didn't seem like much of a life but still it interested me, and at the age of six it drew me in, like it was a future worth considering. Perhaps it was because I already knew something of poverty, already knew the basic things you needed to survive.

'Food and water,' I whispered to myself, 'and fire for cooking and warmth.' I imagined myself walking the wide stretch of that particular far-easterly beach, looking down at the tideline, my eyes searching for the tiny knots and squiggles of driftwood that would do for kindling. I put my hands out between Mum's bare feet and pretended to arrange the wood, lighting it with one flick of my fingers, something I'd been practising, like the Fonz on TV.

'I'm lighting a fire,' I told her.

'Better move this sheet then.' She laughed, and I waited for her to fold it up completely before the cave slowly drifted from my imagination, its dark wet walls slipping into light and the sound of the iron retreating, no longer waves but a vestige of domesticity to be put away.

★★★

21

I liked to sit on the side in the kitchen, watching Mum make her potato and onion soup, the speed of her hands as she wielded the sharp knife, finely slicing the vegetables and adding cloves and the bay leaves we'd helped to pick, which hung by a piece of string from the ceiling to dry.

The soup was famous in our household, because every time she told us that was tea for the next few days, we'd cheer, happy to be heartily fed, looked after by the simple act of being provided for. Sometimes I'd just sit and tell stories while Mum did the dishes, and she always loved this, called me her 'little writer', but my favourite time of the day was strip-wash time, the scrub of a warm, soapy flannel that was everyday necessary because I'd either scuffed and dirtied my knees playing football in the field in front of our house with Dwayne Collins, the boy from Number 1 Brenton Terrace next door, or because I'd got tar on the soles of my feet, the sticky black globs left over from oil spills that always got stuck in the clumps of bladderwrack that banded the beach after a high tide.

In those early years I felt my mum's arms around me daily, and in that gentle rocking, lullaby, she always had something of the mermaid about her. She was mysterious, secretive, and everyone on both sides of the river Tamar knew that behind her long dark hair she was incredibly beautiful. Oceanid, Naiad, Kelpie, she was a water nymph, always watched us play at the edge of the ocean, standing in the shallows and the surf, watching from the shoreline, her feet dipped in with the limpets and starfish, her eyes flitting between us and the Seaview pub, Dad. How much she kept from us when we were young I don't know for sure, but I still remember the look in her eyes as they flashed between close comfort and distant fear.

Underwater she was me and my sister's anchor, digging in deep. She kept us steady and rooted to the one place, no matter how my father's storm weighed us down and rocked us.

That pub, that coastline, the bay of Whitsand that cuffed the far-reaching corners of the bay from ear to ear. My home peninsula on the south-east coast of Cornwall was all I knew and, for those first few infantile years, was all I wanted to know. The way it curved from east to west like a half-moon, lifting the sun gently over the distant ridge of Freathy Cliffs and high above Rame Head in the morning, then travelling across the bay of water until finally setting safely behind Looe and Looe Island to the west, the rest of Cornwall out of sight but down there somewhere, a far-off place buried in myth that I was yet to discover, until later on foot.

Growing up, those two known points of reference, Rame Head and Looe Island, were the only ones I recognised as pillars of home, with fifteen miles of cliff between and the Eddystone Lighthouse somewhere out there in the far-flung sea. That was it. Three points that, looking out from Downderry beach, pegged the wide expanse of land and water to the corners of the earth, like a sheet put out onto the wind.

Like any child, I didn't know anything of distance or space, nothing to clasp me to any true sense of knowing except to look at this from afar, the same head-shape peninsula to the left, Hannafore Point and Looe Island to the right, and the all-encompassing ocean with the flashing night-time lighthouse out front.

Through infant eyes my home-turf triangle was beautiful, the horizon that stretched out in front of me like a painting that I could only look at, trace from a distance, my chubby fingers strained wide to catch the constantly shifting tide and the bright, moving light, and in the middle of this triangle, always, my mother, the calm balancing point where all things meet, merge and make sense.

Me and my sister are the children of a mermaid, or *morvoren*, as we say in Cornish: part human, part otherworldly, made of all the elements, she is belly-fire and warm wind and all the earth's water, full of gold dust and inner grit, like digested sand, and growing up she was the best part of the ocean. Her nurturing underwater love meant we were the lucky ones, because at that time in our young lives, we at least had one emotionally accessible adult, someone we could hold on to, look up to, rely on.

No matter if we were playing in the back fields or down on the beach, we had Mum's hands to lead us through bramble and across dangerous rocks, point out all the small natural things and catch us if we fell. Our mum always squatting down to our level, no matter what; she was always just there, by our sides.

Kneeling in the sand, Mum was a mermaid complete, her long dark hair covering her face as she leant forward. 'Girls, come here and have a look at this.'

The three of us crouched to look at the dark brown disc lying flat against the palm of her hand.

'It's like a conker,' said my sister.

'Only bigger,' I added, 'flatter, like a heart. What is it?'

'This is a sea bean,' said Mum.

We started to laugh. 'Big bean!' we shouted in unison.

Mum passed it to us. 'Sea beans are very lucky, and for Cornish girls like you, they are the luckiest.'

She continued to tell us the story of how fishermen used to thread them on leather cord and wear them around their necks to protect them from drowning, that some folk said they were gifted to them by mermaids, but in fact they were tropical seed pods that had travelled thousands of miles to our shores from the rainforests of the Caribbean, brought into our hands on warm ocean currents.

I loved the idea that this beautiful beating heart was a gift to us from our mother, but the story of how such a small, perfect seed could travel halfway around the world to find its place with us was the first time I truly envisaged the magnitude of 'out there'. My eyes lifted from the familiar bay and looked out towards the half of my world that was filled with just ocean, sky, a wide open divide that spoke to me with a yawning mouth full of words I was yet to hear.

I looked back at my mother, my sister.

'And when we get home I'll make a hole in it and thread it with a bootlace so you can wear it for protection,' she closed my sister's hand around the bean, 'for luck.'

'What about me?' I asked.

'You were born lucky.' She smiled. 'You pooped on the nurse when you were born. That's luck. It's what they all said anyway.'

Luck, maybe for me, maybe not, certainly not for that particular nurse. Luck is sea beans and four-leaf clovers and horseshoes right-way-up. It is also the unconditional love that comes with the words 'good mother', something that should ensure a child never suffers. But they do, and despite her love, we did too.

Fortune is how you look upon something. It is the spin that shines things nice and bright, makes them all right. As children we are naturally positive; we make colour with the paint we are given, mix the hues in the hope that we might create something new. We had our mum, but the opposite of that was we had a father who, when not absent, was either distant or violent. I often think about the concept of care. In its truest sense it means upkeep, maintenance and repair, things my father did to other people's houses before he gave up working, basic things he should have done for us. The provision of what is necessary for the health, welfare and protection of someone or something is what drives us as humans, as beating hearts, but not, it seemed, my father. He appeared more interested in the maintenance of his own hedonistic lifestyle, the upkeep of self.

***

Down on the beach, burrowed among rock-pools, I could create the most incredible fantastical world away from the people and things I couldn't understand, slipped down into a place of my own making where I could trust in the outcome, the happy ending.

The rock-pools were where I would tell myself that I was lucky, because my dad was loud and devious, what fairy-tales perceived as bad, with his drunken sneaking around in the dark; I automatically recognised that my mum was the opposite: she was quiet, loving and honest, all the things that meant good, and because of her goodness I took comfort in taking care of myself.

Those tiny pockets of ocean water were where I was always happiest, taking my time to collect up the little litter-bits of flotsam to create a new world built from the detritus washed in from out there, other worlds; how many boats I must have constructed from polystyrene, a lollipop stick and red Walkers crisps packet for a sail, like the boats in our bay. How I wished I could shrink down and climb aboard, shove up against the winkle passengers, help out at the helm when the limpet captain got tired. Sometimes I'd sit out on the rocks for what seemed like hours while the other children swam and played in the surf, waiting for the tide to come in and lift my boat, point it towards the hazy skyline and sail it out. Aboard my imagined boat my father receded on the shore as I drifted further out to sea, safe distance, growing smaller and smaller until he disappeared and I entered the world of mermen, sirens and new-world domains.

As a writer I spend the greatest part of my life floating around in a land that is soaked through with fiction and fantasy and the possibility of maybe. My head is burrowed deep in sand or floating furious in the clouds, but this is the fibre and fabric of me. It is a cloak, but at least I know that every stitch and colour and thread running through it has been invented and created by my hand.

In its truest sense, writing is the adult version of play, making stuff up, and to all the world it often seems like we're hiding ourselves away – perhaps we are – but all I know now of my childhood is that the world of fantasy and make-believe was where I was free to do what my imagination asked of me.

The setting was mine, the characters were mine and the shape of each story I acted out in the rock-pools was mine. If I wanted to wait for the tide to turn and sail my boat away from safe shores then so be it. If I wanted to turn it into the wind and watch it crash against the fallen boulders that was okay, too, because it was my world, my story told.

It is not unusual for children to create fantasy worlds to escape trauma: it's a way to keep the pain and the confusion at bay, dissociation, detachment, severance from the things we are yet to understand. It is the same in adulthood, spacing out or splitting off to find the things that make the most sense over many years. I know I have got used to seeking the remnants of good thought and blissful reminiscence, sewing them back together so I might find a way to build myself and my future better, but the edges are still a little frayed, and there are patches where I have tried to repair myself too often. Maybe that is why so many of us who suffered trauma in childhood, who lived through poverty and the uncertainty of where your next meal was coming from, or if you could afford coal for the fire or money for electricity, why so many of us make good writers. We learnt early on how to create new, better worlds for ourselves and those around us. We've got good at lying to ourselves, pretending to others, building an ideal universe that circles us and holds us tight, no matter how shaky the foundation.

We look to the future with unrealistic hope. Crazy maybe, but our writing is good.

Hope is my resilience. It's me now and it was me then, aged five, six, seven, piecing together what I thought a perfect life looked like, on home turf and out there somewhere beyond the unreachable horizon. I can't imagine that vista without water, my mind returning to my mother and her calming, guiding, immersive love.

Over the years I have perfected the act of keeping my head just below the surface of the water, clear focus. It's easier to dive deep into the shadows, face the dark, easier than just going along with the drift, swimming things out. The thing is, we know we have to come up for air eventually, let the flotsam and the tide-trash wash over us, then find a way to recover from the chaos. Many times in my childhood I raised my head above the surface of the ocean to see the silver sun suddenly gone and the storm abruptly returned, a storm that made me feel like I'd taken up a pebble and pushed it into the back of my mouth for the shut-up, one single word that felt wrong on my tongue . . .

Dad.

3

Hurricane

My father rolls into my memory like a hurricane. Before I knew the word for him as a small child I realised his character was strong but flawed. He was a boulder of a man, but with cracks and fissures that on certain days you couldn't help but fall into, feel the dark depth of the gorge as it bound around you.

Hurricanes have three main parts: the calm eye in the centre, the eye wall where the wind and rain are strongest, and the bands of rain that lash out from the centre and give the storm its size. My father was a short, stocky man, but his reach was far, long-lasting. I don't remember much of the calm eye that sat at the core of him but my mum still talks of it being there – early days, perhaps it was. When I crawl into the mind of that child of five, six, though, I can hear only the shouting, can see only the holes the size of a punch in the doors and walls of our four-roomed home, my mum clearing up the mess, she, too, as strong as thunder, shouting back.

Some memories return to us as adults, like shards of smashed glass, shattered. Others come in the shape of a full bottle: if you're lucky the message tucked neatly inside is easy to find, but the younger you are, the harder it is to unravel and decipher the reason behind the scattered or broken pretty things.

If my mum was an ocean of clear stars, underwater, then my dad was the black sky rain that fell upon it. It's easy now to word-away the reasons for his heavy drinking, his violence, his continued promiscuity that lasted throughout my childhood. To a young child the very first things you know are the animals in your den, your siblings, the supposed love that is meant by the words MUM AND DAD.

In hindsight, how are we supposed to deal with fear when we have not got over original trauma? What are the skills we need to level out instant, constant high alert? When our baby-bird body is built for only two things, fight or flight, either way we intuitively crouch, heart hitting hard in our tiny bird mouths.

One minute you're sitting up at the table playing with your Fuzzy-felt, the next moment you're being asked to go and play in your room, just for a minute. You know from your limited short-life experience that a minute might go on for an hour and that your hands might still be designing your Fuzzy-felt circus while you sit on your bed, but your head no longer resides in childish fantasy but swings and flails in a hundred different directions.

You hear voices. Whispered, but close enough to the perimeter of what is classed as raised so that, as a child, you have to decide if this is panic or performance: you don't yet have the skills to think things away – you are still so much of an instinctual in-the-moment animal. The words that went up the wall into the upstairs flat where Dad sometimes slept, then crawled back down into our bedroom were the worst. If you stood at the door it sounded like the tide was in, crashing close, and sometimes it sounded like the TV was on, but not *Tenko* or *Roots*, Mum's shows, but the late-night news, full of riots, shouts, strikes and picket lines.

Sometimes me and my sister would be safely together, but being four and a half years older than me, she was often at a friend's house, or school, or just not there that day, and I'd have nobody to look up to, nobody to tell me it was all okay. If she was there, she would go to the toy box and pull out something silly, tell me to make up a story about our teddies, her Tiny Tears and my Action Men, and I'd sit them all together, all shapes and sizes, and decide that today we'd play schools, or sports day or, although strange for a six-year-old, post office. But when I was on my own it was just me and the four walls for company, the one window and the door, and I couldn't help but listen and try to work things out. Why was Daddy always angry? Why did he hate our mum, our house? And the one question that every kid who lives through this kind of family disturbance asks: Why did he hate us?

My father was not the kind of animal that any child wanted living in their den, no matter if he provided for a while, or that I had one okay memory of him, that time he taught me how to tie the laces of my white plimsolls.

I often wonder who taught him the small, delicate, human things, the seconds of almost love when he stopped for one brief moment and forgot about himself. I wonder what he was like when my beautiful sister was born, a cheeky lad suddenly thrown into manhood, the responsibility and solemnity of being someone's father and the 'Fuck, I'm a dad!'

The burrow my father grew up in was constructed with

sharp objects, sticks and thorns and briars. His parents, although I barely remember them, fought constantly. His dad was a silent bully, his mum a Jehovah's Witness, and together they brought up their children at the point where Heaven and Hell crossed paths. I suppose this was how they saw it anyway.

My dad left us before I had chance for the words and ways to ask or wonder about his upbringing, but I know the story that Granny used to tell, the one she declared one Sunday, that her youngest son was illegitimate. Perhaps this was a lie, spat out in a malicious moment to spite my grandfather, who had returned home late after another all-night game of poker, but I know Polly Carthew liked the company of men. My memory of her having sex with a bloke from the village on a table in the storeroom at the rear of our flats is testament to that. I can still see her red leather boots stuck up in the air as me and my sister took turns to peek through the hole where a Yale lock used to be. I have many Granny stories.

I've no doubt that my father's relationship with his parents was complicated. He would have been witness to arguments and violence between his parents from a young age. There's no doubt that, like me, he was a child who lived in the den of flight or fight, the dangling place where you spent most of your time stepping forwards, backwards, sideways. I would stand and stare up at his bloody fist after he'd made contact with a wall or a door, the moments after when he'd leave for the night, the trail he left behind him, sometimes large, sometimes barely anything at all, my mum on her knees with the dishcloth and his mug of tea running wide on the carpet.

Because of his turbulent upbringing my dad chose the path of familiarity, surrendering to the inevitable, violence and harm, the same way I did.

***

I am my father's daughter I know. The scars and stitches on my arms and fists are testament to this. The whirlwind anger that was never far from childhood drove in deep beneath my skin and I can feel it now, another animal wild as winter, so wild I sometimes find it hard to leash, muzzle, control it.

As a child I feared the unknown. I feared change and the chain of certain memories: the noise of shouting and Dad's fist hitting plasterboard, glass, wood, the way one sound carried and connected to the next, a sequence of uncertainty banging, hanging around my neck. I am not an anxious person. I jump into each day boots first, with a strange mix of attitude and curiosity, but some days the chain swings just a little, not too much, but enough to pull me off balance.

Volatility goes hand in hand with creativity but, really, it's just an excuse for bad behaviour. My father wanted to be an artist: every inch of whitewashed chip-paper wall in our cramped flat that wasn't busted up showcased his canvases and I knew each palette knife crease of hard oil paint, each ridge of hate and occasional dip towards love. I never saw my father paint or create – he certainly never painted at home in our tiny one-bedroomed flat, perhaps he did it elsewhere, or before I was born – but his abstract paintings of hooded figures, churches, Mum naked and headless, existed early on in my memory, the same way the easel that was propped up against the landing wall outside our flat existed, and the splintered dint in the wall downstairs from one night when he'd picked it up and thrown it.

I knew those paintings because for many years I stored them in a large cardboard box beneath my bed, reminding me of his inadequacies, until one drunken night I pulled them out and cut them into tiny shards, my one and only connection to him slashed and cracked, pretty pieces.

My mum was an artist too, far better than him, but she didn't have the time for frames and borders, didn't have the energy for her own grandstanding. Where my dad's art was expressed in greys and greens and yellow-ochre oil peaks, abstract, Mum's was fine-lined and sketched to perfection, still-life flowers, faint fossil leaves and late-opening buds softened by pencil, watercolour, pen and ink. Unlike my father, my mother didn't have to act like an artist: she was one. Moments of beauty caught between the cooking and the cleaning, the early-morning and late-night jobs. Art that sketched itself into the hideaway corners of home, the backs of cereal boxes and across the grey lines of our jotters, our mother's art was healthy, vibrant, lived in a world of design and a desire to create, a place that wasn't meant for aggression, speed, or the frenetic pace of too much hard work.

When I was six, around the time that my dad was at his worst, drinking heavily and disappearing for days on end, something clicked inside me, a way to be that I now know was my true nature: I became protector. Every time my mum had a conversation with someone, I'd stand in front of her, guarding, distrustful, my fists stabbed into my pockets and a no-shit game face waiting at the corner of my mouth in case I needed it. At the age of six, arguments and fights grew over me like a second skin, a seventies jumpsuit I found easy to slip into, zip-up, what-the-fuck. On one occasion I told the neighbour who had driven over Mum's bin lid to fuck off; another time I got into a fight at primary school with a girl who was mean to my big sister on sports day. In retaliation for her bullying I stole her plimsoll and threw it into the stream that ran in a gully beside the school. At the time I thought nothing of my behaviour, and my mum never saw it as anything other than normal, but I know at home I was quieter, more abiding, and maybe this was because I wrongly thought the threat of the world was outside, not in our flat where the space around us was taken up with my father.

I realise now that my violence and anger were big, and for a little girl, they were the biggest. For the most part people thought my outbursts were funny, and goading me became the village sport. It also became my family sport and I remember my sister, aunt and uncle, all similar in age, winding me up so tight that I picked up a boulder the size of a buoy and threw it at them. This was the start of my wild nature, the part of me that is still uncultivated, uninhabited by human self, my father's daughter for sure.

Some days I was a secretive fox, while on others I became a stowaway wolf from my sister's *Grimms' Fairy Tales* book, wet teeth. At night I became an owl and flew out across the ocean to lose myself, and in the morning I grew magnificent ears so that I could listen to Mum's silent sobs when she thought we were still asleep, but I could always hear them.

This, then, was the beginning of me, angry, protective, on high alert. Was violence in my nature because of what I witnessed? Was it in Dad's, passed down through what he saw?

The punching that came easily to him gifted me with an easy fix: feel that way, do this.

In the context of nature versus nurture, perhaps my father gave me the biological, genetic predisposition to kick out, his fizzing blood 50 per cent mine. But learning from his behaviour was easy on my child's eye and I accepted and learnt it easily as it was all I saw when he was present. Those first steps to survival, like animals in the wild – the seal that learns how to swim by riding on its mother's back, the lion cub that learns to hunt, and the baby bear that studies how to filch fish out of streams – we are all influenced by our environment and our genes, no matter what side of the sex or gender divide we sit upon.

Female violence, the violence that is just violence but not 'male', is complex. While boys are meant for quick fist fixes, girls are meant for tears and to run away. I was not that girl. I was pretty in a sulky kind of way, a brooding tomboy with long eyelashes, all muddy jeans, cuts and plaits. Not the stereotypical image of what a good girl looks like, even though I strove to be good, always. I just liked to fight and, looking back, I now see how that wolf-seed nature was planted firm in my foundation from early on. Growing up I never felt like a girl or a boy, I was a child trying to make the best of what I had with smiles and laughter, but the origin of my identity meant I was also destined for kicks and stones, punches and hits.

Poverty and violence often have the same root causes, and the stress that comes from living without frequently manifests in aggressive behaviour. It's a cycle, a series of cause-and-effect events that strike and strike, directly sparking off each other until the end result is fire. The cognitive, behavioural and emotional effects on children who have lived through violence is long-term, stamped on us for ever: as adults we function, try to live loose, carefree lives, but we still have our faces pushed hard against the heat of fear, insecurity, rage.

The effects of violence on children are a minefield, and the explosive fallout hits every one of us differently. Young children become anxious, have trouble sleeping or start to wet the bed. Older children express their distress outwardly by becoming aggressive, uncommunicative and disobedient. In those years I'd have nightmares that all through the night filled my head with paralysing terror. Some nights I'd wake in my bunk-bed and try to call out to my sister, only to find I couldn't open my mouth. I'd try to pull back the covers but couldn't lift my arms, my legs flat against the mattress, useless. At that age I didn't have the words to explain what I was experiencing, how the fear not of what was happening around me but of what might meant I spent my early first-memory existence in a state of high alert.

It wasn't until years later, when we moved to Number 9 Hillside Terrace, our council house that nestled in a small estate on the far eastern side of the village, that I realised other kids had similar nightmares, similar fears of loss after their fathers left, and stories of violence, abandonment and abuse far worse than I could have imagined.

***

Throughout my childhood I would protect my sister and mother at all costs, even during the few months when Dad seemed to disappear completely, his cord jacket gone from the back of the chair and his pack of fags and Zippo lighter no longer on the table. Those months I remained with my eyes wide open and my ears pricked, a fearful hare, or on softer days, one of the rabbits that lived in the daffodil field up the back lane.

The daffodil field was our other ocean, a sea of gold and yellow. It was our silent sanctuary far away from domesticity, time, years, even the century itself. It was a place that only we knew existed, a hidden part of wildlife that you could get to only by bending and crawling through the gorse and briars, the kind that cut without you knowing, that grab you like a bully and pull off your bobble hat. Quiet, except for the down-there out-there sea, the daffodil field was wild and wondrous like the beach, except it was special, occasional, only visited in spring.

Easter Sunday, our boiled eggs already stained pink and green with food dye and the chocolate egg each already found, it wasn't long before we had our wellies on ready to head up to the daffodil field that stretched out across the high hills above our flat. A ritual the three of us did every year, a way for me and my sister to do something for Mum, to shower her with bunches of a million smiling orange and yellow faces, petal-perfect, friendly flowers for free.

That particular Easter, Mum had been reading *Watership Down* to us at bedtime, and she had decided that, before we headed out, we should write a letter to Fiver, our favourite rabbit, and leave it at the entrance to his burrow up in the daffodil field.

We sat at the breakfast table and thought about the questions we should ask him while we dipped our soldiers into our colourful eggs and waited patiently while Mum wrote down the questions in her beautiful handwriting.

'Ask if he likes living underground,' said my sister.

'If he likes chocolate,' I chipped in.

'What it's like to live in the daffodil field.'

'If he eats eggs, chocolate eggs, does his mum hide them?'

'Too many questions, Natasha.'

We watched her neatly fold the letter and we got out our pencils so we could decorate the outside with drawings of bunnies and pretty flowers before we set off.

The lane that led up to the field beside our block of flats was steep and could only be climbed by a head-down hands-in-pockets kind of determination. Deep breaths and strictly no speaking until we reached the top. I was always first to get to the summit, and I'd sit on the broken briar-rooted gate and wait for the others who sometimes forgot the rule of no stopping and talking. I'd start back down the lane to find them picking other wild flowers when our trip was all about daffodils.

Up in the high hills it didn't take us long to push through the undergrowth until finally we found the perfect burrow beneath the golden gorse. For some reason we never questioned how or why Mum was privy to this secret information, how she knew that those rabbits, almost in our backyard, were the ones in the book, but she just knew, like she knew tomorrow there'd be a letter waiting for us, written to 'The Girls', with all our questions answered, in the same beautiful handwriting. Us two, wanting so much to believe in beauty and fantasy and unexplainable stories, believed, every Easter that followed, that Fiver the rabbit wrote to us and us alone. That was our mother, a storyteller, gifting us this incredible world of literary rabbits that meant freedom, fleeting. Our trips up to the daffodil field were the colour of sunshine, the taste of buttered gorse and sea-salt-sucked blackberries. More than anything, it smelt of love.

It was a lightness of being, a family at liberty to run and play and sing how and when we wanted, our hair worn crazy with sticky sap and our T-shirts flecked with golden drops, the petals of gorse, narcissus and buttercups. Free to wear our coats like cloaks of natural wonder, that particular visit to the daffodil field will always be remembered as a moment of spring blue-sky madness, a brief instant of freedom, liberty before one black cloud drifted onto the horizon, with the weighted threat of a rainstorm, getting closer, closing in.

4

Savage Water

My dad never laid a hand on my mother. 'Never laid a hand': isn't that what bullies say while they hold someone's head underwater? Isn't this what their enablers say to protect them? Never laid a hand, never laid a finger, and never ever touched her. But what about the things they do touch, hit, smash, destroy, the damage they do to their families psychologically, the deep wounds of trauma they cause by abandoning them, their weakness suddenly our impairment, our inability to trust others, to feel worthy? When we love someone, we either love too much or not enough.

And what about the damage they do with their thrashing, thieving words, words that steal the dignity from another person and are never given back? Words hurt just as much as muck-slinging, sticks and stones: mean words are collected up and carried around like dead weight.

The harm my father did to the three of us goes a thousand leagues deep. It is not just unfathomable because of the things we know but the moments of doubt, the not-quite-remembered minutes that, while not uneventful, were full of silent drama. I have too many 'almost memories' scattered around in my head, like rainwater after a storm. They stick as individual moments and gather in corners to make surprise puddles, waiting for the right moment to go deep, sink you.

'What are you looking at, sweetheart?'

I stood at the open window and stretched up onto my tiptoes so I could see the tail end of the road that ran in front of our flat. 'Daddy.' I looked back into the small front room that doubled as my parents' bedroom and waited to catch her eye.

'What is it?' She had heard the confusion in my voice. 'Is he coming home?'

I shook my head and waited for her to crouch beside me. 'Why has Daddy got his arm around that lady?' I looked at Mum and felt her hand on my shoulder.

'Nothing, sweetheart.' Her fingers pushing into my skin. 'That's just a friend, now come away.'

At that moment I knew without a doubt that the thing I had just seen was not what I was meant to see. I could feel the heat of my mum's anger coming off her like flames, could smell the damp embers, the way rain smells on hot summer tarmac, and most of all I just knew my daddy's arm should have been around my mum's shoulders, or my sister's, or mine.

The right kind of hand, open, comforting, reassuring, not punching holes in the walls and doors: no, my father never laid a hand on us, not even the loving kind.

Along with similar memories my sister will have different ones, better ones for the simple fact that she is older than me: she has good thoughts stored from before I was born when he was a better man. She once told my mum how she liked to follow him on the beach as a small girl, trace his footsteps in the sand with her own, but there comes a time when the person you follow no longer makes any kind of sense, and the journey they're on is directionless.

That is how I think of him when I think of him at all, directionless, without a rudder and no anchor except Mum, the only person who, at least for a while, could hold him down.

How much at the age of five and six did I truly know? My early memory is sometimes good, a childhood scrapbook of scenes as clear as the recipes and make-your-own-clothes templates that Mum cut from outdated magazines, the periodicals that old rich folk, whose houses she cleaned, gave her once they'd finished with them. In my mind I have clipped and stuck my recollections into a million oversized mental notebooks, each one as vivid as the next despite having no context, no beginning, no end.

At the time I knew nothing of the girl my dad walked arm in arm with, except that she lived in the upstairs flat, and that I often ran past her as she came along the downstairs hall, because there was only one door leading to our three flats. Occasionally she pushed past me as I played, climbing with my Action Men on the banisters, skinny black jeans, long reddish hair and the smell of sickly sticky patchouli, the perfume everyone wore back then. Sometimes she smiled and I'd look away quick, wanting to protect Mum's honour, but guilty for my rudeness too.

This was around the time that Mum started to cry a lot, the time when she couldn't reach for things because her arms were heavy and wouldn't move when she wanted them to. The moments when I'd see her stopped, staring out of the kitchen window at the rock-wall outside, tears in her eyes, mid-toil.

I know now this was the start of my mum's breakdown, but at that time the girl upstairs was just 'Dad's friend', his acquaintance, until a couple of weeks later when he moved in with her, and Mum told us that Dad's friend was his girlfriend now.

I realise that his leaving was a slow drift away from us, that me and my sister wouldn't have noticed so much, but Mum had known what was going on for the longest time.

I have no recollection of him packing bags, but I imagine it happened while we were out, not because he cared but because Mum's instinct would have been to protect us, again. Truth was, his belongings would only have been a few items of clothing, hidden cash and his prized packet of fags. I have a specific flashpoint memory of my mum, always so calm and measured, losing her rag and running upstairs to Dad's girlfriend's flat not long after he had moved up there. I know the story well, how some kind of altercation played out above our heads, but years later Mum told me the truth, how she'd stood over the woman, Janice, who was sitting cross-legged on the floor, and pulled her hair up with one hand and threatened to cut it off with her sharp kitchen knife, the one she'd brought up from our flat, in the other, shouting, 'Is this how you all want me to act?'

This sudden image of Mum totally threw me because when we were growing up she was always so calm, so measured, like a soft, soundless tide. She said she was never going to do anything, but everyone who knew about the affair had kept saying to her how well she was taking it, how incredibly controlled and gracious she was, and that made her flip.

That was how his mental health affected hers, his fuck-ups slowly chipping away at her positivity and lust for life until finally she tripped and fell into his world of fire and ferocity.

★★★

45

Dad no longer lived with us, but he lay above us with his new girlfriend. Every day we'd hear his boots on the stairs and the landing as he passed our door, no longer stopping to turn the key but turning his back instead. In those early years me and my sister had to learn to cope with a new level of trauma. It didn't scar or bleed or make a mess, didn't make a sound, although its silence was deafening, but for us it was way worse than anything one person could inflict on another. He ignored us.

Abandonment makes us prone to depression, co-dependency and issues linked to borderline personality disorder and attachment anxiety. Feelings linked to childhood abandonment trauma can be overwhelming, excruciating and difficult to bear. They can give rise to feelings of isolation, loneliness, emptiness and rage. Depending on the age a child was when they were abandoned, feelings related to fear of death, survival as well as loss of identity can be triggered. Abandonment can underlie other emotional issues, such as depression and anxiety, jealousy and insecurity, low self-esteem, emotional caretaking and addiction, and can leave a child with the message that they are not important or loved.

For me all I can equate it to is feeling absolutely fucking worthless.

You have a parent, a father, and you know what a parent, a father, is supposed to do, how they are supposed to love and protect you, but instead it is exactly as if that parent holds you in their arms, carries you to the highest height, walks to the very edge and throws you.

I don't remember ever being in my father's arms. I can't remember a time when I saw his hands outstretched, coming towards me, or the warmth of muscle and skin touching my small arms and legs. Strangely I do remember his watchstrap: it was wide, made of brown leather, similar to the one I wear now but his had a little cap that went over the face of the watch, and I remember it clearly because it was speckled with a fine spray of white paint. That would have been from his days as a painter and decorator, the time I couldn't remember, the time before he announced that he was going to dedicate his life to socialism and gave up work for good.

My mum tells me that Dad's socialism reached its pinnacle when he announced that he no longer wanted to rip off old women so he made himself unemployed instead. We lived with Dad's political rants and declarations daily. It was a fact of life that we didn't think about except that sometimes it caused misery, like when my sister wasn't allowed to join the Brownies because of the pledge they had to make to Crown and country. Sometimes it caused excitement too, on the many occasions we were driven to Plymouth to walk the city streets to give away copies of *Socialist Worker*, and the drive back to Downderry, occasionally stopping to spray a black fist onto road signs through a stencil that somebody had got free with a Tom Robinson Band *Power in the Darkness* album.

I've no doubt Dad continued to do small cash-in-hand jobs to fund his drinking, but his money was his own, while Mum's earnings, along with family allowance, went on everything else.

I've thought about my dad's hands a lot ever since I bumped into him outside the village shop when I was thirteen. I was waiting outside for a friend who had put me in charge of their dog, and suddenly a man I didn't know started to pet the animal. His hands told me that he was my father without my having to look up.

My hands. His hands. Our hands.

I don't remember much more than looking up, saying, 'Dad.' We probably spoke politely and he would have asked me the basics, how I was, how school was, for the pretence. I know he smelt of drink, remember him saying something about coming down from Plymouth for the day to see a friend at the Eddystone Country Club but all I really remember were those hands: strong, tanned, like mine, hands meant for working, for doing or, as it turned out for him, not doing much at all.

Once my father had moved upstairs to Janice's flat my nightmares increased in their ferocity. Every night I found myself looking down into a bottomless cavern, my arms and legs bloodless and incredibly heavy, like falling and dying were inevitable. Some nights I'd dream that I'd gone into my mum's room and found her dead in the bed. I'd wake up screaming, crying, but relieved that it was just a dream, again.

Other times I'd think I was under attack from strange big-headed beasts. I'd imagine them crashing up through the floor-boards to get to me. Sometimes I dreamt that it was me who had stumbled into their territory, the small cluster of indigenous trees across the road where we sometimes played now suddenly a forest of low-limbed pine where I'd find myself running, my bare feet and legs disappearing into the scratching needles, my hands outstretched to catch the side of the trunks. Big heads running behind me, big heads coming towards me, and each one some version of the wild, the stags jumping out, their antlers nose-close, and the wolves creeping near with their teeth in snap-touch distance, everything oversized, their shadows in the forest militant, forceful, somehow pushing me towards them.

This is trauma. It is voiceless, stealthy, damaging and, above all else, it is exhausting and long-lasting.

Abandonment and the subsequent fallout from neglect and rejection is a disease: it is contagious, like algae crawling across still water, heavy, dark, infiltrating the far reaches until it commandeers every bit of clear water. It's not like its violent cousin, rage, which everyone considers when they think about domestic abuse, but is closer in nature to silence. It is a ticking clock, a stopped watch, a family photo turned to mush on the shelf. The needling control of one person over another, whether from a distance or up close, mute or deafening, is still abuse.

When I was growing up, my mum was an incredibly strong woman. As much as she could, she pushed my father to go away when he was in one of his destructive soapbox moods, the one in which everyone and everything was wrong, when he'd stand in the middle of the front room and shout at the top of his voice. No doubt my flamboyant brand of activism I unwittingly learnt from him, but to me as a child it was frightening: shouting, sweating, swearing, banging the table and asking why, turning on my mum, who, also a socialist, was a champion of equality, selflessness and community, hers a crusade with a conscience. She was all for free speech, but not this.

When he didn't go she physically pulled us away, down to the beach, up into the back fields and one time, not long after he left, she packed a bag and the three of us went to wait at the bus-stop in the centre of the village. He'd moved out, but he hovered above us in the flat, returning occasionally to hurl abuse at my mum for the things that were still going wrong in his life. He blamed her for his shortcomings, his transgressions; everything he did was somehow her fault.

Scrapbook memory. Mum not her usual self, her eyes all over the place, her soothing voice too fast.

'Where we going?'

'Berry Pomeroy.'

My maternal grandmother lived in an ancient gatekeeper's cottage that she rented in south Devon, and Mum was usually happy to bring us there, a few snapshot days in the school holidays when she managed to get a little time off work.

'Like a holiday?' asked my sister. She looked at me and we shrugged, because it wasn't a holiday, just another normal weekend.

'Just like it.'

'How long?' we asked in unison.

'Couple of days.' She looked up the road, where we had just hurriedly come, towards home. 'Maybe more.'

'Is Dad coming?' I asked. I knew the answer was no, but I couldn't help asking about him, have her reassure me, us. I sat down on the tiny bus-stop bench and thought about last night, Mum, Dad, a 'used to hearing' fight.

'It's your fault,' Dad shouted from the hallway.

'Nick, whatever it is, it's not my problem. Please leave.'

We sat on the couch watching *Doctor Who*, my prized Dalek in my lap, listening.

'She's found out!'

'Who?'

'Janice.'

'About what? You're not making any sense.'

'About Orla.'

'Who's Orla?'

'Don't tell me you don't know. S'pose you love all this.'

'Nick, I've no idea who you're talking about. You've been drinking – you're drunk.'

I turned my Dalek towards the door, just in case.

'She's a friend.'

Mum started to laugh. 'Another one?'

'If I find out you've got anything to do with this . . .'

'With what? I'm busy working all hours, raising enough money to put food on the table for your children. Would you like to see them, say hello?'

My sister shook her head furiously while I put my Dalek onto the back of the couch, battle ready.

'If I find out Janice has left me . . .'

'What? You'll come down here and smash the place up?'

The door slammed and I heard Mum crying in the kitchen, kettle on.

'Tasha, come and sit down here with Mummy to wait for the bus.'

I got off the bench and joined my mum and sister in crouching behind the low wall.

I could tell she was looking for him, hoping he wouldn't shout at her in the street, stop us going.

'Now quiet, good girls.' She gave us the overnight bag and told us to push it down behind the wall between us.

'What is it?' asked my sister.

'Quiet.' Mum turned to us and put a hand to each of our faces. 'I need you to both duck down tight and be as quiet as mice until the bus comes. Can you do that for Mummy?'

We nodded.

Heartbeat. The noise it makes in your ears when fear is at full force without you knowing why. That look in Mum's eye. Quiet, PLEASE.

Danger, terror, eyes closed tight. What it is to be asked by your mother to hide from your father. We were told to keep quiet, keep still, be small – the normal day-to-day passing by on the usual sea breeze, the regular village noises that were friendly voices, the ding of the shop-door bell down the road as it opened, and my mind stumbling over the penny sweets, the chop of the butcher's cleaver across the road cutting through nasty meat. The shock of silence and the transference of our childhood shifting, making room so it could accommodate this, a new shape to handle, to carry on our backs, trauma taking up space between us.

Something in me, the kid that couldn't be kept down, eyes peeking, and I looked up to see him, the bully man walking by, my father.

'Keep your head down,' Mum whispered. 'He's going to the pub.'

'What if the bus comes?' asked my sister.

'Then we'll jump up, get on and be gone.'

The world is full of these intimidating men, and in the country it's no different, except here there is next to no escape for the women and anyone whose life is spent in controlled captivity. Domestic abuse contains all the stages of drowning: struggle, submersion, aspiration and, in severe cases, it can mean unconsciousness, cardiac arrest and death. Bluntly put, it means an inability to stay afloat, to breathe, to hope.

The National Rural Crime Network states that rurality and isolation are used as weapons by abusers. Their victims are isolated, unsupported, unprotected and failed by the system, local services and those around them. Domestic abuse lasts, on average, 25 per cent longer in most rural areas and exiting abuse is harder, takes longer and is more complex for rural victims because there are significant additional barriers in such communities compared to urban areas. Close-knit rural communities facilitate abuse, enabling the abuser to play out their captive-and-control lifestyle unchallenged, often because traditional patriarchal communities, including the Church, control and subjugate women.

More often than not, the best some women can hope for is to be abandoned, left to their own devices to look after their children the best way they know how, but sometimes trauma, abuse and poverty comes back to haunt those most affected.

I don't know where my mum got her hope from. In those crazy escape moments she probably didn't look for it at all. Fight on the one hand, flight on the other, and around this time she was probably sick of fighting, sick of shouting back, questioning and picking up all the bits of shit that he dropped or threw her way.

Water is savage at the best of times, but when you're out of your depth and submerged to the point that you have no air left to breathe, it is relentless. Imagine, too, that you have children, a hand in each of yours pulling you down. There comes a moment when you might see a glimmer of light and you know, underwater, that now is the time to swim for your life. Letting go, moving forward so not to sink further into the remote ocean: this was my mum in that moment. It was nothing but hope.

After the weekend we spent at my grandmother's house, and during the weeks that followed, Dad moved out of the village. His departure meant Mum could start to revel in a lightness that wasn't the usual kind of quick-lit, then swiftly extinguished flame, but a smooth brush of brilliance, her smile and laughter like gold dust sprinkled into the eyes and ears of everyone who was in the vicinity, looking, listening.

Her care for us in that brief moment was as consistent as it had ever been, but with Dad gone she could finally start to care for herself.

To care – the urge in us to consider others – comes naturally to most of us, but self-care can often seem like the last thing at the end of a long list of things to do, especially for women, and mothers, and single parents living on the poverty line. Care is not always found in the places that we are meant to find it, and for children growing up in rural poverty, it can mean the difference between illness and health, and sometimes life and death. During the 2020 lockdown, Cornwall saw the largest increase in children taken into care in the whole of England and Wales, a massive 17 per cent jump. Official reasons why so many Cornish kids ended up in the care system include abuse, neglect, breakdowns in family relationships or the family being in acute stress, but there is nothing to say why Cornwall saw the biggest jump of all counties. There's no report that digs deep into the findings and nobody asking why. I'll bet anything that greater factors are at play, like access to health and care services, transport, education and leisure, all of which have a hand in making this statistic what it is. These factors are the undercurrents that move in and around society without ever being properly recorded, the influences that mean the difference between points that either break through weakness or become galvanised through fight. These elements in a young person's life mean the difference between love and loss, emotional availability or fuck-off.

That day at the bus stop, when my mother escaped with us to safety, we hadn't recognised it as such straight away. We just knew our small minds were running towards something. The smell of diesel and the warm feel of faux-leather seats in the sun, the three of us sitting hand in hand in hand, the bay opening up as the bus left the village and embarked on the steep hairpin climb, the sea fading into insignificance below us, quieter now, my fingers pushed up against the window to hold the gently rocking waves, not so frightening, no longer savage.

Knowing what I know now about the statistics around children in vulnerable homes, I see what we were running towards: it was salvation, protection, a chance at security.

5

Teach a Kid to Fish

If I could capture the best part of childhood, the smell and the feel and the taste of it, without doubt it would be fishing.

Cornwall is a port county. It is also a poet county, with a language all of its own and ways with words that, through diaspora, have roved the world. If I could find one Cornish word for the spirit of those people, it would be *devisyek*, resourceful. We are practical thinkers, inventive and definitely imaginative.

We Celts have inhabited Cornwall for thousands of years, since the two Celtic tribes, the Dumnonii and Cornovii settled a thousand years ago. These early hunter-gatherers found a diversity of sea creatures on our shores and in its shallow waters, and since then fish and shellfish have been important food for us Cornish.

Fishing remains a vital part of our economy. More than £30 million worth of fish is landed every year in Newlyn alone, and the total value of the industry, when seafood processing is factored in, is worth almost £100 million to the Cornish economy. We have the largest fleet of 10-metre and under vessels in the UK, boats that mostly operate within twelve miles of land and are polyvalent in their activities, which mean they can easily switch between gear types in the same day, like potting, netting and hand-lining.

The Cornish fishing industry is well managed, highly regulated and more sustainable than ever before. We are also blessed with up to fifty different species that are landed around our coasts every day.

Every job seems to find its feet in the tide and we have more than enough folklore to do with the sea: smugglers, sailors, pirates, mermaids, sea monsters; some stories we grew up with stick in our blood; others we forgot. Every coastal town and village has its fair share of local legend and our twin villages of Downderry and Seaton are no exception. Part of me realises that in the seventies and eighties we were the ones creating the stories, taking the fabric of old legends and ripping them up, stitching them back together to make new stories, a patchwork of lore to pass on to the next generation. I doubt now that the rich second-home owners are even aware of our ancient traditions, not much of that droll-soul remains, but during my childhood, when there were still plenty of us working class around, we were the story-makers, living legends, our heads and hearts forever hankering in, around and over the sea.

There is a Cornish saying that goes 'More rain, more rest, dry weather suits us best'. It was meant for mining and farming but in our village it was used for fishermen to green-light their sit-and-watch at the Seaview pub, one eye on the horizon, the other on their pints. Many times during the summer months a gang of us kids would hang around the pub garden, waiting to catch a glimpse of one of the men and beg them to take us out in their boat. My favourite was a bloke called Pat, a man of indiscernible age, who didn't seem to do much of anything but had heart enough to notice us and say, 'Okay, one hour, two tops.'

Pat's boat was always red with a blue trim, no matter how much repair it needed. When he had to buy a new second-hand one, he always painted it the same blood red, blue trim. There was only ever one life-jacket tucked away beneath the boards of the boat and I guess whoever was the youngest of us four or five children got to wear it. It didn't seem to matter to us or Pat, or even our parents: we were Cornish, and by that definition most of us couldn't swim. To outsiders that might have seemed strange, but to Kernewek kids it was natural, like drowning would somehow have been a rite of passage. Besides, why drag out the inevitable? A quick death during smuggling days would have been just that, cold and quick, and I always held those rogue forefathers in the forefront of my mind as I stood beside the men, older kids, keen to help, be seen, be a part of all this.

I could imagine heading towards our pirate ship out to sea, like in one of the many pirate stories we were told on long dark nights around the beach fire. The story of the Barbary pirates was my favourite, how in 1625 they raided the nearby town of Looe, seized eighty mariners and fishermen and led them away in chains to North Africa to be enslaved, torching the town to the ground. All along the south Cornish coast, crews were taken captive and the empty ships left to drift.

Those buccaneering stories were never far from my mind as we pushed Pat's boat down the slipway, pretending to help launch it into the waves, wading out into the water until waist deep. That feeling of control on the water has never left me, the underside of the boat as it lifted from its ridge in the sand and started to float, causing us to jump quickly onto the gunwale and swing ourselves in, winded, delighted.

The sound of the water hitting against the bow of the boat as the engine kicks in is everything, eyes scanning the near horizon and your heart in your mouth until you see something, shout, 'Rock!' the emmets looking on, pointing.

Pat turned backwards as he crooked the rudder, shouting, 'Fuck 'em.'

Pride in the way we sat, sticky shoulder to shoulder, a tribe of mini warriors. We were our own swallows and Amazons, like off the telly, but without the picnics and stuck-up voices.

There were only ever three ways to go once we'd negotiated the valley of sand that reached out beyond the rocks and on towards big water: left towards Whitsand Bay, right toward Looe Island or straight on towards the Eddystone. You only ever went straight if you had a bigger rig, a trawler, deep-water fishing, and Looe was cool but I preferred Whitsand Bay, basking-shark country. Basking sharks love warm water, and for some reason that bay always seemed to hold the sun in both its hands, maybe because it was less rocky, or perhaps because of the yellow sand that replaced Downderry's silver rock remnants, or perhaps the fragments of periwinkle shells reminded the sharks of eternal summers. Either way, that part of our bay was big and blue and beautiful.

We never caught anything other than mackerel when we went out fishing, but Mum said that was all she ever wanted. It was a pretty fish, like a blue and pewter rainbow, and it was the only fish we ever ate, stuck bones pinning open the backs of our throats for an instant shut-up. Fish dinners were an integral part of growing up and we often had mackerel with pretty much everything.

Food for free, sea food, food to make Mum hug us, job done.

For me, because it meant sustenance, fishing was a job of high stakes, and if I was in the mood for dramatics, it was a matter of life and death.

***

Food poverty is commonly defined as the inability to acquire or consume an adequate or sufficient quantity of food in socially acceptable ways, or the uncertainty that one will be able to do so. Access, health, worry, struggle, higher percentage of income on food and less choice from a restricted range of foods, especially when you factor in the only shop in a six-mile radius and no transport to travel to others anyway, let alone the bigger-town shops, ten plus miles away.

It is more than the lack of money to buy food and ingredients: it is also the inability to afford electricity, water, a cooker that works. In my mother's case, money also meant the ability to stay strong, keep her head up while others patronised her, pretended to help. There were many rich older women whose houses she used to clean, like the one who used to give her giblets to take home to boil for stock, another who gifted her cooked carrots and peas, leftovers tipped into a plastic food bag 'for the girls'. Sometimes they gave her old magazines, and I used to love sitting up with her at the table in the flat with a pair of scissors in my hand, helping to cut out the money-off coupons, 20p off Daz or 10p off Andrex toilet paper, all known brands, but that was all Tom's Store, the one shop in the village, sold anyway.

We were poor, so the coupons were welcome, but my mum was proud, and we girls never got to see those cooked waste-offerings, because Mum always threw them into the outside bin on her way home from work. She cooked with what we had, often seasonal food: potatoes, onions and cabbage fresh from the field, left on the doorstep in a cardboard box by the farmer whose uncle Mum sometimes looked after for free. She cooked with herbs and berries and wild garlic and, more than anything, we lived on mackerel, our ocean bounty.

On average, earnings in Cornwall are 25 per cent below the UK national average. In addition to lower wages Cornwall also has some of the highest costs of living in the UK. Housing is some of the most expensive outside the south-east and London with ten times price-to-earnings ratios in popular locations.

In 2021, 3.87 per cent of adults in the county suffered from hunger, 9.49 per cent struggled to access food, 11.11 per cent worried about not having enough food. Laid bare, the number of people using food banks and children claiming free school meals continues to rise. Prior to Covid-19 there were more than 11,500 children in Cornwall claiming free school meals, but by January 2021 this had risen to more than 14,000. This represents 15.7 per cent of primary-age children and 14.4 per cent of secondary-school children – much higher than the south-west average.

According to the Trussell Trust, the national charity that supports some 1,200 food banks throughout the UK, including Truro food bank, there was an increase of 11 per cent in the use of food banks in 2021 compared to the same period in 2019, making Cornwall the worst unitary authority area in the south-west for food poverty outside Bristol.

It's hard to compare socioeconomic challenges in the 1980s with today's, difficult to evaluate what it means to a kid growing up in poverty now with my own childhood experiences.

To that young girl sitting by the driftwood fire with nothing but a couple of fish that she'd hooked with her own hands from the sea, and the spuds she'd dug from beneath the earth in the upper fields wrapped in foil and slow cooking in the hot embers, her poverty was the difference between surviving and thriving; the difference between living and existing; the variance that is danger and hardship, prosperity, fire or fortune. Perhaps not so different from growing up in poverty today, after all.

***

Out on the ocean I'd settle myself up in the bow away from the others, who always seemed to be messing around, and tentatively thread my hook through the thick pink fleshy foot of my chosen limpet. I'd prick my thumb with the barb just for the sake of feeling, being in the moment. Then I'd find a lead weight, knot it tight to my cat-gut line and waiting patiently for the engine to be cut, silence, and then the slow drop, the line green and silver, going under, no other sound but the soft slap of water, just us.

Time thrown out to sea moves differently from the shore. Apart from deep-sleep night it is just day, blue, green, grey. In the boundless space time finds itself fully folded away, a peaceful pause in which it can finally forget about itself in the bounce of the hull and the balance of the keel. Your world reversed, but also flipped upside, hands turned into fins once submerged, face so close you could almost believe yourself down there, part mermaid, my mother's daughter.

Out on the forever ocean you are left alone, no noise but nature, nothing to bother you but the gulls, which Pat called 'fishermen's lost souls', the drifters who hung around dangling on the wind, waiting for the first fish belly to be slit, gutted, offered up.

Alone, not alone, peace put upon the earth without having to ask or look for it, the ocean provided everything I wanted before I knew what that was. The horizon and the 'out there' were as big as my young mind could ride, and yet I'd still have loved to travel as far as the lighthouse, wipe away the fog and climb up to the cupola, get the chance finally to spy France.

Happiness as a kid was the freedom of the ocean, the scatter of kids and some raggedy middle-aged bloke. It was catching fish for the home-show and sometimes it was the fire up by the marooned boats on Downderry beach. Those nights were the ones that came alive with the warmth of brackish flame and the unruly sparks of fireflies. When the sun set west and took the wind with it, we were allowed to take turns at the helm, steering the boat towards home beach, that big salty tower of smoke, that tiny glow.

Our beach was never short of damp driftwood, but it was our community's collective thinking that gathered up the sea-sculptured stubs of trees and runaway planks and stored them on the banks beneath a couple of lengths of tarp until a warm summer night. Nothing was ever planned, but weekends in August were fire and fish and stories told sideways, skimmed in the water, drunk.

I loved fishing, loved the catching and the gutting and the smell of seaweed that you wore on your skin and took to bed with you at night. I loved the burnt-briny taste of fish cooked over fire-stones and how the stars looked on a full stomach. The sound of laughter, the way grown-up voices punched out, crept back, the hooking-up whispers and the breaking-up shouts and our made-up shanties sung too loud, proud until tears, too much love, hate, drink.

On those nights our mum was always around, always the first to call us, check what we were doing, how far we'd strayed from the circle of wet sand, warm light.

Some nights Dad was there too, early on, but the longer the days and nights extended without his swagger, his nonchalant manner, the more I didn't look for him, and the further any kind of binding that might have been tied between us was severed. I don't know. No child can know what a parent is. A dog can recognise its parents as long as they were together during the critical socialisation stage, so I wonder. My father was the man who taught me to tie my PE shoelaces. All the rest is a knot of fear and rage, destined for the snap.

The last good memory of my father was sudden, like a gut-punch.

He had returned home to us and the flat the way a season falls in without you noticing. One minute he was gone, his wintry shadow dragged behind him, like a dead weight; the next he was beaming down on us two girls like summer, a breeze. This 'rock-up' was connected to some kind of 'starting over' between my parents. This is what I know now, but when I was six, he had been in my life, then gone via the upstairs flat to a place called Torquay. It sounded exotic, like somewhere found in my sister's *Animals of the World* book, definitely not in Devon, the next county along. He'd moved there to settle his girlfriend into a flat. Perhaps he was hoping to have two lives, maybe more, because everyone who lived in our village and the surrounding ones knew that he had cheated on his new partner.

That day he had washed up onto the beach, like foreign flotsam, on a beautiful warm day, the week before the start of the summer holidays, mid-July, the week when the weather gets going good but the tourists are yet to descend, and you could kick a ball across the main beach without it hitting a baby or a dog or one of those stupid sun-loungers that emmets used to lie on so they didn't get sand on their pale sticky sickly skin.

He had persuaded one of his mates to take me and my sister out in their boat. Maybe he wanted to reconnect with us, but more than likely it would have been to gain favour with Mum. This sudden advent was a problem for me, whatever the reason. I loved boats, but I didn't like him, and I hated that he was about to steal one of my happy places, the space where I was most content, the place without noise, without thunder.

As usual we were joined on the beach by other kids and it wasn't long before a good-sized crowd of us were assembled and bundled on board the bigger-than-usual boat and headed out towards Looe Island. There were a few adults, too, as I recall, the circle of eager faces the perfect stage for a man like my father.

The brilliance of the stranger who stood in the middle of the boat I will never forget. He was striking, berry brown, as muscular as a stoat, grandstanding in cut-off jean shorts and the usual cocky smile. The stranger who had obviously been happier away from us returned now, not as a drunk or a cloud or a storm, not even a man, but an unrecognisable, mythological animal. Already a thing of legend, the shock of him, the jolt of how I felt to see him like that, was akin to something hard but shapeless that lodged in my chest and refused to budge, an unexpected thing bitten too big, too fast, swallowed. It felt strange, an unused-to thing, like when you get something right, but this wasn't right. I know now what that feeling was. I can even name it. It was pride.

I still don't know why I felt it. I don't know what factors led to this feeling except perhaps some sense of belonging, a reciprocal link perhaps, but for one day in summer, once upon a time, I looked at my father and felt something close to love. A memory not good or bad but different, something unlike anything I'd felt for him up to that point: it existed within an in-between place, but perhaps if he'd stuck around, gradually becoming the person he was supposed to be to me, Daddy . . .

But it didn't last.

***

That moment of near love for my father was a moment of weakness, a slip into the fantasy that was to imagine what it would have been like to have what other kids had: Mum, Dad, sister, me, four corners that made up the walls of a happy home. But the more I became aware of Mum's increasing absence because she had to work so much, the more I hated him.

Every morning she would cycle the mile from our flat to her job as chambermaid at the Wide Sea Hotel in the middle of the village to get the 'still' on for hot water, the water that meant every room had a pot of tea waiting for the occupants at 6.30 a.m. She would then return to us, get us dressed and make breakfast, toast soldiers and a dippy egg each. Dad was usually still in bed, and my memory of him during this, his last return, is of a mere shadow, not quite there.

After breakfast Mum would pack our school bags and drop us off at the other end of the village, then return to the hotel to strip beds and make up the rooms for the tourists. Afternoons she spent cleaning the homes of the old rich folks.

The less I saw of my mother, the more the sentiment of hate pushed firmly away every other emotion I might have had for my father.

The moment Mum picked the two of us up from school to walk back through the village and home to our flat was the best time. Sometimes she brought us a snack from home, a couple of pieces of homemade flapjack or toffee in a plastic tub, or if she'd been paid for the hotel job we were allowed to go into the sweet shop at Tom's as we passed and fill a small paper bag each with penny sweets up to ten pence worth.

'What you got?' I asked my sister excitedly.

'Sweets.'

'Swapsies?'

'Why would I swap what I've just got from the shop?'

School always put her in a mood, always just before and just after.

I looked at Mum and we both smiled, knowing.

'We're going out for tea tonight,' said Mum.

'To the pub?' I asked hopefully. I loved chicken and chips in a basket with ketchup, a rare treat, but a good one.

'Barbecue on the beach. Spuds and mackerel.'

'Again?' we asked in unison.

'Again.'

'I love baked spuds,' I said, taking my mum's hand so she didn't feel sad. 'I love fish too. So does she.'

My sister shrugged and popped a gobstopper into her mouth. Good.

'I love all the things you cook for us,' I continued. I was on a roll.

'Well, tonight is Friday night so one of the men will be cooking on a driftwood fire, down by the boats.'

'Free food?' I asked.

'Exactly that,' smiled Mum, 'food for free.'

'Will Dad be there?' asked my sister.

'Of course.'

'Does he have to come?' I looked at my sister and she shook her head, her way of telling me to shut it.

'He's trying Tasha,' said Mum.

He wasn't.

'He's always in a mood,' I continued, 'always angry.'

'Does he get angry with you?' she asked suddenly.

'No, Mum.' I wanted to say more, wanted to say how he didn't talk to me so he didn't get angry, that he ignored me when I showed him the pictures I'd drawn, ignored me when I said I wanted to paint on canvas, like him.

'You tell me if he ever gets angry, won't you? Both of you, are you listening?'

We nodded, the happiness of sweets and laughter and fun suddenly fading, the closer we got to home.

6

Sink or Swim

The ocean glimpsed through the wood smoke and flames of a summer fire is all the best bits of Heaven and earth picked up and thrown. There is nothing better than fishing and foraging and finding food for survival, if you have to, but the return of my father should have meant more money for food, new clothes, fuel for the one and only fire in the front room instead of blankets, but any money he made from his hit-and-miss cash-in-hand painting and decorating jobs he spent on drink. There was money, stashed in punch-holes, like the one in the bathroom wall, the dark space where Mum discovered rolls of cash tucked into the crevices.

She worked hard: every available job in the village she took on and shoehorned into the day. During the duration of my childhood she cleaned holiday cottages and private homes, worked at the crab factory in Looe and cleaned the Eddystone pub and the Wide Sea Hotel where she was a chambermaid until it turned into a nursing home and, by default, she became a care assistant.

All hours, every day, every penny spent in Tom's village shop. It would have been understandable if at weekends or between shifts and during school holidays she had left us to our

69

own devices or packed us off to play with other kids, but when she worked we went with her, and any time she managed to rattle free she spent creating and exploring the coastline and surrounding countryside with us.

Whether our mini-adventures were more about getting away than going to I will never know, but for us and our dog Leo it was a chance to learn about nature and the beautiful land that circled the bay.

Behind our stumpy block of terraced flats there was a steep incline of Devonian rock and, running upwards through it, a narrow lane that led to fields that banked around the village, like a bruiser, protector. Two muscular arms that stretched both sides of the village and hugged it close, a proper father to go towards, not run away from, a father like the other kids at school had, good bloke, nice fella, someone to buy you a Coke, an ice-cream, Daddy please, someone to walk over, walk to.

In those early years the three of us must have walked miles, our wellies stomping up the cracked tarmac, our heads in the hedges, Mum's well-worn copy of *Food for Free* poking from her cagoule pocket: 'Look at this, girls.'

The hedgerows during spring and summer were bountiful, with buds, leaves and flowers. Young nettles, sweet violet, sea beet, our favourites were wild strawberries, gooseberries and the elderflower rosettes we'd pick for frying in the old sticky-toffee-coloured chip pan and dip into sugar later.

In September and October we'd collect beech nuts from beneath thick ridges of fallen autumn leaves found in the tiny woodland pockets that tucked neatly away in the creases of fields, and we'd dare each other to eat the cheek-sucking sloes and fill baskets to the brim with lavender-tasting field mushrooms and quick-to-eat blackberries. We were forever making up silly songs as we walked, and we told stories too, especially me, Mum's little writer, the three of us wandering beneath the broadening, brooding Cornish sky. For a brief moment we forgot about Dad, forgot to wonder if he was home or down the pub, if he was in a mood and if so which one, the silence that was sometimes worse than the noise, the noise that was sometimes worse than anything.

The more our father stayed around that second time, the further he started to sink into his own self-dug pissed-upon mire. Something about responsibility, or the pretence of it, made him madder, resentful, returned to wild. His reappearance had started to unravel all the healing my mother had done, and despite her being positive by default, she began to become increasingly depressed, not like the last time, big and busted, but mini-moments, soft and silent.

I know she would have missed the light touch of being that she'd felt while he wasn't around, existing in the moment of recovery, the past a distant reminiscence, while the future blasted out in front of her, new shoots. She never outwardly showed it or, rather, she never meant to show it, but there were times when I'd catch a cloudlet fragment of the dark, bullying storm that had coasted into her eyes. If she saw that I'd seen it she'd take us out for another walk, or tell us to think about what we saw up in the daffodil field or down in the rock-pools, get out our colouring pencils and sketch it, shade it, remember it.

She tried so hard to pull brightness into our lives in all the ways you could sing it, paint it or wear it with a smile and one of her colourful hippie-skirts, but all the while I could sense

her edges being worn down, her instinct for standing up, pushing on, no longer naturally gilt, but tarnished, fading fast.

Nature was our friend, our ally. It never jumped away or hid
or questioned us. It just watched and offered up what we
recognised as beauty, sensory, mucky and everything for free.

Perhaps during that time Mum was preparing us for later
life, for a lifetime of poverty, the hand-to-mouth and foraging
way that would always be food, next meal.

'Mum?' From where I sat on the floor, drawing in my
sketchpad with newly bought felt-tips, I could see Mum was
crying, one tear, but enough for me to know she was sad, one
tear, but the reflection from the window made it sparkle, like
a rare jewel held up to the light.

'What, sweetheart?'

'You're crying.'

'Nothing. Mummy's got something in her eye.' She leant
forward from where she was sitting on her bed, which in daytime
was just the place we sat, and asked to see my drawing.

I ignored her. 'You're sad.'

Mum shook her head, looked towards the window, closed
her eyes, and suddenly we both heard the ocean crashing.

'Cus Dad?' I asked.

Mum shook her head, rubbed her tears away with her shoulder, her arms gone heavy again. 'What are you drawing today?'

'Us.' I smiled. My drawings always made her happy, and I
knew this one would for sure. I finished off colouring in the
yellow sun, replaced the cap and held up my pad towards her.
'Us,' I said again.

When Mum's tears became heavier I sat up against her, like
I did when she played classical music and cried with her eyes

closed, teaching us to hear the music, how to conduct. 'It's beautiful,' she said at last.

I nodded, my small finger pointing out the characters in my life, and I pulled the page from the pad. 'For you.'

'Thank you sweetheart, I'll put it up on the kitchen wall.' She put out her better hand, the arm that wasn't so numb and weak because of the effects of anxiety, and took it from me.

'Put it up now,' I said, and together we went into the kitchen to find some free space on the wall.

For Mum, the giving-up part was never going to be a factor in her story, no matter how ill she felt, or how debilitating the anti-depressants the doctor gave her, the ones she flushed down the toilet one morning because she forgot to pack my plimsolls for PE and hated feeling out of control, which was worse than the depression.

Even without children Mum would have blasted a trail towards her own history, her terms, her destiny. She was incredibly resilient and resourceful, finding ways to make a living and keeping a clean, comfortable home, all the while inventing dishes and mending and stitching and fixing things, the stereotypical 'man jobs'. Me and my sister knew the difference between a Phillips and a flathead screwdriver and 'lefty loosy, righty tighty' before we could read, could change a light bulb, wire a plug and fillet fish way before any boy our age.

Poverty demands resourcefulness, an any-means-necessary approach to having fuck-all. This level of ingenuity and resilience is a kind of survival strategy, looking for good deals, hustling for extra working hours, thinking up all the ways to make food, water, electricity, heating stretch that little bit further.

Mum's resilience became our resilience, the trick of reaching down into your gut to find the fucking fearless fist that instantly you grab, hold inside, pull yourself up, push out, words tattooed on the knuckles that spell 'I am invincible'.

Nature has a say in all of this. It is the freedom afforded, the escape that makes the difference, the variance between fight or flight, just so long as you don't sit around and wait.

Resilience in the animal kingdom is the capacity of an animal or plant to be minimally affected by disturbances so that they can return to normal as soon as possible. I learnt to turn around and move on early in my life, find nature, discover the nature inside me. I was the seasons, the elements, made of shrub and water, my natural pliancy to negativity meant I could be the earth beneath my fingernails and the hot air in my lungs, big mouth.

We Cornish are known for our resilience. We live remotely from our English cousins, and we have always had to endure a lack of resources, long miles and harsh sou'-westerly storms to survive. It is no wonder that we have always looked to nature to survive: one moor in which to mine, two oceans in which to fish, and a million fields to farm.

We are not a modern people. Our culture is Celt and our heads are full of folklore and tradition. We are superstitious to the point that nothing is done without complete thought, circular discussion, but our hearts are always full of love. There is an old saying that 'Nobody loves the Cornish more than the Cornish,' and this is true: I love our strength in conviction, our rebellious nature and our pride, and most of all I love our ability to turn every story back around to be about ourselves.

The more I studied nature the more I found my true nature, my personality developing and unfurling, opening up like a fern. No longer did I feel soft-blue sad for my mum, but white-hot anger for my dad.

When my father packed his one bag and left for the last time he'd barely been around anyway. He'd hooked up with a big busty woman with curly red hair who lived in a chalet in the Seaview pub car park. Whenever I saw him from afar, or in passing, I no longer felt sad or confused, but angry. I hated him. Years later, when I found myself sitting a couple of feet away from him at the back of a bus in Plymouth, I hated him all over again. I didn't want to speak, but couldn't help looking across at the man who was my mirror image, and yet he didn't recognise his face in mine, his younger daughter. This was the moment that, during my early thirties, led to my own break-down, a moment in time that concluded with my cutting myself so badly with a kitchen knife that two police cars and an ambulance came to my home. I was taken to hospital and had eight stitches sewn into my arm. The calming nature of my incredible girlfriend saved me then, and the nature of my immediate surroundings, walking, writing, and connecting, just being, protected me from my dangerous self.

Determination is a powerful thing. In the natural world it means the difference between survival and extinction. Too young to comprehend all this, I knew I wanted Dad gone for good. I wanted to be that bud, that flower, that leaf expanding without the threat or damage of another's boot. I wanted to survive, and not just survive but thrive. More than anything I wanted my mum's incredible light and lust for life never to burn out.

The instances we saw her sad were few, minute moments of silent sitting, staring, or standing at the sink, one hand holding a mug or a plate, the other mid-wipe, stopped. Despite her suffering, our mum's instinct to protect us was incredibly strong. No matter what, she always greeted us from school with a smile, always woke us up in the morning with her tears wiped away, ready to 'put on my face', blusher, eye-shadow, bit of kissy lipstick. She always pushed for happy, despite the sadness, and announced the day with an 'up and out' style of therapy.

It's no wonder that I learnt to take fear, madness and the remnants of trauma outside so that I could shout it out, disseminate, write it down in my tiny notebook. It's no coincidence that I've written all my books in the countryside, that I'm writing this memoir outside, beneath my favourite hazel tree, the one I planted from a tiny kernel, incredible nature.

Wild writing for me has been the difference between success and failure, the change between truly opening my mind and heart to the ether as opposed to sitting and staring at a screen, wondering 'how I felt' when I could have been out in the elements, just feeling.

I am more than grateful that my mum took us outside when the storm of Dad came crashing. No matter what the weather was doing beyond the flat, the ocean washing in dark blue and the horizon inking jet-black, she'd dress us up for the rush of elements and take us out on a wild adventure, making up songs and stories to carry with us, fantasy versus reality.

I am a writer for many reasons, but the practice of wild writing is my escape, a way of finding, connecting, nature in the detail, the detail of nature in me.

Nature has a way of pulling us through. It has a profound impact on our brains, bodies and our behaviour. We are of the lines and the lights between elements; we are air and water and fire and earth; we are planets and natural satellites, and every plant and living thing that comes to us through each of our senses to kick out at anxiety, stress, attention capacity and inability to relax. Biophilia is in the nature of all of us, pre-birth; it is native to our blood and bone, a genetically determined affinity with the natural world.

Nature is dissemination, the capability to connect with our surroundings and to meld with others. It is what I think about when I consider the look and cut of Heaven – it is all this. There's no doubt that the natural world has a stabilising effect on children's emotional wellbeing and cognitive functioning. How children notice nature, and how they interact with it and appreciate their natural surroundings, no matter how small, is a critical factor in preventing stress and keeping their heads above water. For rural kids it is one of the things that is a constant, that sense of belonging. It is a calm tide when your life is anything but, a cool breeze when your world is full of fierce fire and another's bullying heat.

The environment was another world I could drop into, a world awake beneath my fingertips that, over time, would snake into my arms, my legs, my feet and guide me away from the minuscule land of weeds and ants under the magnifying-glass and upwards towards the oceanic horizon. It was my escape, my breath, the sea air in my lungs, my ears, my eyes, my heart, a concentration of peace and hope and love.

7

Immersion

My parents never taught me to swim. I never got to lie in their arms or hold their hands beneath the waves and lean into my fear of letting go, but from that summer when my father briefly returned, then permanently left, I decided what waves got to wash over me. I made up my mind that I would learn how to gulp air, how to swallow it down into my lungs and hold it there, stamp my feet into the sandy-silt ground. This village was my land, my corner from which to discover the things that were free, all the small things I could pick and pocket and place around me, float beneath my skin so I could carry myself beyond fear, learn how not to sink but immerse myself in nature so that I might at least give the appearance of surviving, swimming.

With my father gone, a little light started to replace the spaces that had been taken up with his clouds and it came in the form of books. For a family with not much cash we always had a good few shelves of books in the flat, an eclectic mix from charity shops and jumble sales of mostly poetry and non-fiction that ranged from farmhouse cookery to the history of Northern European Bog People. My favourite was on the artist William Turner, and before I could write, I sat up at the table with Mum and memorised those paper imitations of art, what it was to take nature and make it your own.

'But how does he do it?' I asked, rubbing my fingers across the picture of a train. This must have been for the tenth time, because Mum didn't just say, 'Observation,' but sighed, took her time.

'You see those apples we picked, the ones in the bowl?' She pointed to the apples in the wicker bowl at the end of the table.

'Yes,' I said. Of course I did.

'Look at them.'

I started to laugh and she told me to sit up straight, not to take my eyes away from them. 'Concentrate now, Natasha. What do you see?'

'Apples.'

'What else?'

'Bowl.'

'Describe what the apples look like'

I turned my head to the side, looked down at the painting of a steam train beneath my hands, then back up. I thought about colour. 'They're green,' I said, 'bright green.'

'What else?'

'Shiny, like there's a light in them.'

'And where's the light coming from?'

'Easy. The window.' I pointed to the outside, the afternoon sun passing slowly across the bay.

Mum moved closer, pleased. 'And what colour does it make the apples?'

I thought for a minute. This game was easy. 'White.' I smiled. 'Green and white.'

'Observation,' said Mum, triumphant.

'Easy as that,' I said. 'Let's do their shape.'

I remember that the description of shape and shade and all the factors that made them up was harder, but always, then and now and for ever, I always think about that word, observation, what it means to truly look at something.

The first time I visited the National Gallery in London I stood in front of Turner's *Rain, Steam and Speed*, and cried. To stand there and feel that childhood memory and connection to self, that lesson in art given by my mum. There it was, my favourite painting, so briefly touched beneath my tiny finger-tips, now larger than life itself.

Since that first visit to the art gallery, I still ask myself, How? That simple transference of beauty, with all its dimensions mirrored and diluted down to one flash moment. How the hell?

I swear I learnt to read by interpreting the captions below the strange photos in books spread wide across my lap. I can still hear the high-pitched whip of my hand as it skated across the page, the smooth serenity of pictures and the patterns of tiny neat shapes racing in lines, the words I was yet to know, saying something, but silently. Of course we had boring Ladybird books too, given at school in Infants to take home for the week, but I'd read these in one sitting waiting for Mum to pick me up at the school gate. They were never any good, contained barely any adventure, compared to our Famous Five collection, *Swallows and Amazons*. Even Winnie-the-Pooh was better than Dick and boring girly Jane.

Every kid who excels at reading gets asked if they eat books, but to me aged five and six it made no sense at all. I get it now:

information is food for the soul. It is protein and flavour and sustenance, immersion, fuel for life. Yes, as a kid I definitely ate words, sounds, stories, books.

My hunger for books and reading was sated once a fortnight when the blue and white mobile library pulled into the Seaview pub car park on a Tuesday afternoon, a lifeline to kids like us. We were poor, had no money for new books even if we could get to the nearest bookshop, which was seventeen miles away in Plymouth. The mobile library was a place we could drift into and dream complete. Like an aquarium of shapes and colours and the promise of something other, it was another ocean, a better one than the body of water we lived with daily at the end of the lane.

This ocean was exotic, especially when the books looked out towards you in the children's section, hopeful faces gazing forwards into the van. I imagined they were passengers on a wild bus ride across Cornwall, visiting villages and strangers' homes to be carried around, petted, loved a minute.

There were always plenty of books in the mobile library that stacked up high, every shape, size, colour and texture. They went from floor to ceiling, filling every space with the possibility of new adventures. I'd like to think that some days I felt sorry for the ugly, dusty books, the books without the picture per chapter or the ones without dust-jackets, the black and blue grown-up books, but I know it never deterred me from searching for my favourites.

We were only ever allowed two books per visit to the mobile library, but that was plenty for us. My sister always opted for big non-fiction books, mostly about animals, of which she now has an encyclopaedic knowledge, but I always

went for fiction, the thick big-print children's hardback reading books that I could saviour throughout the fortnight:
Huckleberry Finn, *The Water Babies*, *Wind in the Willows*, the
librarian raising a disapproving eyebrow as I stood with the
covers stretched wide open, ready for the stamp. These were
the books I'd return to month after month. They became my
beloved, like old friends, and at the age of six, seven, eight,
the only true, reliable friends I had. I hated it when the librarian asked me to leave them behind for somebody else to 'have
the chance to read'. She'd sit up tight behind the desk and
point to my library card, run her finger down the column of
authors and titles. 'See?'

I didn't see, not yet, didn't understand that there might be
another child in Cornwall who loved these books as much as I
did, or worse, that there were others who were yet to read
them. I gave her my saddest long-lashes face the first time I was
refused my favourite books.

'If you love these books so much you should ask Mum to
buy them for you.' She smiled. Mum smiled too, agreed, but I
didn't: these were my books, and anyway, I knew at that time
Mum wouldn't have been able to buy new books. I still hate
how that must have made her feel.

Sometimes when I noticed there was a different librarian, I'd
jump the tiny aluminium steps and search the shelves to find
them, and sometimes I'd find them gone, but the moment they
returned to me, their rightful place in the palms of my hands,
was pure heaven.

I've no doubt that at such a young age those books were all
about the soft protective plastic library-book covering and the
cosy woodshed smell, the odd linocut etching of 'Mr Toad in

his car' and 'Tom Sawyer by the river', but over time I read them and by the age of eight I'd read everything in the library on wheels, including *The Hobbit* and John Steinbeck's back catalogue.

I couldn't wait to get home and find a secret place to read, curled up on my bed or in summer out in the field across the road from our flat. I'd find a tree to settle under and dream, like Frodo or Huckleberry. Sometimes my sister came with me, climbing the trees to be with the birds or traipsing in the marshy undergrowth with a jam jar hanging from a cord of baler twine, looking for tadpoles, caterpillars, shield bugs, anything living.

When I got to the end of a chapter I'd look up and call after her, 'Found anythin'?'

'Yes,' she'd shout back.

'What?' If it was something interesting I would be tempted to put my book down.

'Beetle.'

'He got any horns?' I went to mark my place in the book.

'Nope.'

'Borin'.' I continued to read.

Sometimes she found bigger things, the things I was interested in, like nests, giant puffballs and vacated beehives, but mostly it was just insects, and I'd return to my fantasy world of books.

When she got bored she'd head home to search for her finds in a book, and she'd tell me to look both ways before crossing the road, and Mum would open the big sash window so I could hear the radio, smell the frying onions that meant tonight we would be having our favourite soup.

As a child the world of words was immersion at its purest. The moment when my surroundings washed away and there was nothing left of me but heartbeat, deep breath, one simple sentence or image stopping me dead. Reading had me swim out with strangers and dive down deep into unfamiliar oceans. It wasn't that I inhabited a fantasy world: my days were full of school and sport and nature walks, but reading is and will always be a window I love to peer through, a half-open door through which I can walk and live vicariously, existing in the moment of another's imagination, their truth. What it is to explore another's mind beyond what we think we know and what we're yet to find, stories outside our own comprehension.

I have learnt to swim in familiar and unfamiliar waters. I look towards the seabed of my home bay, see my reflection and know this replication is my work, my writing. I have dived into unknown rivers and read the books of a million strangers, and it all comes back to propulsion, moving forward, learning to navigate the undercurrent. That is what books were to me growing up and this is what they are to me still, water, escape, immersion, oblivious to anything other than learning.

The role of literacy in combating social exclusion is the difference between merely getting by and getting on. To make sense of words is to understand information, to share with friends, to open up the world. Extensive research has shown that people with poor literacy skills are significantly more likely to experience poverty, live in poor-quality housing, be unemployed or have low-paid jobs, become a perpetrator or victim of crime and have poor physical and mental health. For the rural poor it can mean being part of a vicious circle that never ends, as each generation not only falls through the gaps at over-subscribed schools, but fails to access bookshops, libraries and literary events.

Mobile libraries are lifelines for remote and rural communities because they don't just offer books: they can improve literacy by running reading programmes; they host online book clubs, develop reading and writing skills and provide advice to help people extend and develop their reading choices. As one of the last truly free public spaces in this country, there is no expectation to spend money in a library. Everybody is welcome and able to use the facilities, whether in-person or online, and they bring people together by fostering connections and community interaction – those brief moments between jobs when Mum would stand in the shade of the library van, or just out of the mizzling rain, and chat to the other mothers and the old dears about what books they'd managed to get hold of, the latest Jackie Collins or Danielle Steel. The community of spirit, the drive to connect, no matter how brief the moment: in the country this fitting together is not just something, it is everything, the bigger communal picture.

Some mobile libraries also carry IT equipment that offers enhancements to the traditional library services of book-borrowing and research, and as a statutory service they provide a point of contact for much-needed council amenities. Connectivity is a key challenge for many of us living in the country: for those families with low or no income, the elderly, and people living with long-term illness and disabilities, the mobile library is still the lifeblood of our country communities.

When I was growing up, there would never be enough books in my life, not enough stories to feed my ever-increasing hunger for knowledge beyond our bay, not enough experience outside the small village and the ocean in front of us. I was hungry for change, needed more than I could see: our flat and the village, the hideaway rocks and caves on the beach where I'd sit for hours and read, draw and think about the want that stretched wide inside me, the wider village community all around me – nosy, messy, splashy, looking at me with my book, mocking but endeared in one simple single breath.

How I must have wanted my life to change in some way, to somehow turn into a new fantastical story, a novel world that I could step inside, let the words wash over me, an ocean of uncharted water that would in time transform me and my life into something new.

EARTH

8

Cave

A house to call our own. Home.

Number 9 Hillside Terrace, Trelidden Lane was a million memories away from Number 2 Brenton Terrace, and an inevitable drift away from the memory of my dad and everything that went with that. Those two homes couldn't have been any further from each other, not just because one was a tiny one-bedroom flat and the other a two-bedroom semi-detached house with gardens and a stream running through it, but they were at least a mile apart, situated at either end of Downderry. When I was eight, they split the two parts of my life so far into two perfectly formed compartments. Each home contained my family and me as the main character; looking back, I can see how one informed the other, like two hands holding, both places a mix of happy and sad memories, the constant contour of the same circular life that overlapped, like crosshairs in a rifle sight.

The day we moved into our new council house was the start of how things were going to be.

The journey to getting it had been a hard push for Mum. She had argued with every local councillor she could find that we were local kids, our ancestors had built half of the village, we were Cornish in blood and bone, and we deserved to grow up in the village that was rich in our heritage. Her persistence paid off, and from the first moment she turned the key in the front-door lock, our home was filled with laughter and the screams of kids we barely knew skidding across the lino-covered front-room floor. The house was part of a council estate that flanked the narrow lane on both sides, twenty-four houses that consisted of two rows of six on one side of the valley and a line of twelve that ran up the side of the other. For some reason mostly elderly folk lived in the twelve houses up the lane. They consisted of ex-tenant farmers turfed, useless, from their farms, ex-dockyardies, and two of our primary-school dinner ladies. On the other side we were mostly families, each with our own stories of love and loss to tell.

From the outside we probably looked like people pushed together because of hard times, dearth and deficiency, but the ties that bound us were not built on that particular foundation but on another common ground. Some things are constructed not on circumstance or education but burnt into the blood and bone of shared heritage, memory and manual work.

Many of our mothers were cleaners, barmaids, carers, workers stitched and embroidered into the fabric of the village, the only jobs available to women without transport.

The men, the ones who stuck around, were fishermen, labourers; they got to travel by boat or were picked up each morning in the back of some builder's Transit. I can't recall much more about them than that, but I know they all liked to drink, all liked to leave the women to pick up every slack cord they'd unravelled. Many, like my dad, just liked to leave. Some returned, but most didn't. I got to know many soon enough when I started to work at a few babysitting jobs. Sometimes they came home early, angry, never had the five pounds to pay me. Some I saw leave hand in hand with their partners, the mothers of their children, but I never saw them come back or anywhere around our estate, and there was one man who took a shower and sat beside me on the couch in his dressing-gown, said he was in no hurry to leave, so I did.

But, still, this community of women was all the family my mother needed. After leaving the isolation of the flat at the far west side of the village, she finally had a front room where she could sit with friends on a settee that didn't double as her bed. She could put the kettle on in a kitchen that wasn't damp, didn't look out onto rock-face but opened up onto a garden ready for our 'all hands on deck' revamp.

Some of these women had been Mum's work friends from the Wide Sea Hotel before we moved in, people she shared a joke with while she vacuumed dirty floors and sweated it out in the hotel laundry. Now she could spend time with them in conversation, sit down and light up, let it all out. Some were new to the estate, daughters of farmers and fishermen, young women who had moved out of Downderry, got pregnant a couple of times, were abandoned by the fathers of their babies and had to move back.

For the first time in my life I began to understand what was meant by the word 'community', and when I think of it now, I see it as an arrangement of intricate shapes and patterns, like the never-ending crocheted baby blankets Mum was always working on, alive on her lap.

Incredible patterns in the natural world can be unexpected when found in surprising places, but it is within these hidden gaps that often the most striking configurations appear: the intricate geometric shapes found in the centre of a smashed rock or the skeleton of a dead leaf. Our community wasn't perfectly pretty, but on close inspection it had all the colour and depth and brilliance of faultless, fractal, natural beauty.

The people who started to orbit around us were like cumulus clouds on the darkest winter's day. They were all dark front, but if you squinted you could just about see the shards of silver, know that, despite everything, the sun was shining somewhere inside. To the untrained eye they were the shape of chaos, all spikes and sharp edges seemingly going nowhere, but those women knew the contour and figure of their lifelines better than anyone. They knew well the plastic spoons they were born with, stuck sideways in their mouths; they knew about back foots and regrets, and what it took to feed and clothe their children on the few quid family allowance and shit jobs, with absolutely no hope of finding a good man or a family to lean into, no 'Bank of Mum and Dad'.

These women are in their late sixties and early seventies now, and because of their sex, and because they had to look after children and take on multiple part-time jobs, they don't have pensions, unlike men or their 'educated' sisters, the ones who went to university, the ones who could afford to move away and live independently, to travel, to buy books, not have to work every God-given hour, the ones who went and got themselves a career.

These women, like my mum, they were what is meant by 'community', and if you were to paint it, create our extended family, it would be a painting that looked just like them.

Laughing, crying, singing, smoking, its title would be *Council House Estate, early 1980s*.

Our community was like a gathering of snowflakes fallen from the four corners of tough luck and gathered up, squashed together, ice melting with empathy and love.

In our cosy kitchen we had a table with two small benches either side and three stools that made their way around the kitchen depending on whose turn it was to smoke near-ish to the open window. Sometimes when something exciting was happening in these women's lives all of the stools would be dragged to the window and others would sit just outside on the four steps that led up to our back garden, smoke in, smoke out, mugs of tea and coffee half drunk in the commotion of 'sorting it'.

'Kick him out,' Mum would say, point-blank, to Mindy, Veronique, Carol. 'Just bag up his stuff and leave it out on the back step.'

Sometimes there would be silence while they thought about what this advice might look like in reality. Sometimes they'd agree, and others, they'd say they loved him, and I'd think about the 'him' and scratch my head with the strangeness of whatever this kind of love was.

I always liked to listen to Mum's advice, and at every opportunity I watched the faces and listened to the voices of the women who used our kitchen as if it were a counselling office. Mum's advice was taken seriously: she'd lived through trauma and separation and had survived it. She'd kicked Dad out before we left the flat, divorced him, and the only thing we knew of him at that point was that he had moved into a flat in Plymouth, the river Tamar separating us for good.

Mum was a winner and every time I heard her advice I felt nothing but pride.

I learnt the art of how people spoke, eavesdropping on those women, learnt to listen out for the gaps in sentences, the soft unsaid and transient silences that when you looked were filled with raised eyebrows, knowing smiles, stuffed fags. Each conversation had the instability of a round of bullets in a gun, words that were held on the tongue like grenades and laughs that went rat-a-tat-tat, explosive. My mum, an accomplished ringmaster in the middle of all this, never aired her dirty laundry with those women. It was my dad who had done that, and some of those women knew our family's history well, two had even slept with my dad, but in our new house my incredible mum, as strong as she was, decided to forgive. Our kitchen became the centre stage for their drama, a ragtag theatre in the round.

This was the stadium where, at the age of eight, I got to love dialogue. How every spoken word had the ability to shock, every uttered word the power to stop, mid-sentence. I swear I learnt everything there was to know about dramatic pauses in those formative years: watching a room full of women, each other as their captive audience, was, for a young writer, the perfect cave into which to hunker down and listen.

'She doesn't think she can stay with him, not after what happened.'

I'd be on my way out to play, or to the fridge for a drink of milk and would suddenly find myself slowing down, turning an ear, listening.

'He said the baby boy wasn't his, but all you have to do is look at it, big fat face, chunky body, then a tiny . . .'

Sometimes I'd pretend I'd forgotten something, head back upstairs and sit on the corner landing, wondering who they were talking about and reminding myself to ask Mum later. It sounded like pretty much everyone in the village was having an affair, and it wasn't just the council-house men and women, but the rich folk up at Buttlegate, the fancy posh estate on the hill that towered above Trelidden Lane. They were at it, too. The difference was they didn't do it in secret but, from what I could glean at such a young age, with wine and nibbles and a bowl of car-keys. I always thought that kind of took the fun out of it.

These women came from all over Cornwall, one from Oldham and two from Birmingham, because of the thing they called council-house swaps. I loved the way they dropped certain letters and replaced them with others as they spoke, made hums and echoes that didn't sound right but were perfect in the pick-up of my musical ear.

Trelidden Lane was not just our home, our cave, but a whole new system of caverns and secrets and people who weren't afraid to speak their mind or reach out to help or be helped.

Our new house was only a couple of minutes' walk up the lane from our village primary school beside the beach, and it didn't take long for the rich kids who lived in Buttlegate and Trerieve estates to see which direction we walked to school from each morning, as they were dropped off in their Jaguars and Land Rovers.

Stigma describes a thing that has no place in our world. It is a shaming word that no human being should endure: the 'you're a waste of space' disgrace and dishonour of being 'other' does irreparable damage. For children it is a confusion of emotion and injustice when you have done absolutely nothing wrong. It is also a lesson in inequality, the first of many to come.

I don't believe all good things come to an end but I do remember my own particular word-punch to the head. Our house was everything to us, and I still don't know why anyone would take that and turn it into a negative, but once the word got around at school that we now lived in Trelidden Lane, it was as if we had been stamped on the forehead. Every kid knew the words for what they had been told we were and it wasn't long before I heard the slur: 'council-house trash'.

I can still see the whispering girls in the classroom, pulling away the boys who were my friends, can still hear their pretend laughter when I walked into the room, jealous because, despite my humble life, I was good at art, good at sport, jealous because I hit puberty first.

I'll always remember years later when my mum was collecting my young brother from school and being asked by one of the posh mothers, 'What do all of you actually burn on your fires up there on the council estate?'

Without blinking an eye, Mum replied, 'Fir cones and old shoes.'

The woman went red and Mum went on her merry way. I love her for that.

What nobody seemed to realise about us council-house trash was that while we were cash poor, we were rich in laughter and tall tales, generosity and love. These women had a way of fighting for each other (sometimes with) and they had a way of connecting despite most of us not owning a phone. The 'Got an extra shift, can you look after the kids?' shriek over the back fence, and the 'Heading up to the shops, you need anything?' shout were their calls of the wild, our tribe.

I was often roped in to entertain a baby while their mother cried on my mum's shoulder, or ran up to the shop with a fiver and a note to plead for Mindy's emergency fags. It didn't matter what job you were pulled into because you saw others happy to help, especially Mum. For me and my sister, it was as if we grew up in the community, like we had always been rooted there, in that council estate. No longer did we live in the shadow of our father in a one-bedroom second-floor flat, but smack-bang in the middle of a new clan of people, our people.

Every day was different on the estate. Some days a mood would descend because of things going down that we weren't supposed to know about, but Mum always told us: somebody slept with someone they shouldn't have, or some bloke had left his wife and moved out. On those occasions I always thought of Dad.

***

Collective intelligence is a way of sharing and creating knowledge towards a community's development and resilience. We working class know we are stronger together; we are a family of many hands, above and below deck. Whales and dolphins bond together for the greater good of their community. They learn from each other in ways that are important to their societies and their survival. Several types of cetaceans live together in close-knit family groups; they pass down knowledge, share songs and hunting techniques. There is also evidence that they provide food for those less able to hunt, their empathy and generosity far-reaching, like my mum's for all the women and their offspring.

As a community we did a lot together, not just the endless hours between shifts and late-into-the-night cups of strong tea, but for us kids it was the shared sandwiches on the beach, and the fields up the back of our estate where we'd play around the ancient lemon-yellow caravan. The older kids from our estate would bunch into it tightly to smoke the contraband cigarettes they'd pinched from the garage down the road, so many of them you could see the smoke rising from the chimney. Beside the van was a Second World War air-raid shelter that soon became our adventure castle. Complete with rubble turrets and overgrown ramparts, the shelter was a place made for gangs and violence and war. It had secret passageways and tar-black dead-end corners where you had to stand barefoot and suffer the cold concrete if the order was given. It had a secret chute, too, that we'd send down messages from the battlement, warnings of imminent invasion scratched in blood, or secret notes scruffily scrawled in lemon juice, which we called invisible ink, and brief, clandestine love letters that contained squashed daisies and campion from the hedgerows.

When Maggie Thatcher decided it was a good idea to sell off council houses with the implementation of the Right to Buy in 1980's Housing Act, she had failed to realise that this would be the end of council-house communities, although she probably didn't care. The policy allowing council tenants to buy their homes at a discount meant that when someone inevitably sold up (often at a profit) a private buyer would move in. This meant that those families living in poverty, needing a roof over their heads, found it increasingly hard to access social housing, a home like the one we moved into in the late 1970s.

Cornwall is still littered with abandoned caravans; it is also starting to fill with them again. On a walk along any coastal path or through fields in any direction you will likely come across someone living among the bracken and briars, off-grid not because of some environmental middle-class yurt-driven want but because of necessity, extreme poverty.

House prices during the coronavirus pandemic rose beyond all proportion to sate a glutinous demand for Cornish homes.

The average property price in Cornwall county is £334,000, the median price is £270,000. The average price increased by £2,500 (1%) between August 2021 and July 2022, nine times the average Cornish earnings. The UK House Price Index shows that Cornwall's house prices have increased faster than the England and Wales average when compared with the same time the year before. Property in Cornwall has always been expensive, in comparison to local average wages, but the pandemic increased difficulties. A surge in 'staycations' meant many private landlords moved into making long lets to affluent Londoners, evicting local tenants in the process.

Working from home during Covid also meant a lot of rich folk from up-country could live their dream of a cottage in Cornwall, while keeping their remote jobs, pushing locals even further towards the fringes of society. As a result, house prices, evictions, homelessness and the demand for social housing have all risen steeply. Meanwhile, the amount of affordable housing has dropped off a cliff, with many families stuck on the precipice of a social-housing waiting list because they have lost their rented home: for the simple reason that their landlord sold up.

What does this all mean for Cornish communities? It means off-season there are entire villages, like the beautiful twin fishing villages of Kingsand and Cawsand, along the coast from Downderry and just the other side of Rame Head, where in winter all of the fishermen's cottages are boarded up, not just because of the battering sea that hits the village hard but because they are holiday homes, second homes, and, except for holidays, nobody is there, the hearth and heart of each house ripped out.

When I think back to my childhood and our council house I think about our community of chaos and care, the small casual acts of kindness and the personalities that were larger than life. I think about the people who washed in and out of my life, and the ones who stayed.

When I was nine, my history started to merge with that of the other kids on the estate and something else happened too: my mum met my stepdad. Until then she had had a string of uninteresting boyfriends, men from the village and surrounding towns whom she mostly met in the pub. There was one called Clive who played bass guitar in a sixties tribute act, and another called Mark, a paramedic, whom she met when a girl from our village, having turned up drunk at the summer carnival as a naked Lady Godiva, fell off her horse and was taken to hospital with Mum by her side. The hippie paramedics didn't believe in chemical pain relief for the girl's suspected broken leg, so they lit a joint, made with weed that Mark's colleague grew in his garden, which they merrily smoked on the way to Plymouth. Mark wanted to marry Mum, but she wasn't ready to marry anyone, and this was great news for us because, although he taught us to surf down at Senna Cove, us girls had decided he was an arsehole.

Another boyfriend called Nate had a Mustang that he drove with me and my sister, Leo our dog, our aunt and uncle who were similar in age to us jammed into the back, along the coast to Millbrook, where we got stuck in the lane and had to be pushed out by lads from one of the local pubs.

Every one of Mum's boyfriends was introduced to us and told we came as a package, including the dog. We had many adventures with Mum who, after ten years of being tied down to my dad, was rediscovering her teenage years and enjoying her new-found freedom in single life. Until she met Catts, who became my stepfather, and offered her a different sort of freedom.

Catts wasn't like the other men: he was kind, trustworthy, a working-class navy lad from Plymouth who came into Mum's life via the Harbour Lights nightclub in Torpoint. A young man of few words (lucky because Mum had loads), he showed up every day, not just physically but as an emotional anchor that kept Mum steady. It wasn't long before he moved in. There were many times when, as I grew older, like every self-respecting kid, I made this man's life a nightmare with my temper tantrums and the obligatory 'you're not my dad' rant, but I can truly say he was one of the very few people I could rely on.

While I grew up on our estate, there was always a part of me, the biggest part, that I kept solely to myself. I was part-wild, detached, an animal that lived mostly in my own remote world down on the beach, but I recognised the big battered heart that beat around me. The voices and the customs and the uneven ground that stretched beneath our feet were mine and theirs, our slowly developing family and

the ever-changing community, circled into the womb of
sand, sea and occasional sun. Hillside Terrace was a place
where I finally started to feel like myself, a beautiful, nurturing habitat where I began to appreciate the world around me
and take solace in everything I had.

9

On the Rocks

At dusk the bay that scoops out, like a wide-winged bird, beneath the fields verging my home is finally quiet. A few driftwood bonfires hitting up the coastline with firefly stars, a few boozy cheers to welcome the dark, but mostly at night peace comes to the stony upper reaches of the beach, the edge of grainy grey sand turned soft and silver in the tiny arched half-arsed moonlight.

My newly discovered beach was a minute's walk from Hillside Terrace, down the lane and onto the path that cut past our primary school. It was a new world in which to explore, no bathing inlets but plenty of rocks to climb, and it wasn't long before I found the perfect outcrop, from then on known as Natasha's rocks. It was a place to think, do nothing except hold my notebook up towards the horizon and draw, my imagination heading out there, then to the lines and contours of the fields as they stopped abruptly at the cliff edge, the turf hanging down like icing, a big bitten chocolate cake.

The beach was a place to sit and watch the colours in the sky fall, the stars come up. At night I could be whoever I wanted to be. No longer was I Barbara's younger daughter, or another strange Carthew character to add to all the others, the ones who, during my short life, had slunk from the village to move to Devon and become reborn Christians. On the beach at dusk I was just another kid, normal enough except for the wondering.

I wondered about the tourists, who every night sat around the barbecues in their fancy chairs surrounded by a circle of windbreakers and umbrellas, no matter the weather, cooking their over-priced steaks and buttering their artisan bread, drinking wine from glasses when everyone knew that glass was banned on the beach. I'd watch them across the wide bay of sand and listen to their gentle bubble of conversation, some songs sung and caught directionless on the wind, echoing. I wondered what their normal lives looked like, what their houses looked like, what jobs they had, and if every family had four corners, two kids and two parents. I wondered if the dads were proper dads, like the men I saw in daylight, the ones who wiped tomato sauce off the kids' faces when they ate hotdogs from their barbecues, the dads who held them gently in the sea, just above the undercurrent, teaching them the basics, life lessons, gifting them the tools to live fulfilling lives, everything going swimmingly.

On the beach in almost complete darkness you can see the map of things. Something about the ocean night tells you all you need to know about direction, route, not just where you're heading but also where you've been, some recognition of well-trodden paths and new itineraries. It's not until you're older that you realise how much the past informs the future, and not just informs it but tells it outright: you're poor, you're working class, this is how your shitty life is going to end up. As a child the map in your hand is ill-defined. Drawn in a light 6H lead pencil, it is less than a whisper. Some things you imagine and you trace them with your fingertip, but mostly your juvenile map is just a mess of lines and vague shade, the faint outline of some semblance of future, but then your hand moves across it, and your destiny is rubbed, a sea of grey, storm-warning.

I know all about the map of my surroundings, the way the bay bent in a beautiful semi-circle and how in the height of summer the sea sloped ever so slightly in a certain light. There were moments when I felt like I lived in the centre of the earth, an eye looking inwards, complete. Sometimes I tried to draw it, illuminate my setting through observation, but it never quite worked.

Drawing for me was a prequel to writing. I was good at sketching but it frustrated me. I always wanted more than I could see, wanted to reach into the landscape and move things about, rearrange hedges and trees and push the ocean back. As a child my mind was boundless in flight, skimming the comforting waves with stories that were yet to make it onto the page, positive in my imagination, contemplation spreading out into the bay, all the things that I could do, maybe, now that we were safe in our new home.

Thoughts good and bad drifted in and around like salt sea air. Memories: those that shone inside me and those that seared me. Flashes of colour and then words, some marked for ever in my mind. Two words in particular.

Sitting out on the rocks that flanked the swimmers' cove in the centre of Downderry, my home village in Cornwall, was where I first heard it. I tell myself to remember this much and then forget it, that sentence: sharp, strident words that stuck in deep and twisted like a fine filleting knife, 'the haves and the have-nots'. A proud Cornish family never thinks of their *gwedren*, their glass, as half empty. Why would we? We live in the most beautiful part of the world, have the sea in which to swim, the fields from which we feed and the sky to which we dream, but that's not the whole story. It's not even the start of the story.

Every year when summer arrives and the sun pulls closest to the earth, it brings with it half the country en route to Cornwall. The population increases by 210,000, many of them in colourful surf-shorts and expensive wetsuits, with blow-up paddleboards and wind-breakers tied to the roofs of their spot-less Range Rovers. They park in laneway passing-places or drive down onto the beach, oblivious to the people who live and work there, oblivious to the nature they destroy, the environment that they congest with the buckets and spades and body-boards bought new each year and left by the side of the council bins at the end of the season.

To a young girl growing up in the eighties these people were a breed apart from me completely. They were not my people, not my kind of animal, but strange city creatures come to sit and sprawl and swim in places that, to a young working-class kid, weren't spaces meant for them.

These creatures stomped across our small coastal village in packs, their tongues and lips forever licking at something, their pelts slick with sweat and the oil of bottled coconuts. Animals but the over-domesticated kind, so used were they to comfort and loping after their own needs they never noticed the chil-dren that inhabited the county's council estates or the folk living in unregulated off-grid caravan sites that sat on the wild fringes of Cornwall, not until the day they noticed me.

When I was growing up, the rocks that circled our bay were always where I was happiest. Tucked away from the noise of crying babies and barking dogs, I could dip myself into rock-pool life and suddenly feel myself slipping down deep into the warm shallow water. Happiest hidden within a world populated with blennies, beadlet and snakelocks anemones and the fringe seaweed that housed the secretive hermit crabs, my favourite. With my age shifting closer to nine, coupled with the recent move to our council house in an area of the village I barely knew, play had slowly started to be replaced with a curiosity that was hard to sate. I mostly liked my own company, sunk deep in concentration, my imagination so limitless that some days it left the coast and stretched out across continents.

Every weekend I liked to get up early and head towards the beach as soon as I'd had breakfast to start my adventure, but that particular summer's day I'd woken up late and, for some reason, I knew as soon as I walked down the squash-guts path, which ran alongside the primary-school playing field and down onto the beach, that the day wouldn't go the way I wanted.

I stood on the sand and looked right towards the main beach, the silver sand already tiled with bright stake-a-claim towels, and I looked to the left, an area of almost pure rock that I knew, by noticing the outgoing tide, would be full of sea-life. I felt in my back pocket and pulled out my pack of coloured pencils and my jotter, the one I kept for recording nature. Even though I could see other children playing there, it was an area of the cove I was yet to explore so I went to it.

There were moments when I sat out on the rocks that I thought perhaps I was somebody: I could do anything, be a writer, a naturalist, no matter how many kids played around me. Submerged in my watery domain I took comfort in their splashes and screams of joy, but separate in my solitary, made-up world, I could explore as I wished, my pencil and notebook in hand, until, that is, the day I heard three simple words.

'She's a have-not.'

I sat back against the rocks and wiped my damp hands on my denim shorts. 'What?'

I wondered if they were talking to me and looked around, hoping to catch the eye of someone else.

'We're not talking to you,' laughed a girl close to my age. 'We're talking about you.'

I nodded, shrugged, and acted like this was an okay situation, whatever. I returned my gaze to the rock-pool where I had been playing, hoping they would continue walking towards the main beach and leave me alone. I didn't want to bother about them, didn't want to feel the increasing cold sweat and the beat of my heart that had suddenly started to speed up.

'You live in the council houses, don't you?' asked a boy. 'Up the lane there.'

How did they know?

'Our cousins live up Buttlegate, up on the hill,' he continued.

I knew well where Buttlegate was: it was the field my great-grandfather used to own, a field gambled away in a game of poker, so the story went. It was full of huge modern houses now, nicknamed the Cornish Hollywood Hills.

'Our mum said we're not to play with the kids from the council estate,' said an older girl. 'She says you're rough.'

I didn't know what rough was, not properly, but these city kids were starting to annoy me. I wanted to tell them to go away, leave me alone. My heartbeat started to slow, which meant I was about to say something I shouldn't, and I wished I knew how to swear in Cornish, my native language.

I stood up and walked towards them, stepping from the rocks as one shouted, 'Run,' everyone laughing, 'the have-not's coming.'

***

That day I learnt the difference between shop-bought and hand-me-downs, and I returned to my rocks to think about this, realising that I and a few of the other council-house kids were the only children to have the imagination to play with flotsam. I understood that the difference between bare feet and shoes made from wetsuits went pocket deep.

I'd never taken much notice of the tourists until then, the emmets as we Cornish call them. Nobody from the village spoke to them and we expected the same level of courtesy that they would never, ever speak to us. That day, happy in my thoughts and secure in the knowledge that we had a new home away from bad memories, was the day I heard the term 'have-not'. I've never forgotten it.

That word will always make my heart lurch and my fists grip fight-tight into my pockets. I should have looked around at my surroundings, the sand and the sea and the cliffs, the routine riches that called out to me. I should have shouted after them, 'Everything, I have everything.'

It's funny: as a child you don't coin yourself anything, good, bad or indifferent, you just are. An animal of your own choosing, you walk and crawl and climb, and no more so than an animal born and raised in the country.

I was not wild in the feral sense, but I had a wild mind, a head for heights and fights and the will to see things through to my own way of understanding, but from that moment on I'd heard all I needed to know to understand my true bearing. In the eyes of others I was missing something. I was without.

I know that what I felt was connected to the thing in me when I had first stood in front of my mother to protect her from our bullying father. I was all about the interrogation, the processing of data, the argument. Justice, injustice, it fits and sparks within me, like nervous electrical blood, those words spat at me from a group of faceless kids who then ran off, their words slowly stinging and sinking in like tiny burn marks on my skin.

I wasn't worth bothering with.

Blue sky, forever ocean, but still, it seems, I didn't have one damn thing.

***

The widespread effect of tourism on small Cornish communities goes marrow deep. Like two sides of the same coin, the side the tourists see is colourful, warm, serene, but the other side, the side we locals experience most of the year, is cold with a draught splintered straight through. It is unforgiving, demanding, painted in all the shades of one colour. Night or day, it settles at a constant boulder grey.

The growth of tourism has an economic, environmental and social effect on counties across the UK, but the doubling of population every summer in Cornwall transforms our lives completely. With at least five million visitors a year to Cornwall, it's no surprise that this 'over-tourism' has led to pressure on infrastructure, tensions with local communities and diminished resources. The overcrowding and congestion disrupt bus-service schedules and make public transport unreliable. Fuel and food prices rise as wealthier tourists provide incentive to local shop-keepers. Seasonal jobs bring in a wave of people for the summer, displacing locals and shifting the culture and traditions of the area. Resources are used to within an inch of exhaustion and then, suddenly, everyone is gone. Nothing left but the plastics piled up in heaps at the perimeter of beaches and the tarmac on the lanes pulled up, replaced with McDonald's packaging and beer cans. Our overstretched police force, hospitals and the RNLI let out a sigh of relief as the last daredevil hiker, non-surfer, weak swimmer is sent back and those of us who aren't rich business owners, the have-nots, are left to count the cost, clear up.

That's before you consider the damage inflicted on the natural environment, from footpath erosion and litter to the destruction of natural habitats to build hotels. Each season, the economic smash and grab of tourism increases the level of pollution and leaves a large carbon footprint in its shadow. From noise pollution and congestion, to additional burdens on water and energy resources, the county is battered by environmental stresses for months every year. While autumn brings a period of recovery, the impact on soil erosion, the harm to ocean health by over-polluting, and the natural habitat loss put pressure on endangered species that causes permanent damage.

Managing high visitor numbers in a sustainable way has become increasingly important because it is the quality of the natural environment that reinforces our visitor economy. Record numbers of people want to visit Cornwall every year, and at the same time, we know that it is more urgent than ever to protect and restore our precious ecosystems.

This far-westerly landscape, the moors, the rivers and hills and the two surges of ocean, is my home. It is where my life began, where my ancestors' sweat and blood is present in every granite tor and pebble. It belongs to us Cornish and to every-one who has chosen to live here, yet every summer we are forced to consider that it doesn't, the times when the tourists arrive, not the ones in tents and caravans who move unobtru-sively from corner to corner, but the disrespectful rich ones who spread themselves across our land and do what they please because of one thing: money.

The effect that the influx of millions of tourists has had on Cornwall's roads, crime, on our council and police services and even our water bill, is not new, but in recent years it has become bigger. This is down to four things: people are holi-daying in Cornwall more than ever before because of the Covid-19 pandemic; more people from out of county are living here in long lets; more people have bought property here as an investment; and more people are building properties because the government has made it easier for developers to do what they like with minimal regulations.

***

I walked back across the rocks towards home and for the first time in my life I was careful not to slip. I imagined all eyes on me, waiting for me to do something stupid, something only a poor kid would do, and I kept my head down, the way you were meant to in order to keep your anger in, but it didn't work. When I hit the hot sand and into the gob of tourists I couldn't help but look up to see every one of them snapping like teeth, the whites of their eyes drunk on heat and the burn of their skin, like gleaming gums, grimacing. I pushed through the insular 'put a stake in the ground' windbreakers that they smacked into the sand every morning in a rush for land, and I thought about our council-house community, how when we went down onto the beach we sat in a group, how we shared our blankets and towels, that we didn't feel the need to break the coastal wind, only bread, together.

As I passed them I realised that this was my home turf and they had stepped onto it, a realisation that slowly dawned on me, a drift of thought I couldn't shake, an insight into my life that suddenly made me incredibly angry.

When I got home that day I was made whole again.

So much of what it means to be Kernewek is about the tiny trinkets of our nature that go unnoticed, the mute pride and the stones we never leave unturned. I knew that those mean emmet kids were jealous – jealous because I had beauty and serenity on my doorstep, jealous because I didn't have to run around in a panic to find it. We didn't have a lot and, more than that, our cash-strapped parents didn't have the fear those rich kids' parents had, the fear of losing their hoards, of not having the latest diving kit, the fear of brushing their immaculate four-wheeler into a hedge and getting dust on it.

We had a larger-than-life family, a community that the tourists would never understand, and it had nothing to do with money or what you did or didn't have, but everything to do with love, compassion and understanding, and for us kids it simply meant imagination, adventure and wild, unbridled danger.

10

Stone's Throw

There are things that exist independently of money and what can be bought, the things that cannot be taught but drift in on the wind and exist in the earth and foundation of a community.

Creativity was gifted to me from birth by my artistic mother but it wasn't until we moved to our council house and the world of new experiences and adventures opened up to us that I discovered the ingenuity of play. Play that wasn't just with fumbling fingers and mud-stomping feet, but living and breathing stories that lived in and out of our imaginations, a place where we could run and jump and break free, kids alone but for our distant mother's call.

As children we were always encouraged to go outside and play, sometimes because it was housework day, or there was some kind of community crisis, but mostly it was because our parents worked long, irregular hours. Whoever was around on our estate kept an eye out for the younger kids, and if us older children, the ones over the age of eight, needed to get hold of their mum, one of the houses at the back had a phone and the numbers of every building and business in our village where all our mums worked - the shop, the two pubs, the hotel, the butcher's and John Fowler's holiday park. They even had the numbers of the arcade and chip shop in our neighbouring village of Seaton.

This casual approach to childcare was not unusual in working-class communities, where the kids were watched from windows and every door was open, inviting. There was always music playing or a play on Radio 4 blasting from someone's house on our little estate, a way for us to have an audible base to touch, even if we didn't realise it. How different we must have seemed in contrast to the posh kids, children we barely saw except in the backs of their parents' cars, miserable faces being transported to the outlying towns for dance class, karate class, bloody boring chess club. Sometimes they looked at us warrior kids, staffs in hand and grubby knees, playing at life the way I read in my adventure books.

There always seemed to be a handful of us sitting, legs dangling, out on the low wall that ran the length of Trelidden Lane. Sometimes we took off our shoes and paddled in the stream if we were told not to go far, a pretty trickle of water that we turned into a dam with rocks so that we had our own pool in which to pan for gold with a garden sieve. If it was a weekend day or the holidays, we were allowed to go down onto the beach or up to the high-stepped field that was only a stone's throw from our estate and ran all the way to the top of the lane. For some reason I always considered the beach to be mine and mine alone. It was a place I visited when I got bored of the others or after tea, a secret, sacred place. The field next door to our estate was something different, a place to share.

Many years before we arrived at Hillside Terrace, the field that stretched far and wide in our imaginations had always been earmarked for housing development. For a long time it remained as it was, four huge steps of earth that went high into the sky, like a giant staircase, at least six metres high and six metres wide. It was a thick-wedged field that lifted from the stream-bed and up towards the potato fields that spread across the utmost reaches of the village.

Each tier had its own curiosity attached to it that drew us kids in, like a portal to another world, a world of mayhem that was brutal and beautiful and mysterious.

The bottom rung was home to the dilapidated yellow caravan, sunk into the claggy earth a long time ago, part man-made part nature-claimed. For a time that little yellow trailer was my sister and her year-seven boyfriend Paul's headquarters, where they made plans and presided over the rest of us younger kids.

The second ridge was where war really commenced, our battleground where we'd stand at one end with our hands on our hips and have the kids that weren't from our estate stand at the other. These were the nowhere-land children, the ones who didn't come from the fancy rich estates or our council estate but from the farms and cottages that dotted in and around both villages, kids who had been invited down to our neck of the bay for a bit of play and a lot of fighting.

This was one of my favourite contests, based on the traditional game of Red Rover, where you shouted and chanted at the top of your lungs to summon someone from the opposite team, but our game was heavily built around attack. We'd throw rocks at the other team members until somebody fell over, somebody bled, or somebody ran home crying, shouting that they'd return with their dad.

The third rung in our sky-high field was reserved for nature. It was mostly filled with gorse and stingers and briars and was strictly reserved for hunting snakes. Our communal obsession with snakes and our self-identified title as snake-wranglers was legendary, and many hours were spent standing around with our socks pulled up snap-tight and our hands gripped around a sharpened two-pronged stick ready to 'trap the serpent's head'. I don't think anyone ever saw a snake except the tiny beautiful slow-worms, but it was an exciting game, a game loaded with rumours and bluff.

'Last week,' said Niall, 'George said he saw a grass snake.'

'George is a bloody liar,' I said. 'He int never seen anythin' bigger than a slow-worm.'

'Earth worm,' laughed Lana.

We all kicked at the dusty auburn earth, looking for rocks to overturn.

'Slow-worms are cool,' said Lana, 'if you can keep hold of 'em.'

'Slippery,' said Dan, her younger brother.

'No they int, stupid, wiggly is all.'

'Adder!' shouted Niall as he lifted a large flat rock from out of the ground; it was where my sister had read that they lived.

We all dropped hard to our knees and moved closer, forgetting about our sticks, safety, bites.

'Grab it,' shouted Lana. 'Grab his sneaky tail.'

'Don't.' I pushed Lana out of the way. 'It'll come off!'

'Good,' said Dan. 'I want a snake's tail.'

'I want the whole thing, finders keepers.'

When Niall crawled into the briars I went after him, followed by the others. We waited and waited, the gritty earth making dents in our bare knees, our breath hot and sticky on the backs of each other's necks.

'You see anythin'?' I asked Niall.

'Not yet.'

'You see the adder?' asked Dan.

'Fucksake, if I did I'd say.'

We all took a deep breath. This was it, for definite, life and death.

I let the others push in alongside me and we waited, the day suddenly turned to night in the wraparound undergrowth.

'Ouch!' shouted Niall suddenly. 'Fuck!'

'What is it?' we shouted in unison.

'Fuckin' nettles.'

We all laughed, reversed, stood and brushed down our scabby knees, game over.

The top and final rung of our play field was where the horses lived, and while none of us rode, because that was what posh people did, we'd line up on the fence that cordoned off that part of the field, eat apples and feed them to the horses, the fruit that in autumn we'd steal from a garden in the centre of the village that you could only access by crawling through a wall of palm trees in the memorial garden, and then through a hole we had made in the fence.

In some ways growing up in poverty gifted us with wings, an ethereal lift that granted us the ability to soar and assemble ideas without thought. Play was exciting, dangerous. We were resourceful and astute, crafty, and we adapted to each day by not focusing on what we didn't have, but what we did. We learnt from nature, but also used nature to our advantage. It was all things and everything we believed in.

This sense of adaptability and ingenuity did not just live in the minds of us children, but was the essence of our working-class parents and relatives too, and it manifested itself in the form of our own special brand of shabby grass-roots culture.

Before I was born my parents and two of their friends founded the Downderry and Seaton art exhibition in our village's Working Men's Club, something that my mum continued to be a part of for many years. I remember the story of its inception, an idea written on the back of a torn beer mat, and how my dad and a few other men spent several hours constructing the boards that would hang the art, boards made out of plywood that they sawed and painted and meticulously drilled with a million neatly aligned holes so that the paintings could be hung freely.

Me and my sister spent many years stuffing the invites into envelopes and running around both villages pushing them into letterboxes, seeing who would be the first to empty their carrier-bag.

Growing up we took part in many creative pursuits, including the Christmas pantomime, the summer carnival and any produce-growing or gardening competition going. All of these things were run by our working-class community, mostly planned in the pub by a few, but with the many different people who lived in Downderry and Seaton firmly in mind. My people had no money and very little spare time, but their energy and lust for life, despite being born dirt-poor, was the mainstay memory of my growing up on that estate. They cared about what community meant to them and, more importantly, what it would go on to mean to us children.

There are two sides to every story and no more so than when you think about what play means to the rural poor and what it meant to the visiting city rich. As kids, our play was always small, collective, unassuming, but the visiting tourists' idea of fun was large, disruptive and always incredibly loud. If they weren't swerving into our bay on speedboats and jet-skis they were scuttling across the beach dragging their chairs and inflatables and barbecues, everything garish, out of place, at odds with the beautiful landscape.

In 2022 nothing much has changed, except the toys; the jet-skis and the boats have gotten bigger, bolder, and everyone seems to own a paddleboard, supersized, of course. Cornwall has become all about the adventure, the speed of things, when everyone who truly loves it knows it is best experienced immersed in the tranquillity of nature, measured silence.

It didn't cost us poor kids one penny to play. We didn't have to buy stuff to immerse ourselves in the countryside, the fields or the beach, we just did it.

When it comes to culture, our Cornish ethos is calm, collected, mostly quiet. We do things with Kernewek pride, our heritage worn like a tattoo of honour inked onto our chests. It is a tiny, intricate design, nothing much to anyone else, but we know it's there, a tribute to our legacy.

Rich folk culture has money thrown at it. It is cultivated and grown from the seeds of others' ideas, usually us working class, because our customs and ways are authentic, genuine, true. Those who aren't Cornish, the blow-ins and the emmets, like nothing more than to plunge head first into our Celtic country philosophy, and while their interests are well-meaning, their idea of idyllic can often disturb our culture. Our traditions are strange: they are dirty and messy and mostly make no sense at all. Don't ask us why certain things are the way they are, they just is.

In the country there's no doubt that there is a lack of cultural institutions. Therefore exposure to creativity beyond your village or market town is the norm for many. The availability and distribution of cultural funding has diminished since the withdrawal of EU financial aid and access to support structures in most places outside the main urban areas, meaning many kids who come from low socioeconomic backgrounds are losing out. The lack of money is the greatest barrier to accessing culture, because the bottom line is you need spare cash to travel to a venue, pay for tickets to galleries, the theatre, concerts, buy laptops. Even decent broadband coverage costs when trying to access creativity that exists 'out there'.

I am incredibly grateful for my community, not just those working-class people who came together to ensure we kids never missed out, but the gift of freedom that they allowed us to have. The fields behind held our heads in imagination, the ocean in front held our hearts in love and the coastal path between always held our spirit for adventure.

★★★

One last memory, a hot summer's day and the usual gang of Dan, Paul, Stevie, Lana, Niall, George, me and a few strays picked up along the way decided we'd set off on the coastal walk so we could spy on the nudists over at Claydon beach.

The walk was long, and because we'd made the decision to go while playing down on the beach, none of us were wearing shoes, and we had no water or food. But, still, it was early autumn, and we merrily picked the ripe sea-salted blackberries as we went on our way, imagining how we would sneak up on the nudists. The path that leads easterly towards the beach along Rame Head is high, and there are places where you could easily slip, the loose rock and grit crumbling under our hot blistered feet, but still we continued onwards until we came to the knot of trees that led to St German's Hut, the ruin that used to be an aristocratic hunting lodge. By then we were getting tired, and the excitement of naked tourists was waning.

'I'm hungry,' said Stevie, the youngest in our gang.

'Just eat more berries,' I told him.

'They're making me feel sick.'

'Just shut up Stevie. Don't you want to see them?' asked George.

'Who?'

'The naked people.'

Stevie shrugged. 'I int bothered.'

'Sex,' said Paul. 'Don't you want to see sex?'

'No.'

'Why not?' asked Niall.

'Cus I've seen my dogs do it, it's nasty.'

Some of us older kids agreed that when dogs did it, it looked nasty, and when our cat did it one time, it sounded like murder, but we wanted to see humans do it anyway.

We passed through the overgrown garden of the hut, which used to be a large house, and down the steep cliff where you had to hang by a rope in order to reach the sand.

Each one of us took turns to swing like Tarzan, calling out words of encouragement until the last one jumped the remaining couple of feet. Together we stood and put our hands on our knees, catching our breath until words started to form and we composed our plan. First we would hide behind the rocks. Next we would set off in twos and threes so it looked like we weren't together (even though we were all around the same age, tanned, barefoot, and wore sun-bleached shorts and T-shirts), and we would stroll along the beach and casually look up.

Me and Lana were the first to go, taking our time to look at the sea, pointing out imaginary boats, laughing and smiling, like two ten-year-old girls taking a turn on a nudist beach was the most normal thing in the world.

Behind, the boys had started to move off, and the image of us kids walking like we were on a school trip will always stay with me. The sight of us would have seemed odd, really odd.

We saw a few boobs, bums and willies that day, but no sex, and when we reached the towering jut of rock known as Devil's Point, our disappointment grew deeper when we saw that the tide was out, and we could have accessed the nudist beach easily by staying on the beach.

This was the innocent bliss of childhood, the joy of coming together in a moment of us, what it was to be local, Cornish, working class.

When we council-house kids weren't playing in the fields or cutting through them on the coastal path, we were working in them, and while we didn't realise it at the time, at the age of eight, nine, ten, we were preparing for the future, a future filled with hard, tough graft.

11

Common Ground

My mum always said this was potato-picking weather. Thirty years since the slip and trip of childhood and still it's easy to close my eyes and let all the early-autumn weather become wind and sink in the bitter taste of sea salt, the sweet smell of manure turned into earth. My memory circles, closes, returns fully formed, landed on common ground. The sudden drop in temperature has me falling feet first into the fields of my childhood, shrinks me down to the size of tomboy, young writer, as clear as any laidback Cornish day, dressed for the chill in jeans and hat, and a hundred homemade itchy-fucker grandmother jumpers ready to pull off, strip down, because Mum said this: it's what you do in September, potato-picking weather.

The uphill ride inland from our coastal village in the back of some borrowed Land Rover: it was like we were travelling to a far-off land, the excitement of doing something other than nothing seeding and blooming wild inside us. We sat squashed together and tried not to breathe in the smell of each other's early breakfast, trying not to feel the melancholy pull that meant the end of summer, the start of school, structure. For some it brought the twenty-mile round-trip bus ride to

124

secondary school in Torpoint, and for all of us the shame of hand-me-down uniforms.

'When you goin up?' asked Dan, the boy from the back of our estate.

'Next year.' I shrugged. I was only ten but already felt the drag of the inevitable, the school 'out there' beyond the comforting walls of our village.

'Next week,' said a kid from Seaton. I'd seen him around, hanging out at the slots in the holiday camp, but I didn't know his name.

'It's shit,' a few older voices from the back said in unison. 'We int ready to go back yet.'

Someone's mum in the front seat told us to be quiet and she passed back a packet of wine gums, saying they were her favourite, but she was willing to donate them to shut us up. It worked.

I shifted my position so I could catch a glimpse of the sky, another late-summer-early-autumn morning when, if you forgot the cooler temperature, you could look out at the flowers in the hedgerows and imagine it was still summer, full on. I closed my eyes and sucked my blackcurrant sweet and gave myself over to the moment, potholes in the road and the buzz of safety, in my blood, my muscles, my bones, the excitement of being, existing in the moment of rural working-class living.

Most of us enjoyed the couple of weekends we gave up to the cause that was potato-picking. Like a rite of passage, we village kids were meant for this. We were meant to learn about agriculture, the cultivation of plants and livestock for sustenance, we were meant to know what to do with our hands from down here, kids of the countryside.

Without knowing it we would go on to learn about foods, fibres, fuels and raw materials, know all there was to know about crops without ever looking it up. This was education without the need for teachers and books, it was learning as you went along, the sweet smell of spuds on the air and the colour of their skins, the snippets of conversation between farmers that made you slow down in order to listen, words that meant good or bad; temperature, weather, maturity, storage, transport. I couldn't wait for the Land Rover to slow and pull into the designated, crop-heavy field, couldn't wait to hear the skid of brakes and the sound of doors slamming, like a circus coming fresh into town, we were loud, eager, full of bravado, wonder, country-kid swagger. The thought of school kept at bay at least for one more day.

The bleak routine of having to leave nature's nuanced nuggets, those pearls of wisdom in order to endure a future of studying the bullying din of nothing was too much, they were the things I didn't care to remember. All I ever wanted to do was sit out in the fields and think, draw, eventually write. I would never be a farmer, but my passion for the Kernewek earth beneath my feet meant I dug and dug until I pulled up unfamiliar words: *aras* was Cornish for plough, *bethan* for meadow, *falh* was an easy kid word for scythe; *godegh* was my favourite – it meant lurking-place, a secret haven for wildlife. Ancestral handouts just for me, these sweet new words were treats to be sucked from the soft, brackish dust, savoured.

In the eighties, girls weren't allowed to choose fishing or farming as a career and poor girls from council houses weren't allowed to choose much of anything at all. There were the cleaning jobs, of course, and in our village you had a good mix of those: the hotel, the many holiday homes and the giant posh people's houses (my mum did all three) and you could chance your arm (and your back) at the harbourside in the neighbouring town of Looe, filleting fish and cracking crabs, but as a young kid I was only ever interested in living organisms: the rock-pool blennies and the spider crabs and the compass jellyfish that turned in the warm incoming current, like yoyos. I was interested in the lizards and the adders and the slow-worms that hid in the sanctuary of the cool mute earth, beneath the purple slate-stones that stepped through the fields and ran across the headland and down towards our bay.

How many of us children rode out on those early-autumn mornings year upon year, sitting on each other's laps, looking out at the verges, singing shanty songs and grabbing at the wildflower hedgerows when we slowed: the going-over pink campion and the sticky goose grass and devil-darts that were ammo for throwing, the stubborn cow-parsley and fingering foxgloves that still held on to something, some sense of summer without the traffic jams, the tourists gone and our Wild West world finally returned to us. We were the kids with sticks for guns and more smarts than all the posh emmets, the city kids who never knew about the badger paths that meant shortcut or that rosehips gave the best itch down the back of the neck, until they got it.

Potato-picking weather: the smell of summer still warm, familiar, yet biting cold, when we got to the fields we could see it had made its mark in the peaks and troughs, the fine dust of dip-down early frost. You'd swear we'd never been anywhere in our lives if you saw us jump from the trucks and vans. It was mostly true. We were council-house kids brought up well but in poverty. We knew the meaning of hard graft, what it meant to stand in those furrows and bend to the rhythm of work. We would never own the land, but for one or two weeks in September we were kings and queens of the spud field, lifting the tubers from the ground like they were jewels to put in our imaginary crowns.

How little we knew then, but how much was subliminally learnt, through our fingers, the glimpse and blink of an eye, our minds on the simplistic act of physical labour, hard grind, how little we knew of the lives that stretched like storm clouds out on the blue horizon ahead of us. There were no prospects out there for me, no notes in the pretty basket on the fireplace lintel where Mum collected up the lecky 50ps and the coppers for Sunday's ice-cream van, ten pence each if we were lucky, high-balls. No prospects back then, yet I was the last to know it, my back fixed, my hands either in dirt or water, it didn't matter; how the mind, despite common belief, never really shuts down to the mindless drill of domesticity but lifts and trips and soars into the ether. The places I was going to visit, the stories I was going to tell, the books I read and was starting to believe I could write despite the weight of pebbles in my pockets and the lone-liness of backwater life, no way to expand, except the vista I could see, the one that sat pressed up against my childhood, that bastard blue window. Despite the fog and mizzle I imagined the colour of some other clearer future, the most beautiful azure shores and the green of freedom fields, the security of commu-nity and the peace that existed in simplicity, our happiness not because we came from nothing, but despite it.

Beneath a sky-high explosion of black and white, the chess-play crows and the gulls that confetti-fed the firmament with fine feathers and cries, where we'd stick ourselves into the bramble and briar hedges and like the start of a long race, we'd find our mark, get set and go down into the rhythm of so many folk before us, picking and throwing – and then the sprint to the slatted crates and the tip of each carrier, the thrill of the 50ps that waited for us once each one was filled, full to the brim.

I can still feel the crack of the cold pink flinty earth, and the comfort of each peachy potato as it teetered within the palm of my hand, their beany underbellies warm from yesterday's sun and the rub of mud, the smell of goodness, the taste of salt and late summer at the back of my tongue, and the sting of youth, lip-licked, eager to please. Easy come but so long gone, like a dream with the bad bits taken out and spat, every day of early childhood paced out, barefoot, shouting and flirting with the future like we knew our destiny was this, mud on our boots and the stain of blackberry juice on our mouths, the drip of new words learnt on the wind: fuck you, fuck off, fuck it. I knew the meaning of words in those formative years better than I knew the kids who said them. Words were music, art, they were the bird bones I kept in a tin, the silver and white gull feathers that meant peace and the flint stones collected off the beach that, when smashed together, made fire, heaven; words were for whispering, not shouting. They were for long autumnal mornings, thinking stories.

The best, as I remember, was when the sea mist finally lifted and Mum shouted for us to take off our top jumper, first layer; when the sun hitched high up on the easterly hills she'd shout for us to take off the other, the heat of day hot on our heels, our backs. All the while I could think of nothing else but those boxes of spuds and the 50p pieces lining up, and they weren't for the lecky meter or the gobbling rented telly like Mum's would be, but all for me, another notepad or a fancy pen with the special ink like the ones in the old Sunday-afternoon films, my dream of being a writer not yet established but lingering around the edges of my consciousness, no matter how many holes I made in my jeans as I knelt to pick up insects and sat and lay down to cloud-watch, no matter how much dirt I had beneath my fingernail, how it slipped beneath my skin and muddied my blood, out in the fields aged eight, nine, ten was where I was happiest, where life began.

We worked all through the morning, through lunchtime, stopping briefly for the slurp of milky tea and warm flat-splat jam sandwiches that, because they were stored in Dad's old plastic packed-lunch box, tasted of his bacon butties, and we went back to work until our backs hurt and our knuckles went wet to the bone, but despite all that we laughed, and even better, our mothers laughed: a community brought together not just through poverty but the belief in the land, common ground. This was a place to grow a part of ourselves back better, if we could make the best of what it was to live in the country in the eighties, late-summer-early-autumn potato-picking weather.

It's funny but when you're a kid you don't think of yourself as disadvantaged, and growing up in one of the most beautiful parts of the world as I did, many people would say I was lucky. But disadvantage in rural areas is often hidden, with the widely applied statistical indicators used to identify disadvantage perceived as inappropriate in rural places.

Growing up in our village community we didn't think about the jobs that were on offer to us. The range of opportunities was limited, and some of our older brothers already worked on town building sites, at sea or in the fields full time, while our sisters worked as cleaners, just that.

The nature of work in rural areas for us working class has always been closely linked to the natural world and the turn of the seasons; whether daffodil harvesting in early spring, fishing for mackerel at dawn and dusk in a June high tide, lifting potatoes in September and broccoli and cabbage in winter. Whilst during the short holiday season, those of us locals who lived in towns relied on the hospitality industry; waiting on tables in restaurants and cafés, serving behind bars and standing in field gateways, fleecing fivers from unsuspecting tourists for a two-hour park.

The seasonal nature of rural employment still causes problems for many. Gang labour, for example, is incredibly poorly paid with pitiable working conditions, and here in Cornwall employers' provision of housing (tied housing) has meant some workers being trapped in unsatisfactory employment with no job-security, no holiday pay and no sick pay. The bottom line is that if you lose your job, you lose your home.

In 2022 many farms in Cornwall have had to install caravans to house fruit, vegetable and daffodil pickers. It comes as the housing crisis continues to rage on, with farms already struggling to recruit seasonal workers due to a combination of Brexit, foreign-worker policies and a lack of housing.

Growing up we simply accepted the things we knew we would never be able to change, like each generation before us, we learnt to manage our expectations at mud level, lower than low.

The journey home from the fields was always the best. It meant cans of cold lemonade and silly songs with the windows down, the lanes finally free of the emmets, and the only traffic the men coming home from a day's fishing, all of us together, being, the moment ours for the dreaming, if only for a minute.

In many ways those early-autumn mornings spent potato-picking set the tone for how we would cope with hardship and poverty in our late teens and early twenties – the single fact that we would always work for someone else, would always be the first to put our backs to hard graft, knees bent, hands in the dirt for a few quid, everything we knew of ourselves and each other, hardship, community, poverty, forever shared on that brutal, beautiful common ground.

12

Pocket Full of Grit

How humble the 50p piece. How that pretty coin meant the difference between cooked or uncooked food for tea growing up, how for so many of us it meant hot or cold water to wash, clean or dirty clothes for school. This sometimes elusive coin on our small council estate was what every single one of us had in common. The humble 50p piece was not about choices, it was about subsistence. For every single reason, that big silver blossom became the focal point for much of our daily existence, and our lives were often taken up with the hunt for it.

Growing up, a day didn't go by when we didn't ask Mum or she asked us if we had enough 50ps in the house. We'd look in the spare-change basket that sat on the mantelpiece and pull out the stool to climb and feel around on top of the lecky meter, shout, 'Got one!' if our fingers stumbled across a cold heptagon, and if I got to sit long enough on someone else's sofa, I'd always slip my hand down the sides of the cushions, in the off-chance that I might find a rogue one.

On our estate 50ps were the best thing ever, better than gold-dust. Simply put, they meant electricity, life force, but to all us estate kids they meant something much more: they meant competition, rivalry and the rush home from primary school to push one into the slot at the back of the rented TV so we could watch *Grange Hill*.

The war for 50ps that ran throughout my childhood in our small corner of Downderry was legendary: we would argue over them, haggle over them, and go into battle if our mothers told us to, just for one. Despite community spirit running deep in our veins, we Trelidden Lane kids learnt early how to shake our heads and apologise if someone came knocking with five ten-pence pieces. It was usually Niall from up the back.

When the knock on the door didn't stop I looked through the side window to see him standing and waiting, agitated.

'What?' I asked.

'You got any fifties?' He smiled. 'Mum said to say please. We just need one.'

I stood against the door jamb and shook my head, 'Don't reckon we've got any left for ourselves, just one for the TV and one for the lecky slot. You tried up the road, Bod's place?' I looked back into the front room. *Newsround* was on.

If Mum was home she'd shout my full name, Natasha Emma, tell me not to be so mean, that we could spare one from our stash, two, even. 'He said somebody just cleared 'em out.' Niall looked down at the front step. I looked, too, and realised he was wearing his mum's slip-on shoes, 'What you wearin' on your feet?' I asked.

'I was in a rush.' He shrugged. 'The lecky's off and Mum's got the oven on.'

I started to laugh. 'What's it worth?'

'Fifty pence.'

I sighed, went into the kitchen, picked up Mum's coin basket to pretend to look, even though it was full to bursting because I'd just collected ten pounds' worth from Bod, letting Niall listen to John Craven from the gap in the door, in case their TV was also out of coins.

'Found one,' I shouted finally, passing it from hand to hand as I returned to the door. 'Give me your money first.' I waited for him to drop the five ten-pence pieces into my hand. 'Thank you.' I smiled and flipped the fifty so he'd have to catch it.

'You're tight you are,' said Niall. 'I know you was up there, gettin all the bags of fifties.'

I smiled, 'You goin fishin tomorrow mornin'?'

'Try and stop me. See you down by Pat's boat?'

'Defo,' I slammed the door and returned to the TV, waiting for the local news and the tide times for tomorrow's next big adventure.

★★★

As a kid living in poverty, so much of your nature is about survival: survival of the cleverest, shrewdest, fittest. Me and my sister were mostly friendly with the other kids, but knew not to trust them with anything, ever.

My mum was different: she liked to share, to give. She liked to feed strangers and stragglers, give away clothes, make blankets. That generosity is a part of me now, but as a kid I still wasn't used to the few things I had, wasn't used to our semi-detached house. Every day I imagined it would be taken away again, like at night when I feared Mum would leave us not just for work but for good.

Something about the 50ps brought out the worst in me, so much so that my obsession with them meant it was my job to hunt them out. I got used to asking for them in the change at the village shop, forfeiting a few penny sweets to make sure I had enough, and I'd hide out in the front garden and wait for the old man our neighbourhood nicknamed Bod to get off the bus from Plymouth, a bag of 50ps slung over his shoulder that he'd got in the big post office in the city. I'd watch him coming up the lane, a tenner from Mum burning a hole in my back jeans pocket, hiding down by the stream as I sniffed out the smoke from his endless fag. I'd move like a wolf, going from hedge to hedge, until the moment when he was safely inside his house. It was then that I'd smile, first in the queue, deep breath, then I'd knock.

'Int got any.'

Bod always said this, standing and shrugging with a new fag, me trying not to blink first, not to believe him.

'What you got?' he'd ask eventually.

'Ten quid.'

He'd take his fag out of his mouth, look at it, at me, nod. 'I'll have a look.'

I swear he kept the bags of 50ps in the fridge, disappearing into the kitchen, but then I'd see the nicotine-stained door open and when he returned the bags were ice cold even though he'd only just got home. He'd grab the tenner and tut as he counted out the coins into the tiny plastic bag, but Mum said he loved it. Looking back, I understand this now: he had no family or friends and those coins were a way to keep him in the community, just about.

If Bod hadn't been to Plymouth and the city post office, there would be an uncomfortable moment when I'd think he was joking and he wasn't, and I'd leave pissed off. Not only did I not get the kill, I had to go back down the lane to Number 1

Trelidden Lane where Victoria Plum lived, also not her real name. She, too, collected 50ps, but not on such a grand scale as Bod. Victoria Plum had lavender-tinted hair that went up in a beehive and purple-blue eye-shadow. I didn't like her because she insisted that you went inside while she looked for her purse, then forgot why you'd come and give you stale cake instead.

These incredible, complex, generous characters, I now realise, needed the 50ps as much as any of us did. They, too, inhabited the cycle of poverty and make-do that was our council-house estate.

Everything other than the 50ps came on the never-never as far as money was concerned. Some things 'fell off the back of a lorry', too, but for my mum and my law-abiding stepdad, everything was good old-fashioned above-board working class. When they met, Mum had next to nothing, and what she did have needed replacing fast. The cooker and the fridge and the washer, everything was bought new, on tick, hire-purchase, the good old never-bloody-never. My stepdad was younger than Mum by nine years, only in his early twenties, but he had a military wage and a good credit score, so hire-purchase was the best offer for them at the time. Like everything when you're poor, you weigh up your slim options and throw a dart at the best one, hoping it holds, even if just for a minute.

I don't know how long it took them to pay off those items, but it was definitely years, and it was the same with clothes from the catalogue, even if just a few quid, for me and my sister: it took the best part of a year to pay off, and sometimes that was just the huge interest.

Some people on our estate didn't have any choice but to fall into the hopeless pit of bad debt. Things cost, and in the country where there is little or no competition between service and goods providers, they cost a lot. Sometimes you have no other choice than to borrow, then borrow some more to pay off the original debt. It's a never-ending cycle of misery that can easily lead to losing your house, your family, what jobs you had. That was in the late eighties and early nineties when, no matter where you lived, loan sharks operated outside the law, charging high rates of interest with little or no paperwork to confirm loan arrangements.

Loan sharks still operate illegally today, and no matter where you live they can sting, but in the country, where policing is at an all-time low, they can pretty much trade how they want, and the sting is more of a bite, with many teeth.

In 2022 the Bank of England warned that the UK was set for the steepest drop in living standards for thirty years as the cost-of-living crisis set in, with inflation rising at its sharpest since 1992. This has led many families to rely on hire-purchase. Nowadays hire-purchase and conditional-sale agreements relate mostly to cars, but for poor people they are also signed for furniture, white goods and TVs. Hire-purchase contracts are different from ordinary credit agreements because the signee doesn't own the goods until they have paid off the agreement. They are a slippery slope into further debt because of their sometimes incredibly high and unrealistic APR, making it extremely hard to keep up with the payments. If someone can't pay, a creditor will repossess the goods, or will hire bailiffs to repossess other goods until the debt and the bailiff's fee are recovered.

There's little wonder that people inside the poverty trap find it almost impossible to get out of the never ending circle of deprivation. It is not just food and rent that have gone up in recent years. Fuel poverty, the condition which means a household is unable to afford to heat their home to an adequate temperature, is caused by low income, high prices, poor energy efficiency, unaffordable housing and poor-quality private rental housing. It is at an all-time high and is still rising. The *British Medical Journal* reports that 'Children growing up in cold, damp, and mouldy homes with inadequate ventilation have higher than average rates of respiratory infections and asthma, chronic ill health, and disability. They are also more likely to experience depression, anxiety, and slower physical growth and cognitive development.'

In Cornwall we rely heavily on fossil fuels because so many of us are off the gas grid, without coal and heating oil, both of which have risen in price in recent times, leaving the homes of the poorest without heating or hot water.

Many homes in the country that rely on oil, bottled gas, coal and wood to heat and cook are facing rapidly rising bills, made worse due to the instability caused by the war in Ukraine. These alternative fuel sources are not covered by Ofgem's increased price gap that has come into force, which means the wider implications are cold winters, cold food, cold water, poor hygiene, dirty clothes and death.

My memory of debt is my incredible stepfather, the hardest-working man I have ever known, who over the years worked to pay for and pay off, and think of all the ways to step up onto the next rung of social mobility, so that my mum might be happy, and secure in the knowledge that what little she had would not be taken away from her again. For so many years she had to scrape by, make the best of what little she had. After ten years of living with my dad, a teenage couple with nothing to them but dreams of something other, something better, she finally got a house with a good future attached to it. No matter that they still had to pay rent, had to pay extortionate prices for essential white-goods, my mum was finally back on track, living the life she was supposed to have, and with a good man to boot. She was happy, relaxed, and me and my sister were happy for her, even if her tranquillity meant that, over time, she no longer worried so much about us.

For every decent parent, fundamental things, like a roof over your children's heads, a machine to wash their clothes (there are no launderettes in the countryside), a place to keep food cool and a place to cook that food, these are the things that so many people take for granted. Basic need is an easy thing not to have to think about, until you don't have it, but to those living in poverty they can easily be thought of as luxuries, we forget that they are needs and necessities, what separates us from the animals.

As children my sister and I had a basic need for nature that transcended money and possessions and this has never left us. We loved the exploratory walks we embarked on when we lived in the terrace, before my mum remarried, just the three of us, up the back lane and into the sunny south-facing fields, her hard-working hands pulling us down into the earth in order to pull up pieces of pottery and bits of ancient clay pipes, the beautiful bare bones of our history. No matter how poor we were, no matter how empty our pockets, Mum taught us never to forget to look up at the horizon and the surrounding countryside, never to take for granted the cliff path that edged the length of the village, a path that as I grew older started to whisper to me. The more I listened, the more I could hear the rhythm of it, words like poetry, hidden riches calling me over, pulling me away from our estate and immediate beach and bay, 'this way'.

13

Freedom Fields

Growing up in poverty and rural isolation we kids missed out on many things, the things that most children would never understand. One of which was we didn't own a car. If I wanted to travel to another village, further than our circle of sea and cliff-path and fields I had to walk, and I walked a lot. Something inside me started to realise what those kids had meant when they called me a have-not. It was true: I didn't have a lot of physical things but there was something else too, I didn't have whatever was out there, the things that went wide outside of the horizon, beyond the triangle of Rame Head, Looe Island and the Eddystone Lighthouse.

I was a curious child. I wanted to know how things worked, why certain things were built in a certain way. I once found a TV dumped in the passing place beside the road and took off the back so I could have the circuit board. My wonder went wide. It travelled beyond the bay, went further than land and ocean, the earth and the water, the sky. I wanted the air of each and every day to lift me, the warmth of the firefly stars to guide me, and more than anything I wanted to be something more than nothing.

I was always interested in 'out there', the horizon and the holding place where the sky met the damp, distant film of

water, and I never stopped thinking about the boats, the trawlers and the ships that navigated their way out of Devonport
Dockyard and the river Tamar on another 'secret manoeuvre'
when they sat out in the bay all day. I wondered about the
lighthouse too, the Eddystone.

The Eddystone Lighthouse is one of nine in Cornwall that
serve to warn mariners of dangerous shallows and perilous
rocky coasts. They are mostly dotted around the treacherous
coastline of west Cornwall, but I'm proud of our beautiful
sentry, looking out for us at night. We Cornish call them
golowji, *golow* meaning 'glow' in our native Kernewek, and it's
all I need to know when I see that sphere, a luminous beacon
of light that is a gift of radiance, security, pure heart.

Local legend said that once way back a storm blew so hard
that when it retreated it took the entire ocean with it. For one
full day and night, so the story went, you could walk as far as
the Eddystone, eat a pasty, drink from your flask and look over
towards France, then walk right back. You could stay as long as
you wanted and still have time to get back to Downderry
before the ocean returned. Like all good stories our lighthouse
yarn had its foundation cemented in oral tradition, and while
I've let the detail slip, as a curious child and a writer in waiting
I never stopped thinking or asking about different factors,
never stopped wondering why every old boy in the village
gave me a different answer when pushed for detail.

That horizon.

I wanted to do more than just stare at the green contours
and the tiny rope of scuffed earth, the muddy path that walked
my imagination beyond the circle of predictability, the shape of
safety. More than anything I wanted to step out of my stifling

seclusion and into that new world, exist out of my depth in the spaces I knew I belonged, if I could just find them.

Little did I know that at the age of ten I would find the battered paperback at the school jumble sale that very possibly changed the course of my life.

Until that moment, I always hated anything to do with school that wasn't actual learning. I hated the discos, the bake sales, the Christmas fair and the summer barbecue. I hated everything.

On this particular occasion Mum had been roped in to run a stall, collecting clothes or face-painting or whatever. It had nothing to do with me, but I remember having to be there. Walking around the two adjoining classrooms that made up the bulk of our tiny country school, trying to go unnoticed as usual, trying to slip beneath other people's radar, ignoring their pleas for me to smile, smile more, commenting on how pretty I could be if I loosened up, talked more. If anyone asked them, I'm sure those women from the main part of the village would have preferred me to think less too. I never would, and the moment I found 'my book' was the instant I knew that one day soon I would leave those narrow-minded people for good.

I had been standing on my own at the entrance to the class-rooms, waiting for my next instructions from Mum to fetch black bin-bags from the boot of whichever Range Rover when I saw a group of posh girls walking across the playground. They were from my class, the mean girls, the ones who thought I was weird for only having boys as friends. I went inside so I didn't have to endure the usual questioning – which lad was my actual boyfriend, which one was the best kisser . . .

I pushed the door closed to buy some time and went around the rooms stopping briefly at the stalls to pretend I was looking for something. That was when I found my destiny book or, more precisely, that was when my destiny book found me.

As I Walked Out One Midsummer Morning by Laurie Lee slipped into the palm of my hand in the bric-a-brac section at that end-of-term fundraiser and, despite its well-worn appearance, the image of a young man walking barefoot on a dirt track into the pages of the book resonated within me. It was as if he was waiting for me to follow him into an uncharted landscape. Ten pence later, I did.

That book, about a young man's travels into the unknown leaving his community and family with no more than he could carry on his back, evoked in me the romance of the moment, exploration in an instant, a flash of freedom. I had finally discovered a way to escape, as all the tiny slip-skin elements of my nature started to fall into place. I still loved to draw and record nature, but I had discovered a new way to express the wonder and the fury that lived inside me and it was with words, my own, poetry.

I was starting to become more distant from my family, a detachment that in part was my fault for wanting more than I could find around me, and my family's fault for letting me do what I wanted and for believing I was safe, with a responsible head on young shoulders.

There was a part of me that thought my loved ones would notice my newly found ethereal qualities, my increasing absence from the house, but mostly I was left to my own devices, which slowly, unwittingly, had me fall below anyone's radar. I started not just to feel but to know I was unnoticed.

I read *As I Walked Out One Midsummer Morning* from cover to cover, and then I read it again, realising that all the times I ran down onto the beach at night, all the times I shouted at the waves and cried, I wasn't waiting for somebody to find me and ask me if I was okay, I was connecting with the elements. Nature was my nature, the outside come in and my inside put out, joined. It wasn't long before I turned my sketchpad into a notebook and began to write everything I could see around me, and everything that cut and scarred within, in the soft thin pages of my sketchpad.

How quick those fire-flash moments of definition, understanding: one minute you're a kid messing around in rock-pools making flotsam boats, the next you're staring down a stormy night making stuff up. Suddenly I realised how to paint the world around me as I wanted to: with words. Finally I had discovered a way to transfer the things I looked at onto a page in a way that might, some day, have meaning to others, a way to communicate contours, texture, colour, light and shade. I was finally the artist I wanted to be: with words, the greatest palette there was.

Not only that, the more I wrote, the more I connected nature with me, my heart the hills, my head the cliffs, my emotions every variable storm and flat-calm run of the ocean. From the age of ten I wrote everything down, like a diary only better, because this was poetry.

The next time me and Mum went to Plymouth on the bus on a rare Saturday she had off, I asked if we could go to the army surplus store so I could buy three things: a tactical notebook, a saddle-bag and an old-fashioned military water bottle, all cheap as chips, and all vital in my plan for exploring that home-turf triangle.

Looking back, I realise I was preparing for some semblance of a near future in which self-sufficiency would be vital in determining how I negotiated the world. I knew that I wouldn't be able to rely on my family in the way others did, knew I would leave the village for good as soon as I could, and more than anything I knew that the person I was becoming, the person I wanted and needed to be, would be determined by how good I was at surviving.

Survival is the difference between forging forward and stepping back. It is the balance that hangs between living and existing. It is the mind moving and turning and your legs walking, the act of escape, the art of it; it is perpetual motion, curiosity at a constant.

Some might not believe that, at the age of ten, a child can head out on a long walk, no matter how far, or climb, no matter how steep the cliff, but in the country in the eighties you could pretty much do what you wanted, and I did. Equipped with my notebook, pen, jam sandwiches and aluminium water bottle that came with its own green jacket and belt, I was ready for anything.

I was a survivalist, a poet, a nature writer, and, yes, to all the people who inhabited the narrow world around me, I was a strange kid. Growing up with no money and seemingly no prospects, my life was always going to go one of two ways, and once I found that book, once I'd chewed on it and swallowed it and digested all there was to think about nature and adventure, I was determined to set a course further than I'd ever been before. No longer was I content merely to look into my wide expanse of bay, I wanted to explore it, properly, not just with my eyes and my imagination but with my two feet stomping.

***

When I was out in a boat I was always drawn to the side of the bay that swung around towards the Rame Head peninsula, but on foot I wanted to see how far I could walk west, past Seaton and on towards Looe. The writer Daphne du Maurier lived near Fowey in an estuary hamlet called Bodinnick, situated this side of the coastal town that I know now is a twelve-mile hike from Looe, but at that young age I imagined (hoped) that it was just beyond our bay. I was nine years old and I'd already devoured *Rebecca*, another jumble-sale find, and had decided that Fowey was where I was heading.

Walking is not just a means of motion: it is the proceeds of knowing. I knew that, by my own power and momentum, I could go anywhere, achieve anything, escape to the wild edges, the fierce fringes of my rural community that, until then, were yet to be properly investigated. Freedom was the upper fields I scrambled through. It was my boots stomping into the flinty coastal path with my head in the clouds, my childish thoughts that perhaps a famous writer might read my passion-poetry and declare me a genius, why not?

By my reckoning nobody was that bothered if I was absent for a few hours every other day throughout the weekends and holidays. I was mostly out there on the cliff-path anyway, thinking, writing, dreaming and, perhaps more importantly, creating a future for myself, a future that would help me figure out the child I was and the person I was going to be.

'I'm off out,' I told Mum, that first adventure-fuelled morning.

'Down to the beach?' she asked. She was standing in the kitchen, baking, something she had started to do more of now my stepdad was around and she didn't have to work so many long hours.

'I'm gonna walk the coast path.'

'St German's Hut?'

That was the derelict hunting lodge out on the cliff in the other direction where I sometimes went to sketch, paint the ivy that had crawled through the windows and doors.

'Not today,' I said. 'I'm heading to Looe.'

'Looe?'

'Why not?' I waited for her to tell me not to go, wanted her to voice her concerns, but she was in love, trying for a baby, preoccupied with her new improved life. 'Anyway,' I continued, 'that's where I'm going.'

'Good girl.' She put one of her freshly baked buns into an empty bread bag, for later. 'Make sure you're back by five thirty for tea.'

'Yes, Mum.' I nodded. 'Always.'

★★★

Escape. How incredible that, without the tools to know or means to show how my childhood trauma had affected me, except for the sudden jolts of violence and desertion, I discovered my own little patch of peace upon the earth, and it was nature, the muddy, dusty path beneath my feet and the beat of walking, power from within.

Knowing without knowing, somehow that one adventurous step out of the village and up the steep hill west out of the valley and away would become everything I knew and all I wanted to know. Through the kissing gate that led from the lane and up past the enchanted woodland on the left, the freedom feeling when all you can see is green and rust-coloured ferns and gold gorse as far as the eye can see, and suddenly the sea, your home ocean, washes back into view, and you're 125 metres in the air. That day I decided to walk as far as I could on the coast path, feeling for the first time like I was winging it with the kestrels and the buzzards, my spirit birds.

The further I walked, the more I felt like I was stepping out of my old skin and pulling on a new outfit, an outfit made from the nature I gathered around me, the soft cliff-top moss to protect my heart, the pink slate rock in place of armour, my mind finding freedom in the fields where I could go, not in the places I couldn't, and free to do the things I knew I could do, not the things I couldn't. Perhaps as I got older, the things that caused me harm I could dig down into my belly, my dad and his violence and abandonment when I was younger, my mum's occasional emotional absence now I was starting to grow up. The more time passed, the closer I found myself walking both physically and mentally towards the cliff edge. I still dreamt of falling, still fought the thought that everyone I loved was slowly dying, or leaving, but by taking myself away I discovered a new route through. By walking and writing I was setting a future course, no matter how small, to ensure that, when the time came, it was me who would leave first.

Occasionally I stopped to note the inscriptions on the way-marker standing stones, the ancient Bronze Age markers that pushed out of the Cornish earth like guiding hands, pointing. I could feel their energy connecting and reaching beneath my feet, the marker stones giving me direction, telling me that my ancestors had walked this way too.

In ancient times folk would stop and ask people the way if they were lost, but travellers in remote coastal and moorland areas of Cornwall would have to rely on way-markers, these ancient standing stones, for directions.

This was my defining breakaway moment, the instant when I finally knew what I was going to do. I had my reading books – Laurie Lee, John Steinbeck, Daphne du Maurier and D. H. Lawrence – in my life for guidance, and I had my notebook into which, without knowing it, I was laying down the routines and rough routes that would ultimately lead to my escape from Downderry and our bay.

Children living in poverty in remote rural and coastal communities face continued struggles because of poor transport, a lack of safe spaces to meet in and poor digital connectivity. Rural isolation means you are mostly on your own, or if you are lucky enough to have a few friends, they are mostly not of your choosing, sometimes not even your age – they are just 'not adult'. Coupled with this you have no outside stimuli except that which you can manifest yourself: no sports coaching, no creative pursuits, no dance classes, art classes, youth clubs, absolutely nothing except standing and staring down another long, dark night.

Experts coin the impact of this as poor mental health, but broken down it reads as depression, low self-esteem, self-harm, drug and alcohol dependency, violence, rape and hate.

I wish I could find a way to show every poor kid the right route to doing it, be a way-marker stone, standing ready to point them in the direction of the horizon, help them to hold it in their imagination and set out the course to charge through the waves and tides, ride out the insecurity and anger to reach it. But you've got to want to do it, and you've got to get over the unfairness of it, because it is unfair: absolutely nobody fucking cares about poor country kids – they don't care about you, your background, or your lack of prospects. I know some things, most things, are easier said than done, but you've got to try to find a way to create prosperity, see your future the way you want it and manifest it.

I was lucky to be me: despite my young age I unwittingly gifted myself the tools with which to navigate, protect, galvanise myself against poverty, hardship, assault, addiction and all the damaging things that were yet to be inked and tattooed into my constellation, but at least for a while, on the midsummer cusp of ten, nearly eleven, the stars were aligning.

14

Solitary Moon

The summer before secondary school was a summer of no return for many reasons but, more than anything, it was a moment in my young life when I suddenly felt the shift in me that slowly slipped towards true temperament.

My family and the community around us always acted in a certain way: they were predictable, their dimensions and mechanisms always moving in the same circular motion. I knew just by walking past an open door what was being said and what was coming next, could sense the air was hostile or friendly or fun just by feeling the currents. Everything was expectable, easy and flat-calm tiresome. At the age of eleven I was bored, really, really bored.

Summers in Cornwall, especially the ones remembered from childhood, are feather-stuffed, full of hot heady days and warm sleepless nights, like a giant duvet had fallen from the heavens and settled between the river and our two oceans. The summer that lodged itself between childhood and that 'something other' age, was no different. I've no doubt that to some extent it was the same for the tourists and the rich village kids who were of similar age to me, but when you grow up in poverty everything is just that little bit harder and the tedium that exists day to day is a vacuum of things you wished you could afford to do but know you can't because of money. No trips to the cinema in St Austell or roller-disco in Plymouth, no video games, except those at the arcade in Seaton, the ones that cost money, money we didn't have unless we got lucky when we stuck our hands among the cobwebs beneath the machines.

Around the time of leaving primary school, the long dusty track that was July and August stretching out in front, I started to spend more and more time alone, drifting away from my family and the boring kids on our estate and looking increasingly towards people I didn't quite know, namely the older kids from the wider village, the ones who already went to secondary school, but in summer, like me, had to endure the boredom of nothing other than sitting, waiting, looking.

I used to watch those kids at night. Sitting on the main beach in Downderry, with the sun finally dropping behind the westerly peninsula of Looe, the moon slowly rising and the summer-night sky washing in, reflecting on the laid-back tide, this was when I'd settle myself smack-bang centre of this new world, a world made up of messy bonfires, not like the ones our parents used to construct, and plastic half-gallon jars of scrumpy, and homemade bongs when the drink ran dry.

The kind of summer-dusk light that slips in without you noticing is my favourite instant, it is neither night nor day, and up until that premium point was the moment when absolutely nothing happened. Meals were eaten, TVs went on and preteens went to bed, but not me. I'd tell Mum I was going out on my bike and she'd always say, 'All right, don't be late.' We never established what late was but I always took it to mean pitch-black and home before they went to bed.

The night was made up of all the colours that eluded the hot midsummer days. It was blue and grey and everything hit through with the violet tint of sunset, like the colours of a mussel shell, hoary and dull on the one hand, pearly-pink on the other. The smell of salt on my tanned skin and on the evening air, everything soaked in seawater.

Down on the beach at night I knew, with relief and reassurance, that I was not the only person in our village who was bored. Although I was younger, I felt like I could attach myself to their apathy and deep-seated despair, find a way to understand my boredom by observing them. By watching from the shadows I realised I was not alone, not so different after all.

I'd cycle through the village and lean my bike against the railings that ran down the side of the slipway and walk towards the main beach at the centre of the village. The pub with the ghost of Dad at one end of the beach, the slipway with the old rusty winch and the coastguard cottages at the other, and at the top end of the beach the long line of boats and upturned dinghies and the memory of fishing. At night, the glow of small impromptu fires and throwaway barbecues lit up the night, the faces of near strangers that flitted about the flames like fireflies, each with their mouths snapped tight, but each with a story tied up inside.

Under cover of the encroaching darkness, I could shrink myself down into the shadows of the hump-back boats, and sit tight and watch, listen. I learnt a lot that summer, learnt what it was to be a girl and what it was to be a boy.

The girls sat on one side of the fire, at a distance, whispering, while the boys sat up close, feeding the flames with bits of driftwood and melting plastic, drinking and pretending not to notice the girls despite their giggling. As a small child, a near-teen and in all the years since then, I have never fitted into either skin. The girls were silly, the boys were stupid, and despite the boredom that we shared equally, they seemed accepting of the long-winded summer of stand and slump, sit and stare. They gazed at the fire and gaped at each other, and when darkness fell fully they moved closer to the flames, the whites of their eyes and teeth hungry for the night, for the cheap bootleg drink, for each other.

***

At nightfall I find it easy to be seen or not be seen. As a Cancerian I am like the moon. Some days I am a satellite, I like to take centre stage, shine bright, send out signals to pull folk into my orbit, at other times I rush to find the clouds, pulling them about me like a cloak, a wolf in sheep's clothing, keep out.

As an adult the beach at night is no longer a place that I go to alone, despite us knowing each other so well. When I look at the sea I still feel like that stupid, humble, vulnerable child, the one I ran from, the one I escaped from in order to be free, but by eleven its briny darkness was still my comfort, not yet a curse, and it was all I had to fold myself into, bundle my secrets tight beneath the rocks and pin my silence up against the cliffs, so if anyone found me, noticed me, they'd find me normal. Maybe that's why I no longer like the beach at night, it knows all my secrets, all the anger and the trauma, it has collected up the best and the worst of me, dug me deep into the ocean and the sand, all of my parts, the mess of me still exist in its fierce, soothing hands.

At that crossroads age, I started to see that the deep black void of boredom didn't just belong to me, all us poor rural kids could see it, we could feel it with our toes as we tried not to fall into it. I could see it in the sleepy slow-burn eyes of those older kids, could see my future reflected in their pupils, could imagine it drawn out in the damp night sand; drinking for the sake of it, sucking on a plume of skunk for the sake of it, getting off with whoever sat beside you, just for the sake of it.

That summer, the one before my first year of secondary school and my self-made prophecy that I would at some point be exactly like those other kids, I'd sit for what seemed like hours and draw the stars around, move nearer when the ocean pulled closer. Water, air, earth and the childish fires joining hands, everyone wondering what they were going to do with their lives despite being only fourteen and fifteen, buried in amongst the monotony of too much time, their jaws fallen in apathy and early-onset addiction, their brief singular sentences dropping like moments of pure poetry.

'School is for fools, hate it.' Two girls nodded, looked towards the sunset, moved towards the fire to decide which boy they'd pick tonight.

'School is a waste of time.' An older boy shrugged. 'I'm gonna work on the boats, with Dad.'

'Waste of time,' a lad with his back turned agreed, 'no jobs, no work, no prospects.'

I moved closer, pulled up into the concave bend of a small wooded dinghy that had been tipped onto its side.

'There's money out there,' the older boy continued, 'way out beyond the lighthouse.'

'France?' laughed one of the girls.

'Close enough if we want, fuck knows they fish in our water enough times.'

'I want to be a lawyer,' said the girl, 'like on the telly, sort out everyone's shit.'

'Good luck with that.' Her friend leant forward and pulled the joint from her mouth and stuck it into her own. 'You'd have to sort your own shit out first.' Everybody started to laugh. 'Anyway, you'll have to travel up country to study for that.'

'So?' said her friend.

'So your dad's a farmer.' She inhaled and looked up towards the stars, blew them cloudy. 'You gotta look after 'em, and the farm workers, cook for 'em and that.'

'That's my mum's job.' She took back the joint and shrugged, but I could see she was wondering about that. Her destiny written, like all of us, because most of us would never have enough money to leave home and study at a distance, never have enough reserve to go after our dreams because of rural duty. The forceful families, the agricultural and fishing invest-ments meant a farm and all its debts got passed down, and dreams were given up for the sake of guilt, duty, toil, good girl, good boy.

I watched their faces drop with the realisation that this was probably it and for a brief moment I saw my dad among them, saw him as a lad, eager eyes and heart for all the things he was yet to discover, then suddenly muted for what he must have known was his future: living in the same small village where he was born and raised, all ambition hammered and blunted, working for his dad as a painter-decorator.

I looked into the fire, and then briefly closed my eyes, made a promise to somehow dig my own path out of the granite so that I could get out. The night suddenly holding its breath, made the flames go low, angry-red, and it pinched into the kids' cheeks, made them look like little devils; horny, fearless, reckless for the sake of it.

Sometimes when I watched those older kids they'd hook-up early, walk hand in hand along the fizzy-white shoreline, and later they'd put a jacket between the boats for a quick fuck, stumbling and fumbling for a respite minute of something other than nothing, a moment to dig out of the sand, pass around before putting back down. These were the moments that I took to be mine, in three or four years, my own prophecy lived and wasted, lost beside wild water.

Boredom for children and teenagers comes with the territory of minimal age, but being bored in the country, and without money to spend on activities and diversions, means there's not a lot to do except wait and hope.

Access to youth programmes is next to impossible for working-class children and young adults. Youth services have a far-reaching and popular appeal, engaging with young people regardless of their socioeconomic status, they provide opportunity for personal development, socialisation and wellbeing, but not when you live in the country, at a distance from anything useful or impactful. Crucially, youth services include a range of safeguarding and early-intervention support services, which are vital to vulnerable and disadvantaged young people, but there was never anything like that for us.

Now it looks like things are starting to get worse again, investment in and young people's access to youth services has fallen across the whole of Cornwall, whilst the needs of young people have increased. Annual spending on youth services have dropped by £1 billion over the past decade which is not sustainable. Hardest hit are the 2.25 million young people living in villages and coastal areas, the areas that are consistently overlooked and are shamelessly missing from the government's levelling up agenda. It is these rural areas that have experienced a snail's slow-pace revival from the pandemic, with the capacity of youth-service support at its lowest for over a decade.

There's barely any provision in rural areas to tackle inequalities and put young people at the heart of the post-Covid-19 recovery. Investment is required for a rural action plan designed with young people in mind, something to build and strengthen youth services that can be readily delivered through strong local partnerships across all rural communities. Analysis of Public Health England indicators finds that young people in rural areas score worse than average on levels of risky behaviour, like drinking, taking drugs, unprotected sex and self-harm. For vulnerable young people in rural areas, support from youth services is the difference between getting by and getting on; where there is a restriction or absence of opportunity in a community, including lack of social and support networks resulting from an absence of places to meet and good connectivity, young people will never be able to move up and out of poverty.

Survey results during the first Covid-19 lockdown showed that young people in rural areas felt worried, anxious, lonely and isolated, and that their main call was for better access to services, specifically mental-health services. Research by the Royal College of Nursing flagged issues with Child and Adolescent Mental Health Services (CAMHS) provision in rural areas during that time. It found 'significant and unjustified' variation in available services to young people and their families. Almost no evidence was acknowledged as to the provision of young people's sexual-health services and clinics in rural areas. One report cited privacy and travel issues in smaller populations connected to the use of services outside the community.

There was no doubt that as I watched those older kids sit and lament about their rudimentary futures I started to think about my own. Looking back this was a tipping point that I didn't realise at the time, but watching those other kids was like looking into a reflection of my future, the drinking, the despair and the desolation, my fate was to become just like them. Because of the lack of support and provision from anywhere, my destiny as a poor coastal child was this, emptiness.

When I returned home I ran upstairs to our bedroom to think about what my future looked like, and I sat on my bed and looked over at my sister's, wishing she was sitting there so she could tell me to stop being such a weirdo always worrying about odd things, but she had a boyfriend who lived in Seaton and was barely ever around. Downstairs I could hear Mum and Catts laughing in the front room, and I wanted to go down more than anything in the world, be a new family, a new three, but I had distanced myself, made out that I was always busy, that I didn't like Catts; I needed to be called down, needed to hear my name float up the stairs and for them to tell me they were putting the kettle on, but that night the call never came.

At the age of eleven I felt the first stab of loneliness. The future I'd been so excited about, with our house and my coastal adventures, now made me fearful, so much so that I had to reach for the nearest shell so I might at least be in control of one thing: the unemotional curl of safe-shelter and seclusion of my own making.

FIRE

15

Hermit

Isolation was the thing that almost broke me. It was a shadow of my childhood and it sounded like the smash of known things and the scream on the unknown, black, void of any kind of joy.

Hermit crabs are known for their mobile shelters, but these temporary homes are not their own: they are empty scavenged mollusc shells that they have adapted to protect and insulate themselves from others, or risk being defenceless. This I understand completely. As a child I wanted to hide away in order to protect myself, but there came a time when, despite my love of hiking and writing and being on my own, at the beginning of my first year of secondary school, I started to notice other creatures beyond my family, our estate, the village and me.

I started to notice something else too: how little we truly had.

Secondary school was in the river town of Torpoint, an easterly twenty-mile round trip on the school bus that brought us halfway around the long winding cliff road of our bay and took the best part of an hour to pick up every rural secondary kid. Most of the year this journey was made in partial darkness and most of us didn't know each other: we were the country kids, and as far as the townies were concerned, we were backward, stupid and smelt of cow shit.

A lot of the posh kids were driven to school by their parents, but a few had to ride the bus to school with us working-class riff-raff, the kids whose parents were cleaners, builders, fishermen and farmers, and I loved that.

Torpoint, an old Cornish harbour town, was first mentioned in records dating back to 1734. Its rapid development was due to the expansion of the navy in Devonport Dockyard across the river Tamar, a place of shipbuilding and repair. It always amazed me that, despite its history with the ocean, the town always seemed to look in on itself. As an eleven-year-old, I couldn't wait to explore my new surroundings, the riverbanks and the parks and modern housing estate that for a young country kid, was like being in a new found city, but my enthusiasm didn't last.

My world was opening up, but at the same time the horizon, that guiding line of stability, seemed to be moving further and further into the distance.

The bus journey always seemed to take forever to navigate the narrow lanes and sharp bends, like a journey that on some days, usually double maths days, didn't seem to have an end in sight. The roads and hedges blurred through the scratched, damp-breath windows, the lights that still worked flickering bright, catching sudden moments like in a play, girls laughing and smoking, boys mid-punch, joking.

Me sitting with a book, fourth wall, pretending to do homework, read, going over the same page while I prayed that I'd be left alone, left to sit inside my shell so I didn't have to shout and fight because if I started to bite I knew from experience that I wouldn't be able to stop, wouldn't be able to keep my violent, tomboy wilderness to myself.

In my first year of secondary school I was marked as different from the very first day I stepped off the bus and went towards it. I can still remember how it felt to have the best bits of me fall away in clumps as I walked and the sound of taunts as I tried not to go too fast in the compulsory tights and skirt. My usual swagger gone in the dress-up and silly shoes that I hadn't known since infancy, my anger boiled down and turned inward, all wrong.

The skin I had to sit in for five years, the covering that was meant to define what a girl was in those character-defining teenage years was not mine. It was borrowed, blue. Somebody else's pelt perhaps but to me it was just bad drag. From that moment on I had two very different lives.

Home time and weekends out with friends I shifted back into my natural state, wild wolf. I was confident, built with a bit of protective arrogance stitched into my heart and fists, and despite there being changes at home too, with the news that Mum was pregnant and expecting her first baby with Catts in June, things at home on our estate were good. They even bought me a cheap 'student typewriter' where I typed up my poems in the evenings and sent them off to local poetry magazines in the morning post, and I'd started to get them accepted for publication, the thin A5 collections of verse that over time became my whole world.

It was only in the classroom in Torpoint Comprehensive School and those long stand-and-stare corridors that I felt myself change into a rabbit, and everything and everyone were probing, searching headlights. Difference is only recognised when viewed through the prism of others' standards and preconceptions as to what is. Before that we just are. Animals don't have an awareness of themselves. They are not self-conscious, and they don't give a damn that their mum likes to hunt and rip the shit out of stuff. They wouldn't blink twice if their dad liked to howl at the moon each night, wearing heels and a pink feather boa whilst doing it.

Every evening when I got home from school and peeled off that nasty skin, I became myself again, returning to brilliant, gorgeous, androgynous, and every morning when I climbed back in I reverted back to ugly, awkward, stupid, clumsy. Between the hours of 7.30 a.m. and 4.30 p.m. I knew nothing tangible about my life except those bitching, blinding lights, lights that were everywhere, glaring out from behind giggling hands, at the back of classrooms, the corridors and toilets.

***

'You don't belong in here, Natasha.'

I stood against the ancient radiator and waited for the door to swing closed. 'I need the toilet.' I shrugged and pointed to the three open cubicles.

'You should go outside,' said the ringleader, 'or, even better, in with the boys.'

I pushed past her, keeping eye contact, goading her to push me first so that I could push back. 'Make me,' I said.

This was what those early secondary-school years were like. Every single day I had to endure low-level bullying, the side-glances and stopped mid-sentence conversations, the fake laughter. Again and again I was told I didn't belong, and yet they were for ever watching me, girls and boys, trying to work me out, the *Mona Lisa* as they started to call me. I asked my mum what they meant. 'Enigmatic,' she said. 'Mysterious.' I liked that bit.

It wasn't just because I was a tomboy either: their animosity against me was also because of where I stood in the dinner queue. The walk of shame was a corridor that took those of us on free school meals past the hungry hordes of not-poor kids to stand with our little pink free-meal tickets. To all the world it must have looked like a village raffle as we stood there and waited to be called, but the prize for us poor kids was a full belly, and for that we had to endure purgatory, under a magnifying-glass and bright lights.

***

I never liked Torpoint and I was right to think it. At the age of eleven I didn't know how much trouble that town would get me into, or that in four years' time it would be the place of my downfall, my alcohol dependence, my rape, and in five years, the place of a near-death experience and a savage homophobic attack. At that time in my life it was just what you had to endure, two hours spent on a bus and seven hours spent in a town devoid of personality and a school that had no hope for a working-class kid from the sticks.

Despite all the chaos that was in my future, it was also the place where I finally got to break free from isolation and, unexpectedly, started to make friends. My ragtag crew of misfits consisted of Jill and Sandra, who came from the council estate in Millbrook, Sian and Kerenza, the hippie-esque sisters from Millpool, the hamlet that was situated beside the Mount Edgcumbe Country Park, just up the road from Millbrook, then Elle, Janey and Nic, who all came from Torpoint. Outsiders, this group of friends from all over our peninsula slowly helped me push aside my shell.

Because we didn't own a car, I couldn't hang out with my new friends after school, or weekends or any day. If anything was going to happen, like a birthday party, I would have to factor in the once-a-day Saturday bus, and if plans changed, I never got to know because we had no phone. This kind of isolation trauma is not unusual for rural children and teenagers, the fear of being left out, forgotten, unfriended. It's tangible: you can touch it, feel it in the way your heart beats faster as you get off the bus in the centre of town only to realise everyone has left.

It took energy and creativity to keep friends in that first secondary-school year, and the four years that followed. I had to be the funniest, the cleverest, and the most attentive at all times.

Children from rural areas live two lives, the one that they are given, their home life, and the one that is there for the taking, the one that is created in a school of wide-ranging strangers. This I realised early on, sitting on the bus with the usual bully from a neighbouring village throwing lit butt-ends at my head and me trying not to hit her (I eventually did), I realised there was a way to make the two lives thing work and it was a word, still one of my favourites: reinvention.

My reinvention started with the growing understanding of the world around me and, more importantly, who I needed to be in that world. If some of my friends wanted a shoulder to cry on or a listening ear, I was that person. If they wanted a good laugh or something to take their mind off, I was the one to do the stupid daredevil thing – climb the swings in the park, disagree with a teacher if I thought it would bring me favour. I got good at shoplifting too, small things like chocolate, or lipstick, trinket gifts that made them smile, even just for a while. My talent lay with the ability to listen, to know what somebody wanted and then provide it. My heart is big and my ability to empathise meant that instinctively, as a kid and a young teen, I found it easy to shape-shift into people's lives and be who they needed. I learnt to do this at a young age, to help my mum, to reassure my older sister, always knowing what space existed around another and stepping in to fill that void with my 'bigger than me' shadow.

There is no doubt that my ability to reinvent was a survival tactic, instinct, born into me from those first early moments of adaptation, the way to work things through in order to shed the bad, blue stormy windows and the volatility that was my dad. Maybe that's why I can handle change: I don't like it, but I find it easy to emotionally load a gun, pack a bag, and say, 'Let's go.'

Reinvention in nature happens continually: seasons change, birds lose their feathers, and snakes shed their skin when it's time to grow a new one. These processes indicate a natural need for change and evolution and it is the same with us. There is a force that prompts us to let go of the past, step outside our comfort zone, and move forward into the future.

This was what I did to survive my teen years: I shed my baby feathers, changed my shade, coloured my blood other than red, slipped from my skin and climbed into another thing – reinvention.

School in those early years was a battle to learn. A part of me thought I knew everything, and the things I didn't I guessed weren't worth knowing. I didn't care to sit and be told: I wanted to pick things apart, get my hands dirty. I didn't want to map out the Royal Family tree. Why would I? They meant fuck-all to me. I'd endure the bus ride, find my seat in class, sit and stare out of the window, or look at those around me, make faces, invent sketches and jokes, anything to distract me from the sit-and-suffer, the teachers who went on and on and on.

I liked the attention too, realising in those first couple of years that with my stories and elaborate observations about the teachers, other kids, the people in mind-numbing Torpoint, I was starting to bag a wider audience. Growing up, I never got enough outside attention, not nearly as much as I wanted anyway. I was my mum's good girl, pretty, attentive, consider-ate and mistakenly thought of as an introvert. That couldn't have been further from the truth. I was thoughtful, but that was only one part of me, Mum, the caring sheep part. The other side of my nature was Dad, an angry, punchy wolf. Two natures that I still find hard to balance, two sides that I endure good and bad days on both accounts. I love attention, like any and every writer if they're honest with themselves. I love praise and I love my work being talked about. I was like that as a kid, and I was like that as a teenager, and those stories and sketches that I created made those first two years of secondary bearable. That was until I discovered the one thing that would give me attention above all else, or so I childishly thought: alcohol.

★★★

When I reached thirteen, I finally, firmly, joined the new cohort of directionless Downderry and Seaton shoreline kids, the kids who when not at school, would do all the same tedious things; mainly lighting bonfires down on the beach, sitting about and drinking. This was what our parents did and our ancestors going way back did and it was nothing like what our ancient Celtic forbears would have you think, no sacrifice or calling to the gods but a simple way to pass the time.

Alcohol was a big part of my childhood, those early barbecues spent on the beach when the drunk grown-ups would forget where they set down one of their half-gallon scrumpy jars. We'd huddle in a cave or under a boat, laughing, whispering into our coats, 'We have it.' Drinking brought us country kids together in the same way that simple pleasures like darts brought Mum and her friends together, or Dad and the lads who played pool in the basement of the Working Men's Club, none of us friends, barely acquaintances, just all of us 'in on this'.

Everything in the village was based around drinking and the beach and the two pubs. Get pissed, stumble around on the beach collecting firewood, dig a pit, add some tinder, light it and soak it in kerosene, almost die, drink more, pass out, wake up with the early morning kittiwakes and guls. This was pretty much the life of anyone who lived in poverty in Downderry and I was no different, but the tug of friends outside of the village that had slowly pulled me out from my shell did it with more permanence, that internal wild that I had inhabited for so long started to fit me better, and with it a new kind of bravado.

At the age of thirteen, fourteen, alcohol was easily accessible, which not only pulled me from my protective fleece, but also, perhaps inevitably, hauled me up and out of any kind of edification and threw me back into barren wilderness. The wilderness that I found myself in was uncharted, unmapped because I didn't know how things were meant to go, the contour lines that signalled the change in elevation that I was meant to navigate was a scramble of tough terrain, the simple act of learning a scatter of rocks, rubble and dust.

I'd spent so long watching the kids who went before us that in many ways it was a rite of passage to become one of them, a passage that was long, complicated, sacrificial in the way we gave ourselves over to the night, like tumbling lambs, blood-ied, blinded by the firelight.

Fire worship is in us Cornish.

Without knowing it, we stand and stare into the blistering abyss and somewhere deep down we know that we are a part of this: heat, light, hope. Fire is the sun come down to sit among us, Belenus, meaning 'Bright One', but I prefer Kowlleski, which, translated from Cornish, means 'consume by fire'. The burning up was what our youth was made of. We'd congregate on the steps that led down to the beach and hang out in a little walled square of concrete that was meant as a bird's-eye viewing platform for grounded fishermen while they fixed their nets and crabbing pots, and we'd keep one eye on the path that came down from the centre of the village for anyone heading to the Seaview and the other eye on the pub door for anyone coming out. Between the group of us young teens, we vaguely knew all the men, and we'd jostle for posi-tion and think of the right way to ask for a favour that didn't sound like we were fuck-up drunks.

Sometimes if they were coming out for a gander at the tide and a quick fag we'd just ask for a sip of their drink, but if they were heading home, we'd follow them up to Tom's before it closed with a handful of our pooled change rattling and glinting in our hands.

'Just a couple beers, please?'

'What you got there?' Geoff would ask, or Mike, or our beloved Pat. These men who worked behind the bar, a backdrop to our growing up.

'Enough for a couple bottles of Newquay Steam,' I'd say, or Dan, or George, or Niall, and we'd wait for the long lament that ended with the summation that they were once like us and 'Don't tell your mums!'

When we had enough alcohol we'd make our way down the steps that led to the beach and walk towards the closest fire and other kids. Some folk we knew, some we didn't, some just sat there in passing, the children of the tourists who hated their parents, missed their homes, their city friends. We'd sit together and pass whatever bottle we had around, barely talking, trying to be casual until drunk, when we turned from being cool to raging hot.

Somehow we looked at each other in the hope that somebody, somewhere, held the secret to how to get off the descending track and lead us away from it.

As kids we all knew the story of Joan the Wad, a naughty pixie from around the next bay in Polperro, who brought good luck and fortune if you asked for it. Joan was famed for lighting fires out on the headland between Polperro and Looe so boats could get to safety, *wad* meaning 'torch' in Cornish. I often thought about Joan in those early teen years, something in me wishing that she would reach inside me and light a fire, so I could find my own way to safety, before it was too late.

★★★

Looking back I realise the damage of no safe passage had already been done, because by the age of fourteen I drank regularly, almost daily. I babysat a lot, on our estate and for rich folk around the village, and it was easy to fill my beloved army water bottle with neat Taboo, Mirage, vodka, gin, anything I could get my hands on. It was also handy that my new best friend Sian's parents ran a restaurant.

The Edgcumbe Arms on the Rame peninsula in the hamlet of Millpool was an old whitewashed building that looked out across the river Tamar towards Plymouth. It had many rooms and various entrances and exits, which for Sian, her sister Kerenza and me were perfect for dipping and ducking beneath the adult radar.

Sian's parents were hardworking people, and similar to my mum at that time, who had become consumed with the bringing up of my baby brother, they were extremely busy and mostly absent in the lives of their daughters. This for us was brilliant: it meant when I stayed over we got to go to bed when we wanted, eat crisps when we liked, and when the restaurant closed meant free spirits, neat.

Me and Sian were meant for everything that wasn't sombre or staid. It was the greatest thing about us and also the worst. We lived life at speed, uphill, forever fast, until eventually it was our downfall, our crash. While Sian was my double shot of tequila, her sister Kerenza was a sip of ice-cold water and I always felt better when I was around her. Together the three of us had a strange relationship: me and Sian were best buddies, and Kerenza was always just her sensible older sister. She was beautiful, in all the top sets at school, and although she often partied with us, she never overdid it, never got into the same level of trouble as we did.

When I fell out with Sian, which was often, I'd slam her bedroom door and go across the hall to Kerenza's room, where she'd put on classical music and go down to the restaurant kitchen to make us a pot of tea. We'd sit on her bed and talk about nature and she'd show me photos of plants and trees she'd taken that morning on the small screen of her digital camera. Kerenza was an easy person to get along with: she was calm, ethereal and interesting, and because I was 50 per cent all that, our time together was almost perfect, like we'd washed into another world together, right up until the door swung open and Sian leant against the jamb grinning, a bottle of wine in her hand and Spear of Destiny blasting out behind her, drowning Mozart.

Every day I wished I was smart enough to cultivate my best side, but for a long time alcohol flattened and numbed all the things I was yet to understand. It was a lot of fun, but within the splash and spill of too much, unwittingly it tipped me head first into a dangerous place.

16

Grains of Sand

Barriers are everywhere when you are working class and live in the country. Barriers to expression and freedom and the all-important wider communal connections, but the biggest is education.

School across those five years was sometimes not having the correct book or PE kit and not being able to pop home for it. School was feeling ill and having to sit in the medical room for the rest of the day until home time, bus time. School was all the sports teams that I loved, but missing after-school matches because I couldn't get home. Being athletic, but having sporting ambition scuppered by the bus curfew. School was no gallery trips, no geography excursions, no days out. School was no chance of cultural enrichment for any of us rural working-class kids. Nothing much has changed.

The UK is one of the world's richest economies, but 4.3 million children and young people are growing up trapped in poverty. This means 30 per cent of children, or ten pupils in every classroom of thirty, are poor. Poverty creates barriers that prevent children from accessing education. It has a significant impact on the educational experience and attainment of many children growing up in the UK, and children accessing free school meals are 28 per cent less likely to leave school with five A*-C GCSE grades than their wealthier peers.

Less than half of students living in Cornwall go on to higher education courses, well below the national average. Going to college and then on to get a university degree is one of the surest routes to a good job, but it all depends on your socioeconomic position, and where you grow up has a significant impact on your chances of moving forward in education. That's before you consider the other factors holding back young adults, including sexuality and the sex you were born into.

Education in the sense of subjects and teachers and sitting in a low-roofed classroom was never my thing and, hand on heart, I learnt next to nothing from the act of entering an ugly grey building and pulling up a chair. The scuffed wooden tables and the tatty textbooks that were given out and looked at, copied down into graffitied exercise books that nobody would ever read again, certainly not the teacher, and definitely not us bottom-set kids. This lack of motivation was definitely exacerbated by the distance I lived from school, family and friends set apart like islands that contained different parts of me.

I got used to keeping my heart in one place, my head in another, but some days it felt like portions of me drifted so far out to sea I couldn't always find what I wanted. Like grains of sand, there were times when I felt the best parts of me had been sunk, forgotten about. My mum would wonder what was wrong with me when I messed about, careless. Friends thought I was sick during those moments of quiet, and there were definitely times when I wondered who I was, what had happened to my personality.

I realise now that this mixing up of character was a way to keep people at bay, like the wolf I always was as a kid, secretive, watchful, working out the best way to shape myself so I might shift seamlessly into any given situation, a way to save myself, a way of crawling into a soft, shielding pelt, protective.

All islands come from somewhere, broken bits of land snapped off, sunk, returned. The older I've got, the better I have become at pulling back all the rocks and fragments. I have planted trees, crops, made space for every kind of flora and fauna, but those early years of school I inadvertently made a mess of myself trying to fit in.

★★★

There was something about being in 'another place', a place away from Downderry and the same stream of blank faces that made me ready to learn something, anything, even if that something was the camaraderie of dissidence. My education, the things I learnt in my childhood, was soon ditched in my mid-teens for wild things gleaned from standing around or sitting on the swings in the town park. I learnt to write love songs and design tattoos with a biro while planning weekends away at Sian and Kerenza's restaurant out on the spit of land in the hamlet of Millpool.

Education was everything learnt at that age, and it was nothing like the clinical classrooms where you had to sit in boxes and lines. Education to me was fractal, far-reaching, and dirty as hell. I know I should have, would have learnt more if I had been noticed, but in a class of thirty kids, whether because I said too much or too little, I slipped beneath the scholastic radar and stayed there. The veil of fog meant that the busy teachers, this the first year of GCSEs, didn't care enough about the strange working-class girl to bother teaching me much of anything, only ever speaking to me to tell me to be quiet or speak up, depending on what lesson I was in.

Sometimes I wondered if they could even see me at all, or if they knew my name: nobody ever seemed to say it. I'd always sit as close to the window as possible so I could look out at the school playground if I was bored, and I'd watch whichever year group had PE that day, critiquing their netball skills, their tennis skills, I loved sport and I wanted to be out there, using up energy instead of . . . I'd look back into the classroom, at the teacher; wonder if this was French, maths, history, glancing at the posters on the wall for clues. Sometimes I tried to do the work, but I always got lost in detail, which meant I'd fall behind and I'd ask to go to the toilet, take my time coming back, or I'd stand outside the library and try to read the titles on the new fiction shelf.

These days, I realise I was probably suffering from attention-deficit disorder, but back then I was called a daydreaming kid or a dumb kid, or a cheeky kid, and absolutely definitely a kid from a rural council estate not worth bothering with.

It's no shock to discover children with ADD and ADHD struggle academically. Attention-deficit disorder and attention-deficit/hyperactivity disorder are associated with poor grades and poor information retention. They're also associated with increased rates of detention and expulsion, and ultimately with relatively low levels of qualifications and post-secondary education. These children show symptoms of inattention, hyperactivity and impulsivity with or without formal diagnoses. They also show poor academic and educational outcomes.

Trauma and traumatic stress, according to a growing body of research, are closely associated with both ADHD and ADD. Trauma and adversity can alter the brain's construction, especially in children – we are grains of sand, slipping – which partly explains their link to the development of ADHD. Growing up, especially in the eighties, where diagnosis was non-existent, this was not a good time for me to be neurodivergent.

I didn't just come from a socioeconomically deprived background, I came from the country and I wasn't alone in this detachment from education. Many of us poor rural kids disengaged from school early on and engaged instead with the local park in Torpoint, or 'The Lawns', as it was called, and through this freeing up of time and energy, we became a strong group of best friends throughout those five years of so-called education.

Disaffection goes deeper than un-bothering, not wanting to do a thing. It has its heart in opportunity, the offering of something other than nothing. In the wild, animals just are, and they do what is necessary in order to survive. The opportunity they look for comes in the guise of what can be found, scavenged from off the ground. Those who know me, those who know what I have gone through, can vouch for my survivor instinct, not a modern sense but buried in the marrow of all things wilderness: food-gathering, fire-lighting, sheltering, creating.

I wasn't bothered about lessons or qualifications, I had already decided that I was a writer and declared myself as one.

My mum didn't mind what I did or didn't do at school, as long as I seemed happy, but she liked the thought of me being an author. It was me, all me. School was a place meant for planning for tomorrow, not living for today. It was about preparing for a future that meant working for another's dream, but I wanted to spend every moment within that moment, the ever-present pad and pen stuffed into the back pocket of my jeans and the curiosity of all things 'other', the things that a childhood spent immersed in nature had gifted me.

School was the biggest gathering of different breeds of animal that anyone could imagine and it was complicated and maddening but truth was it brought me out of myself. I had friends and I was a friend to many, joined together in an intertwined circle of drinkers and fighters and fuck-ups. The best thing to happen to me was brilliant, perfect and sometimes tragic, but that was fine because at that point in my life, by meeting Sian, Kerenza, Jill, Sandra and a whole group of other kids like me, I had finally found my tribe.

My love for my friends and the desire to be loved and bothered about was huge. This desire has never left me and I know it is because of childhood abandonment. My father left me almost daily in my childhood and there were times, like many daily minute moments, when I felt like my mum left me on and off over time – not physically but emotionally, because she was so busy, and maybe it was partly my fault for pretending things were always fine, but the older I got, I was anything but.

Every time I wanted to talk about my internal turmoil during my last year of school, I would suddenly remember how Mum had cried on her bed in the flat, enough for me to swallow my complications back down into my belly, my heart bellowing with sadness, then stop. Suddenly I was back to being that tomboy kid, standing in front of my mother and my sister, and shouting at myself to shut my shit up in order to protect others.

Protection. Protection for everyone but me. This was how I was with my friends too, a solid mate, shoulder to cry on, boot to kick, ear for the billion hours that I spent just listening.

A year on from school I was still the one to hike the ten-mile coastal path to meet up with friends who lived in and around the Rame peninsula, Torpoint, Millbrook and Millpool. The writer's saddle-bag had been replaced with a rucksack stuffed with warm staying-out-all-night clothes, my denim jacket and flasks of mixed spirit, the contraband stolen the night before from whichever rich family I'd been babysitting still going strong. My beloved guitar housed in its incredibly heavy case in one hand, my other free for the thumbing for when I heard a car heading in the same direction.

Hitchhiking in the late eighties was a big thing in Cornwall when I was growing up, and it still is for the rural poor. If you want to get from somewhere to somewhere else, village to town, family to friend, home to job, there comes a time when you live in the country that you're just going to have to say, 'Fuck this,' and put your best thumb forward. It's not about taking chances, not about safety, it's about living.

When I reached the park at Millpool, Mount Edgcumbe as it was called, me and Sian would go out into the formal gardens, pool our stolen drink, and I'd get out my guitar and teach her the words to my latest poem that I'd decided could easily transfer to lyrics merely by repeating lines over and over. I wanted to be a country-music star, which meant Sian had to be my back-up singer and we spent many hours singing and drinking and laughing among box hedges and rhododendrons, then just laughing and drinking until drunk.

Transport only gets worse as you get older, and the fear of missing out is the single most terrifying thing when you are a teenager. This paranoia can lead to quick decisions, wrong decisions and decisions that are based on just wanting to see friends and then go the fuck home. The longer I was away from home, the more urgent it became to get back there. I'd been sending my poetry off to magazines I'd read about in *The Writers' and Artists' Yearbook*, the only gift I asked Mum for every Christmas, and I was eager to check the post. I loved to feel the weight of the A4 envelope, hoping it would be lighter than the one I sent out, a couple of poems missing, which meant they'd been chosen for publication.

I longed to get home to regroup my work, type out new poems on my red Olivetti typewriter and cut out the stamp on the return self-addressed envelope, the one I'd covered in Pritt Stick so that I could wash away the postmark and reuse it. Sometimes I felt like my life was spent in two simultaneous places: when I was back home in Downderry all I wanted to do was escape, get drunk, lose myself, but when I was away I wanted to get home, set my career as a writer back on track. It was no wonder I spent most of my time on the road.

As a young teen I was happy to take my chance at the bottom corner of the hairpin bend that spiralled up the cliff and away from Downderry and walk my hope up the hill. The possibility of a friendly villager lecturing me on the dangers of strangers was worth it. Sometimes they asked why I didn't order a taxi. 'Money,' was always the answer. There was one time when, aged sixteen, I got a taxi to drive me the eleven miles home from Millpool to Downderry. I'd been feeling ill, too much alcohol and not enough food, and I was nursing another broken heart because Kerenza had a new boyfriend, which meant we had to put a hold on our flirting – and I'd borrowed money from Sian's mum, from the restaurant till, to get me out of there, even if just for a minute. I remember that feeling you get when you're almost back on track: you have a plan to get your head straight and not mess up. I'd been sitting in the passenger seat for no more than five minutes when the driver turned the cab into a gravel-pit layby and pulled out a hip-flask.

'Want some?' he asked.

I looked across at the small metal container, wondered if he knew me. If he knew about my misdemeanours, my drinking. 'No,' I said. 'I want to get home.' I could feel my heartbeat start to increase, the headache from my hangover kick in with new vigour. I'd heard about these situations from other girls, alone with a strange man three times my age, a confined space, him with all the power, me with none. I knew you were supposed to be polite, try not to make them angry, but I was not that person, would never be.

I waited for my heart to slow, cleared my throat. 'You need to bring me the fuck home.' I pointed towards the road. 'Now.'

He put the flask away, did what he was told, in silence, not even breaking the speed limit.

Lesson learnt. No taxis.

***

186

My disengagement from school and education made me feel like I was flying out among a flock of the most brilliant birds. We were free to follow the clouds and the wind and everything that meant freedom, no matter that each day we somehow started to lose a little bit of ourselves along the way.

17

The Sea or Suicide

Growing up, career options for poor boys weren't too many steps up from the girls and pretty much consisted of fishing, farming or nothing. For us rural working-class everything comes down to what you can do with your hands. Pick up, put down, every day the same routine until the cold or the wet or the too much of everything seeps in. Some say working with your hands is the secret to happiness, but without the veil of middle-class idealism it's just hard work, not the art of carving beautiful wooden spoons or the hobby of embroidery, but hard, bloody, dirty, sometimes dangerous work.

The lads in our village, the ones who grew up around me, either fished or they didn't, they worked at sea with their young hands prematurely aging in water or they worked at getting the dole in order to get pissed, get high, get away from the monotony of beauty viewed from the bottom of a barrel.

There was a period in my life, before Mum met my stepdad, when, newly settled into our council house, Mum's generosity of spirit reached beyond the women of the estate and out towards a collection of young villagers known simply as 'the lads', young men mostly in their late teens and early twenties. Unique to their own brand of nature, it was as if my mum had run out into a forest and rattled a biscuit tin, shouted, 'All back to mine for free tea and chat.' Of course they came, and not just because it was a safe space where they could congregate, but because they could be looked after by my mum, who wanted to look after everyone.

At weekends the lads arrived in ones and twos. They'd sit in the front room, listen to prog-rock, laugh and smoke dope. Every weekend our front room became their little burrow of wilderness, the walls crawling with bug-talk, the conversations about the meaning of life and all the shite that lads with long greasy hair and drug-addled brains talk about, sitting on the floor in a cloud of forest smoke, laughing, then staring at the fire, asking again, 'What's it all for?'

If you don't have many prospects open to you, you could ask that question over and over, then think of something, maybe, some day, but if you smoke dope you ask the question, then shrug and pull the duvet back over your head. The lads who inhabited our council house at the weekends when we first moved there fell into the second category, and I'm not quite sure what Mum was thinking except that she was sharing our safe haven with others, the village waifs and strays she'd happily picked from out of the fabric of our rural wilderness.

One of them, a lad called Marley, I knew from when we played down at Seaton Camp, the place that was meant for the tourists. Marley was a punk. He had a huge bleached Mohican, ripped leather jeans, and most of his clothes were held together with safety pins. Marley wasn't his real name. Like pretty much everyone in our twin villages of Downderry and Seaton, he was known by his nickname, maybe his second name. Marley was closer in age to us than the rest of the lads, and all I remember of him was he originally came from Plymouth, and that one day he just washed up on our shores, like a rock star off the cover of *Smash Hits*. He was the lad that I'll always remember as the one who gave us younger children ten pence each to kick off our gambling habits in the holiday-camp arcades, although he was only fifteen.

'What's it worth?' he'd ask the crowd of us who had walked from our council estate in Downderry and along the beach all the way to Seaton.

'Double or nothing,' said Dan.

'That's good,' said Marley. 'That's clever.'

'That's gambling.' I stepped forward and put out my hand. 'If we win you get halves. That's the deal.'

Marley pretended to think for a minute. 'OK, deal.'

We all nodded.

'And if you win, I'll be outside the Smugglers Inn having a pint.'

We all agreed and waited for him to give us ten pence each, our hearts already on the sweets and ice-cream we would buy with our riches, even though our small minds knew they would be spent on the one-armed bandits within five minutes.

Small memory moments of generosity despite poverty, the gift first offered to him by my mum, returned via us for all the nights she had sat up and talked him down from an emotional cliff and out of the wilderness. In the end Marley lost the will to find his true path, and his love for getting high soon shifted from skunk and mushroom tea to heroin.

I wish Marley had found what he wanted to be, some path to draw out who he was. Each of those boys was a creative, talented, smart person waiting to unroll towards something. It wasn't that they didn't have talent, grace, style and power, they just didn't have chances.

One of the lads, Vole, was an incredible artist, and I remember him sitting quietly at our kitchen table, a small animal with black hair and haunting eyes, like the creature he was nicknamed after, drinking tea and drawing Mum a CND poster with crow's feet representing the emblem. It was beautiful, a gift from him to her, a gift of thanks for the time and space she gave him to figure out who he was and who he wanted to be. For many years it took pride of place on the kitchen wall.

Some of the other lads were musical, and for a while they had a band, the Prophets. Us kids used to watch them practise up at the air-raid shelter over on the easterly cliff edge, where there was still free power although the building had been condemned and was mouldy and damp as hell.

One of my fondest memories is of sitting outside the shelter on couches that somebody had found in a skip, listening to their loud guitars thrash out something close to music, the sun on my face and the smell of sausages frying, our own little free festival in the cliff-top clouds. For most of us this was about as close to Heaven as we could get, and for the lads that were in the band, as close to escape as they would ever know. Maybe for one or two of them this was their dream, but as anyone knows, growing up in the country, even with money, it can be hard to map out your ambition and point it towards reality. There are always barriers in your way: distance, travel, and for us in the south-west, the opportunity that a big vibrant city can provide. Factor poverty into the equation and you can see why giving up often seems like the easiest option. Poverty is hard, but rural poverty is the hardest thing of all.

If only the lads had anchored themselves to doing something with their hands longer than one or two summers, something other than drinking, smoking, injecting, even if it was just fishing. Life on the trawlers, the bigger boats that left the harbour in Looe and stayed out beyond the bay, was hard, and a beam trawler can be out on the ocean for a full week in weather up to force-eight gales. It is not an attractive job for lads who are creative, think too much, smoke too much dope, think they know everything until they realise, too late, that they don't.

The money you can earn as a fisherman is variable and the hours are long, but it has to be better than doing nothing. Fishing, the trade that was predestined for working-class lads, was meant to be if only they came out of their self-medicating forest, could see the wood despite the hindering trees.

As a kid all I ever wanted to do was go out to sea, sit at the rudder of my own boat and set my sights beyond the rocks, out towards where the gulls circled, best catch. I didn't understand, when the lads could have had anything they wished for, why they chose nothing. I was only eight, but even at that age I couldn't understand why they didn't make more of the band, why they just sat around and did nothing. Once I hit their age I knew everything there was to know about that dip in nature and the jungle of teenage emotion, how hard it was to keep your head up, keep your dream alive when every door seemed closed to you, and not just closed but chained and padlocked, buried underground. I could feel that suck of bog earth, could see the depth of void that hung around all of us like a muddy mine shaft, almost hidden and mostly forgotten until you fell headlong into it. Over the years I watched those boys slip away, one by one.

***

Many lads from Downderry and the surrounding villages have died either from suicide or accidental overdose. Some of them were those thoughtful, bewildered lads sitting in my mother's front room. The young men who thought they were nothing definitely nothing now. There is nothing to commemorate their insignificant lives except a couple of handmade memorials and benches overlooking the sea, something to remind us of the people they might have been.

They were lost souls drifting in and out of the leaden horizon like makeshift boats, bits of them nothing but found wood, hammered together, without a rudder to guide them or a sail to catch good in the wind, a push to help them get the fuck out of the fog.

Rural isolation and depression have a direct link with substance abuse, and the recent plague of county lines and the increased trend for gangs to target vulnerable young people in country towns and villages has driven drug-abuse in the country to an all-time high, with new drugs circulating in Cornwall and a sustained rise in drug-related deaths.

The county-lines phenomenon is nothing new and has long contributed to Britain's illegal drugs trade, a means by which dealers transport large quantities of crack cocaine and heroin into smaller communities from larger inner-city drug gangs, using dealers to exploit children and vulnerable adults into moving and storing the drugs and money, often using coercion, intimidation and violence. Drug trafficking, through county lines, is a category of crime that has seen the highest and quickest rise in Cornwall in recent years, with the number of reported drug-trafficking offences in Cornwall up 100 per cent in 2022 compared to 2019.

The movement of young people across county lines has been supported by an increased use and diversification of social-media platforms to groom vulnerable disadvantaged young people. There is a distinct lack of adequate youth provision in many county towns and rural areas, and little or no coordination between youth services across county borders. County lines activity and the associated violence, drug-dealing and exploitation have a devastating impact on young people, vulnerable adults and local communities. The Office for National Statistics calculated Cornwall's most recent drug-poisoning mortality rate as being 9.8 per 100,000 of the population. For a sense of scale, the south-west average mortality rate is 8.2, Devon's is 7.9; for London it is 5.4 and for England it is 7.6.

Socioeconomic disadvantage is a key risk factor not only for alcohol abuse and drug addiction but for suicidal behaviour, revealing suicide rates to be two to three times higher in the most deprived areas of the UK compared to the most affluent. A new Samaritans survey (2022) discovered that men in rural areas (43 per cent) are less likely than men in urban areas (51 per cent) to reach out for support or talk to someone if they are struggling with their mental health. Two-thirds of men living in rural areas (66 per cent) also said a variety of factors would stop them seeking support even if they were struggling. Samaritans discovered the top three barriers are stigma around mental-health issues (18 per cent), not knowing who to turn to (15 per cent) and lack of awareness of support available (15 per cent). Evidence suggests suicide rates are higher in rural than urban areas; rural-based occupations, such as those in agriculture, have also been shown to have an increased risk of suicide. Men in the lowest-skilled occupations had a 44 per cent higher risk of suicide than men as a whole, but the risk of suicide and undetermined injury is high in farming communities due to isolation and ease of access to guns and poisons.

When I reached the age the lads were, I realised how festering their depression must have been. I have never suffered from depression, but it must have been incredibly hard for those boys, being stuck in a rut as a teenager with seemingly no hope of change, coupled with misery and despair. It's no wonder that the negative consequences of rural poverty on quality of life lowers many people's self-esteem and diminishes their sense of control over their life to such a degree that all that is out there is misery, and all that exists inside is the drip and seep of constant melancholy.

The prevalence of depression is significantly higher among rural than urban populations and this is partly because of the low visibility of mental-health service in our country communities, which has led to a culture of self-reliance. We Cornish are a proud people. We like to think we are self-sufficient. We tuck ourselves in tight and we're tough as fuck, but that hard pride can lead to some folk not seeking support when they need it or only pursuing help when they have already reached breaking point.

Folk say men don't talk enough but those lads never stopped talking. They'd sit on the couch and on the floor in front of the

NATASHA CARTHEW

fire, and as soon as they'd decided what music from my mum's collection of vinyl to play (King Crimson, Led Zeppelin, Jethro Tull, Yes), they'd settle down to 'listen'. I always liked to listen too. From a young age I was a talented guitarist, and was eager to hear what they thought of different dynamics, the chord changes, riffs, whether they were playing rhythm or lead, but past the first bar, their discussion became incredibly boring. Perhaps it was that they talked about the wrong things, superficial stuff to keep from personal turmoil, but there was something else too, something closer to home.

Those with a recorded history of cannabis use in general-practice records are at a much higher risk of developing mental-health problems as well as severe mental illnesses. Using primary-care data drawn from the IQVIA Medical Research Database (IMRD-UK), researchers have found that, following the first recorded use of cannabis, patients were three times more likely to develop common mental-health problems such as depression and anxiety. In addition, they were almost seven times more likely to develop severe mental illnesses, such as psychosis or schizophrenia.

Regular cannabis use can increase the risk of anxiety or depression, and there's a link between using stronger cannabis and developing psychosis or schizophrenia. I know this to be true because of those young men men sunk in a sea of anxiety and depression because they spent their formative years high on skunk.

Downderry, Seaton, as I say, it's close to home.

Perhaps there's something in the sea air that makes us risk-takers, something blustering wild on the wind that draws us towards unfamiliar light, like the cliff-fires that used to lure

196

ships onto the rocks during buccaneer years. Perhaps there's something about the crash and burn that we love. Or maybe it's the wild hitting within that we are born with, a beast that manifests itself in the bay and floods into our veins so that from the very start we are battle-ready, the need to lash out firmly in the flesh before we have time to give listening and reasoning a chance. I know this to be true because I know the men who are full-time junkies and I know the ones who are dead: Willy, Big John, Dwayne Collins, Marley, many others.

18

Heart Hit Hard

By my mid-teens I became the wildest of animals, no longer a fox or a wolf or a hare, but all of them combined. A younger version of my dad, perhaps, but there were other factors too, and it had nothing to do with being poor or childhood trauma, but everything to do with my sexuality and the thing we now consider as gender.

As a primeval being I had found in my youth how easy it was to slip the skin I was born in and shape-shift into other pelts, a way to survive, perhaps, or a way to assimilate the drift of nature that I felt inside. I had no problem changing into whichever animal was expected of me, to be good, clever, creative, athletic, as long as I could wear jeans, T-shirt, battered boots. I found it easy to assess what was needed of me, a way to pacify and inject calm into a situation before any potential storm. An instinctual way of pretending to put down my guard when all it ever was, was up, a way to placate the difference that others saw when they looked at me, the look that said 'It's such a shame, you're such a pretty girl'.

I knew I was gay as far back as I can remember, and while everyone will tell you that you just know, way before you have a word for it, I was always aware that there was a word, but I just hadn't found it yet.

I have never wanted to be anything other than who I am in regard to sexuality or my particular brand of gender, but growing up in Cornwall in the eighties I could never understand why I had to wear a skirt to school, or why we were directed towards certain subjects. I'm still incredibly proud of my sister who fought to study metalwork and woodwork as her chosen subjects, the first girl at Torpoint School to do so, and for many years the last. Our mum brought us up never to take no for an answer, and if the answer was still no, to question why. I loved football but at school I wasn't allowed to play with the boys. I never got a straight answer as to why not.

I was a tomboy, which suited me and everybody else fine, except for the 'pretty' thing, which I still can't quite get my head around. Perhaps folk thought it was a waste: so pretty, could make someone a lovely wife some day, make pretty children. Throughout my teens I was asked why I didn't wear make-up, that it would make me even prettier - God fucking forbid!

I was gay, but growing up I didn't need to name it, and I have never felt fully one of either gender. I balance somewhere in-between and that to me is brilliant and beautiful and perfect. I've never felt I needed to name or label myself so others can find a box onto which to stick it. The thing is, no matter how happy you are in your own skin and head and heart, others are always going to push in with their opinions and prejudices and the question of 'What is normal?' when in truth nothing is. This then is why, as teenagers and young adults, we have our heads filled with questions that lead us to look for answers.

To say there was a lack of resources available to me as a young LGBTQ+ person would be an understatement. Adolescence is a tough time for most kids, but for gender and sexual-minority youths, it's even more challenging. For those living in rural areas without resources or support, life can be a very lonely place. Isolation, social acceptance and visibility, emotional support, safety, gender and sexual-minority-identity development aren't easily accessed in the country, and for those growing up in poverty, they are pretty non-existent. Emotional support and social groups are in large towns and cities, and the only way to get to those places is to travel, necessitating cost and time. What excuse is there when you need to travel to the nearest large town or city to talk about your sexuality, gender and identity? It's not as easy as jumping on a bus: you have to involve others by asking for a lift, or your train fare, or a lift to the train and back again, and this leads to making up stories, excuses. It's why lying becomes a way of life.

I was lucky because my mum knew I was gay from a young age, and my neutral gender was never up for questioning, but the lives of so many young people in rural Britain are monitored, presided over, the community and often the Church still held in high regard. You are watched because you are different, a bit camp, a bit butch. When you're the only gay in the village you stand out like a sore thumb.

I only ever wanted to be myself, but there were times during those school years when honesty made things worse, and I know this. I was a romantic, a poet, and the times I fell in love with the wrong kind of girl were epic. In the eighties there were no gay clubs or groups I could go to as a young person anywhere in Cornwall, and there's not much on offer for young folk now. Homosexuality in the county is still seen by many as a sin. By default we Cornish are Methodist, which means a certain style of hellfire and brimstone is applied to anything outside what is considered 'the norm'. During my lifetime Methodism has declined in Cornwall, but in recent years there has been substantial growth by its stern cousin the evangelical church sector, with many new churches planted around the county.

In the country religious faith is still very much connected to celebration and the farming calendar, a way for communities to come together; not just at Christmas and Easter, but harvest festival and May Day celebrations. By nature we are a suspicious race, and I think this is what sometimes lies at the root of why we are wary of what is considered 'other' or 'not the norm'.

I was confident, and what folk deemed 'like a boy', in the eyes of the older people in Downderry. I never wore anything other than jeans but they still wondered what I'd look like in a dress, in make-up, and they'd often ask Mum in front of me if I had a boyfriend. I didn't fit their narrow view of what a girl or young woman looked or acted like because they never got to see anyone other than what was defined as 'gender normal'. That 'normal' is what's in the Bible, and it's the 'normal' I had to listen to in morning assemblies every day in our Christian school. I was a child, taking in everything I was told, learning that being gay is incompatible with 'Christian teaching', a sin revealing the devil sunning himself somewhere within.

★★★

My fire-fuelled desire for other girls was made worse by their curiosity towards me, and I'll never understand why I couldn't just wait to stumble across another gay girl, but the wolf in me loved the chase of those secret, unobtainable 'straight' girls and I suppose they must have enjoyed the chase right up to the slow-dancing, long-looking, near kissing. Looking back those girls had been the best part of school, the best part of that last year, aged fifteen, when I didn't have any direction except drink for courage, fall in love, drink to forget.

Girls together have a synergy like no other, the combined effect of not just what is said but what goes unsaid. The finite detail of a glance or an accidental-on-purpose hand touch is one of the most incredible flashes of sensitivity and desire, an undercurrent of emotion, especially for teenagers.

Female desire is complex, and at the age of fifteen it was all about love. The girls on the periphery of my gang had boyfriends and Saturday nightclub sex, that weekend evening a time for drawing away from each other to the lure of boys. But those weekdays, all together, a couple of warm ciders in the park brought them around to wishing for other things.

Friday afternoon drinking started with hanging around outside Johnson's shop during lunch break. Most kids were there for sweets and crisps while we pooled what little cash we had and waited for the shop to empty of first-years. Then whoever looked old enough (me) or didn't look like they were wearing a school uniform (Sian) went in and bought a couple of cans and fags while 'others' nicked the wine. That Friday-afternoon routine ran like clockwork, and it wasn't long before we were in the park, first wrapped around the swings, laughing, then sitting on a patchwork spread of each other's coats, river watching.

'My boyfriend thinks I should lose weight,' said Nic, as she passed me the first bottle of wine.

'Why?' I asked. She was a swimmer who swam for the south-west and was proper fit.

'Fat ass.'

I looked at her and smiled. I wanted to tell her that I didn't think she had a fat ass, but there was no way to say it except sleazy.

'Why you with 'em?' asked Jill. 'Why bother?'

'Boyfriend just . . .'

Everybody sighed, except me.

'He just wants you for sex,' said Sian, 'and I bet he's shit in bed.'

'We've never had sex in a bed.' Nic shrugged, didn't argue the toss.

'Up against the harbour-lights wall then,' continued Sian.

'And she's gone on the pill.' Jill put her hand to her mouth. 'Is it a secret?'

'Not any more,' said Nic.

'What about STDs?' asked Kerenza.

'You should dump him,' I said, trying to put an end to the subject, 'find another one.'

'Like who?' asked Sian. 'They're all dicks.'

'Agreed,' said Kerenza. 'We should just concentrate on our GCSEs.'

I took a big swig of the nasty warm wine and passed it to Sian, wishing there was a way to change the subject away from boys, school, boys. These conversations made me uncomfortable, like I was going to be asked why I'd never had a boyfriend, that somehow I was about to be found out.

'Is anyone goin' back to school?' I asked.

'Nope,' said three of my companions.

'I've got double maths,' said Kerenza, and we all laughed because she was in all the top sets and crazy clever. I loved that about her.

'But you're drinking,' said Sian.

'One can,' she shrugged, 'and I've got Polos.'

Sian always thought Kerenza was a square, but I thought she was perfect, and when she caught me smiling at her she smiled back.

'Anyway,' said Nic, 'I've got to stop eating,' she held up the can, 'and drinking.'

I necked a can of cider and lay down. 'I think you're fine just the way you are.'

'Do you?' Nic lay down beside me and propped herself up so she could look at me. 'You're very kind.'

I smiled and looked at the clouds.

'Wish more boys were like you.'

Here we go, I thought to myself.

'So considerate, complimentary.' She turned to the others. 'Don't you wish more boys were like Tash?'

I smiled inside, looked towards Kerenza, and she looked away.

'Fuck no,' said Sian and I reached across and punched her in the arm.

'You're pretty with your hair back like that,' said Nic.

'She's lying down,' said Jill. 'Everyone looks better on their backs.'

'It's just the light,' I said, and I put my hands behind my head. Nic was a bit pissed, something I always knew from the way this kind of girl got close.

'Such a shame.' She put her head on my arm and snuggled in.

'Anyway,' said Kerenza, and by the time I looked over to her she had gone.

★★★

I am definitely not the only gay girl in the history of gay girls to have other girls tell them they wished they were a boy, or that they were pretty, or whatever, and every single time at that young age I'd pretend it was a compliment, then go home and cry. It makes you think you want to be a boy, when in truth you just want all the girls to be lesbians, problem solved.

When you are a teenager, especially when you have experienced the uncertainty of childhood trauma, there is a moment when nothing seems to matter but the drink. You do not know when this transition happens but one minute you're hanging onto the right side of it and the next you're freefalling from off the other.

My story is like many, and some of us get lucky and find ourselves in time or someone finds us before we spin into oblivion, but at fifteen I had a drink problem. Me and Sian drank most days, and when we couldn't get our hands on a bottle or a can all we could think about was how best to beg, borrow or steal. We drank at lunchtime down the park, then hung around school until the buses arrived for home time, or slipped into strange foggy lessons, unengaged. There was one occasion when we went back and sat, pissed, through an hour-long presentation in the school hall by the police about the dangers of alcohol. We were fearless, reckless, and that unruliness led to the only regret of my life. That weekend in spring we went on our usual pub-crawl around Millbrook, the large village that was nearest to

Millpool, where Sian and Kerenza lived, then continued to the only club in south-east Cornwall at that time, the Harbour Lights in Torpoint.

The Harbour Lights was a rough little nightclub that didn't preside over any pretty harbour but looked across the river Tamar at the warships and cranes of Devonport Dockyard. Established no doubt with the yardies in mind and the new recruits up at HMS *Raleigh*, it was always full of fresh-meat navy recruits: the women, also known as Wrens, who annoyingly kept themselves to themselves, and the men, locally known as matelots, who had more money than they knew what to do with, which was mostly buying everyone drinks.

The Lights, as we called it, was a place to dance and get pissed after the pubs shut. That was it. It had a sticky carpet from spilt dregs, the air was thick with the smoke of cheap navy fags, and a few flashing lights were enough to make you think you were having fun, until maybe you were. Then I'd go back to wherever I'd left my rucksack that night. Nothing much ever happened, nothing worth remembering until that night, when certain snapshot scenes and words and sentences wash towards me like river water, murky, tidal, finite.

Snakebite and black, tequila slammers, our drinking went around in a circle until I started to spin so bad that someone took me outside.

Fresh air. Walk it off.

I remember lying in dog-shit on the pathway at the side of the river Tamar. Naval helicopters circling above my head. I remember passing out.

The following Monday morning was one of the last times I was back at school. Double science and I couldn't have cared less. My one regret in life was that I went out that night. I was drinking too much, getting so pissed that I dropped my fists. As usual I had wanted to get drunk enough that I could tell Kerenza that I loved her. Looking back, I realise I should have taken that moment as a warning, found a way to get myself back on my feet, study, be good, but I was fifteen, and I realise now, I was just a kid.

Not long after the rape Kerenza told me that she thought she was falling in love with me.

I'd waited a long time to hear her declaration of 'almost' love, but by then I was angry, destructive, the best part of me completely demolished, shamed, the warrior side of me hitting out, my heart in flames.

19

Rock Punch

I hated everyone, everything, and I certainly had no ambition to complete my education and sit any exams. Aside from English and art, which were portfolio-based, I left school with no qualifications.

At the age of sixteen I hit a wall, both fists firmly out, figuratively and quite often literally too. Lack of opportunity had always been something I recognised, knew about, but still, once you notice the shadow of inequality you realise it is a figure that will tag and follow you for the rest of your life. When I finally looked around me to see what I had got, it wasn't a lot. Mostly what I had got was into trouble: at school I had cut the outline of myself from the fabric of bunking off, drinking when I should have been studying and doing damage by tangling myself up with the never-ending string of straight girls, falling in love.

Some might say this comes with the territory of youth, but without the structure of going somewhere, of going to school, without connecting study with a future other than that same beautiful, tragic peninsula, I was floating out into unknown territory without a lifejacket.

What followed was rage. Rage for the things I wanted to do and rage for the things I was doing. I knew the destructive forces that were all around me, which I had grown up with, were the reason for my self-destruction, but I hated myself and didn't know how to stop.

The first time I punched out at something solid was down on my home beach.

'You can all fuck-off!' I shouted.

I sat on my rocks at the far easterly ridge of Downderry beach where the cliff towered above my head and the rocks scooped up to greet it before crashing down into the sea.

I moved closer to the waves. 'All of you,' I screamed. 'Every single one of you.'

It was raining, my favourite weather for the mood I was in. I closed my eyes and faced Looe Island so I could feel the full force of the violent sou'-wester completely. My hands gripped against the barnacles, hating the tears that I knew were merging with the rain on my face. I hated everyone, my friends for being shit, my mum for not noticing my destruction, and most of all me for literally everything.

I punched out and I punched down into the rock, and when that wasn't good enough I turned to level the slate rock with my fists. I punched and punched until my knuckles splintered and bled with the tiny shards of slate and my shoulders ached with exhaustion. That moment of release, of letting go and giving myself over to pain in order to numb all others, was an incredible and powerful moment, a moment akin to losing myself and falling into the ocean, finding myself washed up in the white-horse draw, returned to childhood, clean slate.

On the outside it might have looked like the loss of all control, but within it was about trying to gain it, attempting to hold on to some loose chain of order, release and relief.

I watched the rain and the splashes from the waves dilute my blood and run it into my clothes, and I bent to a rock-pool to immerse my hands in the salty water, a stop-clock moment, suddenly calm, the best of my childhood returned.

Punching is a form of self-harm and as a teen I discovered that hitting out at walls and doors and rocks and whatever else was solid had a way of calming me. It centred me back towards Tash, that small girl walking alongside her sister, looking up at her mum, hand in hand in hand. Perhaps it was just shock, a slap to wake me up and stop me thinking about my traumatic childhood, my drinking, the homophobia that was all around me, the questions about my gender and sexuality from those who didn't know me, the rape. Maybe my silent ferocity was all I could use, all I knew to use to keep me being me.

The irony of this kind of fierceness is not lost on me, the worst factors of my violent dad having crawled into the knuckle-bones of my own fists, his moves my moves now.

How easy it is to make a bad situation worse when you feel totally, unreservedly alone. But self-harm was a way to cope when I didn't know how to cope. It was a shout, a scream, a way to let my boiling blood spill out.

It's amazing how in our youth we try to cover a fuck-up by making the hole bigger. You dig and dig and get so hooked on the pit that you forget to look up. Those hands again, no matter how damaged, working hard, but at what? The things we do because we are bored, the situations of risk and the destruction we do to ourselves in order to feel something. No other animal has that sense of emptiness, no other living thing looks into that dug void and thinks how best to sink lower, how best to spade down another few feet. Animals do things and they survive just doing. But, still, when you're bored and disaffected and confused you go along with the quick instant fixes to ensure you're still alive.

The summer after I left school the emptiness I felt inside stretched wide, a cavity that, no matter how hard I tried to fill it with drink and fights and unrequited love, the angrier I got. Every single night and every single week I tripped up and fell headlong into destruction, rage, stumbling towards the edge. My search to feel something, anything, meant I pushed myself further and further towards the precipice, and there were times when I came close to finding it.

One of my very worst moments was a near-death experience in the winter after I'd left school. Me, Sian, Kerenza and some other mates had spent several hours drinking in the four pubs in Millbrook, moving up and down the narrow lanes and ducking in and out of the low-ceilinged rooms until the barbell rang out in every one and we were kicked out. That was always the moment when we all just stood around in the street, listening out for the chip van with the ice-cream jingle, wondering if once again it had forgotten about us. That particular evening we noticed that somebody from somewhere had ordered a minibus that would take us all the way to the Harbour Lights in Torpoint.

I'd never liked the place, and by then I absolutely hated it, but for some reason I just couldn't get out of that destructive, deceptive snare.

It must have been winter, because the road was icy, slippery, especially on the main road around where the speed-limit was 60 m.p.h. I knew that stretch of road well because it was the route the school bus took, but I was about to know it a whole lot better when, during a singalong, somebody opened the sliding door of the minibus and I partly fell out. I distinctly remember how the road looked up close, how the ice-crystals fizzed silver from within the double yellow lines, how close my face was to that beautiful moment of impact.

It felt like summer, hot tarmac, luminous, carefree limbs dangling, flying, my compulsion to touch the edge of real danger, like a re-visitation of who I was, who I had become through disregard and damage, until somebody pulled me back in.

Carelessness, which I proudly wore like a flag of self-sabotage, the destructive colours that indicated to the world I had learnt the rules early on in infancy, childhood pain, not just the bust and blast of my adolescent disaffection.

Self-destruction by its very nature is down to one's own failing, but very often that failing leaves you vulnerable and open to destruction targeted towards you. It's hard to expect others to value your life when you barely value it yourself, and there were several times during the course of my teenage years when my risky didn't-give-a-shit behaviour pulled me way out of my depth, including a homophobic attack when I was sixteen.

I had been staying over with my friend Janey. She lived in Torpoint and she was a different kind of friend from Sian and the Millbrook crowd. She was respectable, had nice clothes, was a dancer and I was absolutely head over heels in love with her. Janey was what could only be described as middle class; she lived in a detached house that wasn't rented, had two parents, a car and a drive in which to put the car. Better than that, she wasn't self-destructive, barely drank, wasn't a scruffy hippie or a punk, like everyone else, and for some strange reason she liked me. We liked each other beyond 'just friends'.

At the time we didn't much notice our differences. Ours was a friendship of similarities, our love of music and creativity, dance and poetry. When I was with Janey I didn't care where the next drink was coming from. I just wanted to be with her, talking, laughing, and planning my future with somebody who had ambitions as big as mine. My other friends had zero motivation beyond getting wasted on the weekend, and Janey recognised the want in me for a better, brilliant life.

When she visited me in Downderry we'd walk together through the fields along the cliff path and lie among the wild flowers. I'd read her poetry by D. H. Lawrence and whatever I was working on, and once I wrote a poem for her that she put in a frame and kept by the side of her bed next to a photo of me. That might have been the moment when her suburban parents started to worry that we were getting too close, which we were. I'll never forget the time they came down to the village from Torpoint to pick her up, the horror on their faces when they waited outside our council house, the shame they felt because their precious daughter was friends with someone who wasn't just gay but council trash to boot.

The thing I liked about Janey was that she didn't care where I came from. Neither did I care that her parents were snobs: she wasn't. There was a period of time, after we'd all left school, when the two of us spent nearly all our time together, time that wasn't spent doing nothing. Instead of lying about the pub or beach, we'd go to the fair, or the theatre, mundane things like clothes shopping on a Saturday morning, spending the little bit of cash I had on things other than alcohol, walking and talking, laughing about everything. It felt like being human, alive and in the world with meaning.

Alone with Janey I was as soft as woven-wool, just cloud-watching as we lay side by side, talking about our dreams, how we were going to make it big, she as an actor who had just been accepted into LAMDA in London, me with my increasing list of literary credits and plan for a full poetry collection. That summer, the summer we both turned sixteen, was my first summer of love.

Shame, then, that I couldn't stay sheepskin soft. Shame I couldn't keep the coarse guard hair of my wolf side from itching, digging in.

One particular night, the night of the attack, we were on the dance floor, messing around with other girls we'd been to school with, when suddenly a woman twice my size and definitely twice my age, pushed up to me. 'You should leave,' she shouted in my ear.

'What the fuck?' My usual response to something I didn't want to do.

'I saw you last week, with that other girl.'

'What girl?' In my mind there were many, jumping in and out of my radar.

'That girl from Millpool.'

'Sian?' Everyone knew everyone else on our meandering peninsula.

'The other one, her sister. You were snoggin' her.'

I started to laugh, smile, remember, but when Janey came closer I pushed the woman away. I didn't want my newest friend to know about this part of my character, didn't want her to know how reckless I was, getting off with girls in the suburban military town of Torpoint.

Janey was having none of it. 'What's wrong?' she asked.

'Your friend here, this dyke, kissin' girls, it's not right.' She turned towards me. 'You're a freak.'

I was starting to get angry. This woman was spoiling my night, and it wasn't long before my fists started to grip tight and I shouted for her to FUCK OFF!

I don't remember much more of that night than that, perhaps I'd blacked out. But I do remember being badly beaten up, carried out of the club. That night I had been repeatedly kicked in my chest, something I couldn't quite get my head around until I woke up on Janey's couch and tried to move. I could barely breathe, and when I looked there wasn't a part of my chest that wasn't purple, blue, green, my favourite colours in nature, a part of me now.

Janey helped me then, as she did on many occasions after, and she'll always kind of be the one who got away, but then again, she just wasn't gay. Janey moved to London to train to be a dancer and I was heartbroken, then nonchalant: she was another person to leave me, which meant I had to force myself not to care about her in order to let her go. We kept in touch for a while after she left, but the hurt of first love and loss was too painful for me and eventually we drifted completely apart. We were so similar in character, optimistic and ambitious, but our lives were too different, she with the advantage of a stable childhood and money enough to chase after her dream and make it into a reality, me with the weight of childhood trauma dragging behind me and my dream hand-typed on tiny scraps of paper, imagining.

★★★

Growing up in rural isolation means you can't be picky when it comes to the people you know or the friends you make, and when you're a teenager in Cornwall it's like standing on top of the highest Bodmin Moor tor and shouting, 'Anybody?' just to see who shows up. If you're lucky, a smiling face might appear out of the dense fog, and they might be a similar breed of animal to you, like Janey.

Punching walls, heavy drinking, getting into fights, doing hot-knives when the drink ran out, all because I was angry, angry because of the bind of country ways that tied me to a rural norm. In the country you are not gay, you are not trans, you are not non-binary, and you learn to live in the spaces that are made for others, places that are meant for everyone but you. Eventually it's inevitable that you'll fall so far through the cracks that you no longer know which way is up. You are lost in the perpetual dark and buried in the pitch, and to anyone who has ever hit the rock at the bottom of giving a shit, it's incredibly hard to find a way to get back out of it.

At the bottom of the ocean there is nowhere to hide. You see the world moving above you, towering in the soak, you see some things you still love, the bodies of basking sharks and the hulls of fishing boats, and you wish you were 'up there', normal, but you're not. You see the mottled skin of arms and legs passing, the limbs of those more capable than you, and you wonder what it must be like to swim unaided, how it must feel to dive deep into things safe in the knowledge that you will find your way back to the surface. This is the kind of mind-set that is built within the confines of middle-class confidence: it is buoyant, not like those of us who are born into or have lived through trauma, who have become derailed and detached. Those swimming arms and legs above our heads belong to confident, buoyant people and, if you look closely enough, you can see them holding hands, connecting, attaching themselves in ways that never fail to move forward, always forward.

20

Undercurrents

I spent most of my time balancing on the back foot.

If the long messy days were meant for melancholy and seclusion, the neat night was meant for unified adventure. I was spending more and more time away from Downderry. Mum was busy with my brother, now four years old, my sister had moved in with her boyfriend in Seaton, and with Janey gone to London and no school in Torpoint to keep me near to any kind of track, I spent most of my time in Millbrook, near to Millpool where Sian and Kerenza lived. Millbrook was a large village, small enough to know everyone, but big enough to get lost in.

We roamed the lakeside village on the furthest edge of the Rame peninsula like a pack of hungry wolves, small groups of scallies looking for something, anything other than the empty void of nothing. A few of us were still at school, but most of us had dropped out at sixteen, some of us had not much in the way of family, and a few of us lived in the shacks up on the windswept cliffs, but something we all had in common was we had little to no money.

Some of us moved between the groups, looking for a place to fit among the childish doctrines of who spoke to whom, and who you were allowed to like; we were already stepping into the shadows of our parents, using gossip as a way to navigate around all the rules and subtexts of adulthood.

There was a pub for every group and ours was the Mark of Friendship, a pub I always knew the name of because Mum had sometimes gone there when we were young to play darts. I don't remember what it looked like because our den was in the back, a pool table, a few stools and a banging jukebox. That was it. Nobody bothered us back there and we got our drinks through a tiny hatch in the wall, no questions asked, which was lucky, because we were all under age.

The Mark was where we hung out every Friday and Saturday night until closing time, whether we could afford a drink or not. Sometimes me and Sian got lucky and someone who'd just been paid took pity on us, but it didn't much matter anyway, because we always rocked up to the pub already drunk, thanks to my babysitting spirits stash and the bottle of white wine we'd steal from her parents' restaurant before we came out.

After closing time, if none of the older crowd had cash to hire a minibus to Torpoint, we stood outside in the narrow street until somebody suggested somewhere better than darkness. That was when our packs would merge and we'd slope off into the four corners of the sprawling village until we found ourselves in the bedroom of some kid whose parents weren't home, sitting on the floor with a sawn-off plastic bottle in our hands, sucking on sweet acrid smoke, every single one of us with one thing in common: the inability to move forward with our lives.

I never enjoyed being high and the few times I bothered I wished I hadn't. I loved the speed of alcohol, not the heavy-head drool that skunk resin heated between two knives made you feel, nothing. I hated the way it had you believe you were partially passed-out, and how it made lads think they could get close, try to kiss you in the name of free love. That was usually the point when me and Sian would stumble back into the street and look for a passing car that might be heading to Millpool, or maybe someone from another gang we could ask if we could stay over, just until we were a bit more sober. But we were always the last to leave a party, always the last to look at each other and ask, 'What now?' We were useless, the worst kind of friends. There was one time that I hated 'us' so much that I punched Sian full-on in the jaw. Another time she stabbed me in the hand with a pen. One New Year's Eve when we were looking for a party we tumbled twenty metres down a cliff. Then there was the time when she was attacked by a swan: it freaked us out so much, because we were both drunk and high, that we ran around knocking on the doors of people she thought she knew (turned out she didn't), which led to trying to open car doors. When that didn't work we walked to the village car park and went to the public toilet, and because we were so drunk and tired, we decided to stay there, on the cold, sticky, pissy floor for what was left of the night.

At weekends we lived like we were homeless, the self-inflicted taste of vagrancy in our mouths and on our lips and skin. Some of us talked about moving to the city, the way country kids do in a knee-jerk moment of how to escape, and there was a time when me and Kerenza talked about moving to France together, away from the needy hands of those who pulled us down.

We sat under one of our favourite trees, the largest oak in the Mount Edgcumbe Country Park in Millpool, she with her camera, lying on her back taking photos of the canopy above our heads, me with my tiny notebook, trying to finish a poem I'd been working on. This was a rare moment when it was just the two of us alone, and we must have realised how simple and how right it felt.

'Summer's coming.'

I looked down at Kerenza and shrugged. 'And?'

'It's going to be the same all over again.'

I nodded, looked out towards the river. 'True.'

'Everyone drinking and fighting.'

'That's me.'

'Waking up every morning with regrets.'

'That's both of us.'

Kerenza sat up and turned the camera onto me. I was used to this.

'You never smile for me,' she said.

'Don't have much to smile about.'

'You heard from Janey?'

I shook my head. 'We're not in touch.'

She put down the camera and joined me in watching a lone gull land on the water in front of us. 'Maybe it's for the best.'

'Maybe.' I looked across at her and waited for her to say whatever was on her mind.

'Don't you ever want to get away?'

'Where to? Truro?'

'Don't be daft, far away, like France.'

I scratched my bare feet into the grass. 'I dunno.' I looked out at the estuary, where the river hit the sea, thought about France the way we kids thought about it growing up, dirty, wasteful, nasty France. 'Maybe,' I said.

Kerenza turned onto her side. 'We could get the Plymouth to Roscoff ferry – it only costs a few quid for pedestrians – then head south.'

'What's south?' I asked.

'Grape-picking.'

I liked the sound of that, and I lay down to think about what a summer in France would look like. Grapes were definitely a step up from potatoes.

'Who would go? A whole gang of us?' I asked.

'No. This is what I mean, just us, you and me.'

I looked at her and felt my heart rise up and beat crazy in my mouth, the words I'd been wanting to hear for so long: 'just us'. I couldn't speak.

'Say something,' she said. 'What do you think?'

I shook my head, said, yes, no, I'd think about it.

In the days that followed I thought about it a lot, and I was right to, because my heart had been broken before. I was wary of it being broken again, and I was right to think it, because a week later Kerenza had started to feel guilty about leaving Sian, her sister and my best friend. She was a lovely, compassionate person, and she didn't want to come between me and Sian, even though there was already a river widening and bursting banks between us.

***

Net out-migration of young people from small towns and villages is increasing not only in Cornwall but throughout rural

Britain. Some leave for noticeable things, like work and education, but many leave to assess a world beyond what they have known since birth. The monotony of infantile safety, especially when you are poor, is incredibly boring when you reach your teens.

Technically my friendship group were becoming adults, but because we lived and turned at such speed in the dead centre of our tiny spiralling world, we never actually moved at all. We didn't have jobs any more complex than skivvies, which meant we couldn't afford driving lessons, transport, rent. The constant state of bull's-eye precision living meant that other people's lives, those who were older, richer, city-dwellers, went on spinning and moving without us.

In the late eighties and early nineties many of our friends sofa-surfed, moving from one front room to the next because they had no permanent place of residence; in summer they sometimes slept in borrowed tents down on the beach at Whitsand Bay, but back then nobody really considered it homelessness. It wasn't living, it was barely existing, and many had no other choice but to go with the flow of constant stopping.

One summer we made friends with a lad called Joe who lived with his dad up in one of the chalets on Freathy Cliffs. He had been home-educated and was a quiet lad, but like all us country strays, he was accepted into our circle of 'kids who sit around and drink too much'. Joe didn't like girls, which was great because I didn't like boys, and we became friends because, despite being complete opposites, we had one thing in common, and that was we were both gay.

Joe liked colour and texture, while I liked black and denim; he liked listening to Stock, Aitken and Waterman, while I liked stomping country music; and he, like me, mostly enjoyed life when left to his own devices.

I'm not sure if Joe realised he was different from most of the other lads, but there were times when we'd sit on a bench in Millbrook and watch the sun rise, or out on the cliffs to watch the sun set, and he'd tell me how his dad was a bully, that he felt trapped, that he wanted more than just working in his dad's cliff-top bucket-and-spade shop. He also said how his dad asked questions about 'us lot'. Joe, I know, wanted to tell his dad that he was gay, and there was one time when I finally gave him my penny's-worth advice to just go ahead and do it. My mum had been okay and I naively thought this was the era of everyone being okay.

'Just tell him,' I said. 'He'll appreciate the honesty.'

'I dunno, my old man's strict.' Joe took the can of lager I'd been holding out to him.

'You're never gonna know his reaction if you don't say.'

Joe shrugged, thought things over.

'What's he like with the TV?' I asked.

'What you mean?'

'Gay blokes. What's he think of Boy George?'

'Hates 'em.'

I scratched my head. Maybe he wasn't a good example. 'That bloke in *EastEnders*.'

'Which one?'

'The gay one, fucksake.'

'Don't watch *EastEnders*.'

'What does he watch?'

'He don't.'

I sighed and took back the can. 'You just got to do it.'

'How?'

'Say, "Dad, I'm gay."'

'That how you did it?'

'Not quite.'

'Go on, then, how?'

I thought for a minute. How had I come out to my mum? 'I was pissed and told her I was in love with another girl.'

'Who?'

'Does it matter?' (Kerenza.)

'What did she say?'

'Told me to wash my hair.'

'What?'

'Told me I'd never get a girlfriend until I washed it more often.'

'That's random.'

'Tell me about it.'

'Just like that? Normal conversation, like?'

I nodded.

Perhaps Joe's dad thought I was a bad influence, I was butch after all, but not long after Joe came into our lives, he was run clean from it. The last sighting of him was getting on a coach that was heading up to London at the high end of Millbrook, alone, nothing but a suitcase and a black eye for his troubles, and no goodbye.

★★★

We know that the combination of an increasing shortage of rental properties and escalating levels of rent are leaving more and more people in Cornwall with nowhere to live. Add to that the impact of the rising cost of living and the additional pressures on accommodation in key tourist areas, such as Newquay, and we in Cornwall are facing a perfect storm.

Cornwall has as many families waiting for social housing as there are holiday homes in the county. The Countryside Charity has highlighted Airbnbs and other holiday sites, showing that in spring Cornwall has 661 per cent more short-term listings than there were five years ago. As well as this, the Campaign to Protect Rural England (CPRE) said there are roughly fifteen thousand families on social-housing waiting lists as of September 2021, with around the same number of holiday lets available. CPRE said this is a sign that families are losing out on a stable home because so many houses are now used for tourists.

All undercurrents, the ones that float just beneath the surface of what it means to live, survive, ride out the life you were born with, they never really leave us. Sometimes we manage, sometimes we fail, sometimes we harm ourselves or others, become addicts, find ourselves homeless, and sometimes these things are our fault, and sometimes, because of circumstance, trauma, abuse, they are not.

Often poverty is not a tsunami but an incoming tide of tiny waves. They hit and they hit until finally you are overwhelmed with water, and with little option you struggle to keep afloat, your head above water, trying to think of all the ways to make some cash so you might survive the next breaker crash, hoping that at one point you might witness the dark in its final dawn retreat, light breaking through and the glimmer of something close to hope.

AIR

21

Wave after Wave

The career options for girls went like this: cleaner, fish-factory worker, young mother. As much as I would have loved to be a fisherman or a farmer, the late eighties were not ready for me. To the entire world I was just a girl, no matter how hard-working, how tough, how much I loved the sea and the earth or wanted to learn about nature as work, and study all the ways to make a living. I loved picking potatoes in the autumn, a future shared with kin on common ground, but it was nothing on a CV, couple of seasons was all, and besides, just a girl.

At least cleaning was physical. It kept me away from maudlin or thinking beyond my station. It kept me locked in, unthinking, and it kept me from my true calling, writing.

Every morning I'd jump on my bike and cycle through the village to whichever house I was meant to clean that day. Throughout my teens and into my twenties my life was spent mopping floors, vacuuming, cleaning toilets and polishing crap knick-knacks that didn't belong to me, radio on, my boots toe-tapping to the local country radio station while I thought up poetry.

The summer I left school I spent doing one of two things: partying with Sian, who had a part-time job serving in the café in

Mount Edgcumbe, or working: either babysitting, scrubbing rich folks' houses or my weekend job cleaning the coastguard cottage.

Cleaning rich people's houses was strange: it was personal, intimate, like I was dropped into a place that I wasn't meant to be. I rarely got to meet the inhabitants, but I'd have my key, 'especially made', and a list of things to do left on the dining-room table or on the counter in the huge modern kitchen. Every house was detached, like its owners, and each had picture windows that faced out to sea, like our flat when I was growing up. Some were three storeys, and some had mezzanines, and there was one particular house that had a fire in the middle of it; the kitchen and the living room and just about every room circled around it. In our council house we had two open fires in two different rooms, small ones, but here the rooms were spacious, white and light, and each of the many bedrooms had its own balcony and bathroom.

Some baths in those houses you had to climb into to clean, others had saunas before they were popular with the partying poor, but each had something in common: an easy acceptance that it was fine to have a sixteen-year-old come into your home and scrub.

Sometimes the job lasted a while; others broke off the arrangement by writing at the end of the to-do list, 'Your ironing is not up to standard', 'The glasses aren't sparkling' (hire someone with more experience, pay them more), 'Here's your £10 and two pound extra, as a thank you.' Thanks, no thanks. Back then we didn't have a minimum wage and on the posh estates nobody had really thought about what history had meant by child labour. I was cheap, cash in hand. That was the start, the middle and the end of it.

The best jobs, as any Cornish cleaner will tell you, including my mum, who for several summers cleaned at John Fowler's holiday park in Downderry, are the chalets, caravans and holiday homes, and my favourite by far was definitely the coastguard cottage. It paid the most for minimal effort, and for those three hours on a Saturday morning I was completely and utterly alone.

The coastguard cottage was every bit how it sounded: a 300-year-old whitewashed cottage on the edge of the cliff that looked down on the slipway and the main Downderry beach. It had a pretty path and a garden that every year gave a little of itself to the ocean. The only people stupid enough to sit beneath the cliffs on that particular part of the beach were the tourists, who never seemed to notice the uprooted dog-daisies and fallen lilies that now grew erratically in the earthy sand.

The floor of the cottage was an easy wash of thick grey Cornish slate and, apart from the ever-present shifting sand, it was the easiest place on earth to clean. If I was lucky and the most recent family of emmets hadn't had kids to make a mess, I'd get the place scrubbed ship-shape by ten o'clock, put the kettle on, couple of leftover biscuits in my hand, and by five past I'd be sitting at the window with a mug of coffee and my notebook.

Writing came above all else. It was my top-shelf aspiration. From the wide snug window seat in the cottage kitchen I could watch the village at a distance, sipping my coffee and wondering, pretending that this was my life.

Within the extremity of poverty you always feel slightly removed from society. It's not that you don't quite fit in: it's that you definitely don't. I've always wondered if it's us or them who first created the divide: those of us for whom growing up in poverty was a lived experience, or them, those who lived in comfort, without concern or burden, happy for the split to exist. Did we pin the underbelly badge to ourselves or was it pinned on for us? Either way it hurts, gets stuck in the flesh, the bone and the marrow. For me, sitting in that seat drinking somebody else's coffee made me feel I could be somebody, the life where I got to relax, eat biscuits, write.

Writing was my best habit, an old habit better than all the others, from the moment I walked the cliff path and started to fill the pages of my notepad with sentences that became poems, poetry that I posted far and wide across the country. I knew that was my vocation, and when I close my eyes I can still see that version of me perfectly. The pen in my hand was always the driver, the charge that was forever moving in on its own game, my eyes on the prize, the future.

I knew, even as a small child back at the flat in Brenton Terrace when not even the simplest thought made sense, that the future had nothing to do with poverty or the haves and have-nots: it was to do with the possibility of maybe. Think it, want it, live it.

Blue windows, the courtyard cottage got its fair bucket-chuck of storms and there were many mornings when I sat and stared out at the sea that filled the pane with its blue brilliance. These were thinking moments, the moments that always brought me right back. Sometimes I stared at the milk-wet flagstones and thought about the one o'clock arrival, and the mud they would lift from the earthy path that led to the front door, but always and every spare minute I wrote.

When unaffecting thoughts knuckle down and slip into memory, they soon bounce back as better, solid ideas, the same original thought but in colour. Sitting every Saturday morning at that kitchen window writing poetry, lyrics, until one particular morning when I found myself staring down a storm and suddenly turned myself over to a new idea: a story that started with a girl sitting and looking out the window of a caravan somewhere remote, Bodmin Moor. I added snow, hunger, trauma, writing the idea in my notebook, one long lazy paragraph. Little did I know that I was writing the blueprint plan that would later become my first work of fiction, *Winter Damage*.

Writing for me is work. I love it more than anything but it is work the same way my mother worked or her mother worked, and all the working-class women who over forever years have worked and pared their hands down to their arthritic bones.

Poverty disproportionately affects women, and options for girls living in the country are even slimmer. They are still the ones working part-time or zero hours for a minimum wage, cleaning holiday chalets, serving in the village pub and mopping up shit in care homes. Compared to their male equivalents, young women often have family commitments thrust upon them: they cook and clean for younger siblings, care for elderly and disabled parents, and are more likely to be single parents. More than a fifth of UK women, 22 per cent, have a persistently low income, compared to approximately 14 per cent of men. Living in persistent poverty denies women the opportunity to build up savings and assets to fall back on in times of hardship.

There is a strong link between female poverty and child poverty. In its report *Gender and Poverty* the Fawcett Society states that women's poverty is closely linked to their family status and caring roles, with women who head their own households – especially lone mothers – at a greater risk of experiencing poverty. One final statistic: 64 per cent of the lowest-paid workers in this country are women, contributing not only to women's poverty but to the poverty of their children, and so the continued vicious circle of disadvantage continues.

My mother was an incredibly hard worker, as were all the women in our community who, simply put, worked to live. The things they worked for run off society's tongue like a shit poem – food to eat, shoes for feet, fuel for heat – but nobody really thinks about what poverty looks like from the inside, how every ticking minute is consumed by how you can get across the village on your second-hand bike when one job ends at 11 a.m. and the next starts at 11 a.m., and the shop has put up the price of bread and called it artisan because it's August and that's just what they do. These are small things, perhaps, but huge when you think about young hungry mouths, bare blistered feet, and winter always lurking around the bloody corner.

Mum wanted more than anything to be an artist, a designer, but when she became pregnant with my sister at nineteen, she had nothing to fall back on, no second plan, and eventually she gave up her dream to work, just that. Minimum wage, no pension, no prospects, your life over before it's begun – rural poverty, rural work, and when you're a woman, you kick it all off from the lowest rung.

Throughout my four-year destructive phase, there was one thing I managed to hold on to and that was my writing. No matter how far I tripped and fell, I somehow managed to find the end of that tangled semantic rope, the lifeline I knew would help me climb my way out. During my wilderness years I never stopped writing. The overwhelming self-hatred and anger I had internalised for so long I moulded into words of hope, my heartland discovery that in turn became beautiful poetry.

Angry words became calm, healing words, and the act of writing every scrap of hurt into my notebook eventually saved me from myself.

22

Spirit of Discovery

Writing was the only place where I felt truly safe, writing and walking and stopping off at all the beautiful catch-breath moments that were nature. For some reason that last summer of destruction, when I was seventeen, I started to question the decisions I was making. I hated it, hated the situation I was in and how I continued to throw myself head first into it despite everything.

Throughout that last wasteland night, the night we spent sleeping on the floor of a public toilet, I kept waking and wanting to cry. I stared at the tiny glass window with the wires crossing through it and imagined I was in prison, the orange streetlight outside the only flicker of colour and the occasional moth that passed there the only living thing worth bothering with life.

The moment I woke up to see the first rise of daylight I knew that this was it, my epiphany moment. For so long I had wanted it. For so many months and days and hours I had prayed for the instant that I would shrug off the mess of self-destruction. I'd always fixated on the things I didn't really want, or need, but in that moment of standing and walking towards the open door, I finally realised that I should have thought more about what I truly wanted, and I wanted out. Out of Millbrook and out of corrosive friendships and out of the vicious mess of continual circles, the roundabout peninsula that I couldn't get off.

I knew in that moment that I had to save myself. I had to physically push myself to get back to the place where it all started to go wrong, so I walked home.

The first step was out of Millbrook. That large hoary village and the spider's web that included the hamlet of Millpool, where my friends lived, and the twin villages of Kingsand and Cawsand would have been the death of me, literally. Those four villages made up an in-and-around loop about the Rame Head peninsula that made it almost impossible to leave. Folk who live there and those who grew up there know exactly what I mean when I say there is a spin that exists within, like ley lines gone crazy. It is a place that you can't untangle yourself from, can't get out of, and at the age of seventeen it was exactly the spin I was in.

As a child in the bow of Pat's boat, I always wanted to head east of Downderry, the beautiful intricate Rame peninsula, and here I was, stuck with what I wished for, east of the bay, yet now all I wanted to do was go home, return west, push the last few years away and start again.

And so I did.

One foot in front of the other even though I hadn't eaten anything in twenty hours, hadn't drunk anything except the usual snakebite and tequila. I walked out of the public toilet and out of the council car park without even saying goodbye to Sian, who sat on the wall that backed onto a road, smoking and waiting for the first tourist heading towards

Mount Edgcumbe to bring her the three miles home to Millpool.

Despite the almighty hangover I was nursing, my body aching from a vagrant, hedonistic night, I walked out of that village along its stifling narrow lanes and didn't stop until I reached the very top of the hill.

The view that bursts across the top fields and filters down into the fissures and fields of Whitsand Bay is incredible. In fact, it is more than incredible. It is my everything: my life-blood, my bones, my muscles and gristle. It is the essence of everything that is me. I know this now, but back then it took a million drinks and fights and several near-death experiences to realise that this was what it felt like to be truly alive.

No longer did I want to look back, not at my childhood or my school years, wasted and gone, or what I had missed out on. I was all for the future, the step in front that meant the difference between dreaming and succeeding, drowning and swimming. From that lowest moment all I wanted to do was push on, push up, push into the fabric of the world, which I had always been told was not for people like me. I wanted to mould it into a tent, a canopy, a big-trussed marquee where I could be free. Like the freshly pressed sheet folded over Mum's ironing-board, I wanted to make a space for me and my dreams, a cave of my choosing where I could be happy.

Never before had I walked with so much purpose, determin-ation and drive. For the first time in what seemed like for ever I was that young kid setting off on a new adventure, but this time I was heading towards the past in order to reset the future. This time I had no saddle-bag or rucksack, I had no hiking boots or billy-can of water, but I still had one thing, the thing that has never left me: the small notebook and pen stuffed snug into my jeans' back pocket, the two things that had never given up on me.

Poetry, my one true friend, the friend who put its hand in mine and said, 'Write me', the thing that waved its pages across the bay and told me to write this, here, today, and so I did.

I wrote what I was feeling onto the tiny lines as I walked, and I stamped my anger into the pages until it softened, lightened, became tiny momentary memories running like footprints across the sand.

When I got tired I stopped and climbed onto a gate or a dried-out water-trough to watch, just that, the sun lifting up beyond the headland and the sea turning red, then gold, then back to blue, my heart in my mouth, full of love.

Most times you aren't aware that you have found yourself until afterwards, but that particular 5 a.m. summer start I knew well: it was what always got me out of bed each morning, what I thought about every night when I went to bed; that moment of new beginnings, purification, the possibilities that were out there, those distant topmost silver waves, like future-fortune finds, promises, waiting for me as they drifted out towards the horizon.

Without one cloud-shadow of a doubt, I knew that by walking away from my destructive teen life, I had found the best part of myself where I had left her, on the cliffs with a notebook in hand, writing everything down. The sun was in me that day. Finally it knew me, and its early-morning warmth was enough to wave me on, this way.

Ten miles of fields and lanes and dirt tracks, despite exhaustion and extreme dehydration I kept my eye on that ocean, and every step and every mile I told myself to remember the jumping-off place that leapt into every wrong decision and every goddamn mistake. I knew it was time to stop blaming others, to stop blaming everything on being poor, because right then and there, walking along the coastal path with no money and barely any qualifications, I knew I would never get out of wrong situations and decisions until I accepted that sometimes things were just not fair. Some of us are born with silver spoons in our mouths, some of us are born with plastic spoons, and some of us are born with crappy plastic coffee stirrers that are no use to anyone. I realised I was that anyone.

At seventeen I knew that the time had come to stop looking at what I didn't have and start looking towards what I did. Nature. Poetry. Words and cheap A6 notepads.

I knew I would keep on walking, and writing, and recording all the beautiful things around me that I could understand, and all the things that were in me, the things about my childhood, my trauma, and the disadvantage of poverty that I was determined to learn to comprehend so that I could hold myself beyond mere recognition and self-regard, and raise myself further than I'd ever thought possible.

Something condensed within me and narrowed down to self-belief. Despite starting to feel increasingly unwell, I was determined to believe that I could make something of my life, so I walked and walked and walked. The further I hiked towards home the more I felt the dehydration of too much alcohol, and absolutely zero water, lower my blood pressure. I knew I was fading fast, but still all I could think about was my home, my bay, my bed, my mum, and I continued to walk towards them. For several hours I kept on walking, slowly trekking up and down the undulating hills, the heat of the relentless summer sun pounding down on my hatless head, digging into my shoulders and my neck. I was exhausted, thirsty, my legs becoming uncontrollable and I started to imagine that I wasn't walking at all, but drifting out there above the surf, floating across the blue, blue water.

When I reached the top road that slowly descended towards my village I started to stumble, my boots no longer able to lift off the tarmac, and I fell. At this point my memory loses its fluidity and becomes sketchy. I remember experiencing an over-whelming thirst and finding an old almost-empty Fanta can in the undergrowth beside me. I know I wasn't thinking straight because I can still taste the warm, flat, sugary syrup, and I remember feeling ill and being sick, then lying in the muddy dust of the passing-place in which I'd fallen, a moment's rest by the side of the road where I suppose I must have closed my eyes.

How many minutes or hours I lay passed out at the side of the busy coastal road unseen by passing traffic I will never know, but it was as if by trying to save the best part of me I'd unwittingly almost killed myself instead.

My epiphany moment was a reflection of everything I was, near to death, closer to life.

★★★

The distant sound of unfamiliar voices catching on the wind brought me round. I'm incredibly grateful to the two Dutch cyclists who prodded and poked me until I was fully awake, grateful for the drink of water they gave me from one of their water bottles and grateful for their company until the next car appeared on the horizon and they flagged it down.

I'm also grateful to the tourists who allowed me to be stuffed into the back of the car. How strange I must have seemed to them – this sick, dirty native – and how strange I felt to be suddenly inside the confines of normality, sitting behind people with ordinary lives. I was grateful that they didn't speak, didn't ask me to explain something that would have taken for ever to expound, how my dad was a bastard, that he abandoned us, that from that moment on my life just slipped away from me and went from bad to worse.

They dropped me outside the primary school at the bottom of Trelidden Lane and I thanked them, because they had returned me home, finally, safely, to Downderry.

When I got home I found that nobody was in, and although I'd hoped it would be that way, I wished my mum was there to see me as I really was, a mess. I poured myself a glass of water, then another, and went upstairs to stand in the bath and pour jugs of water over me the way I'd learnt to do by way of survival: cold water inside and out, soothing, cleansing, healing. Then I went into my room and climbed into bed.

Small chances, and this was the smallest, but if it wasn't for those cyclists, it might well have been my last, all because of dehydration, physical exhaustion and finally heatstroke, all because I didn't think enough of myself to care for myself.

I never told my mum about what had happened. I never told my sister – she was long gone out of my life and we barely talked – and I never went to see the doctor. I just told myself that enough was enough, that I had choices, and I was determined to find the right route to finding those choices so that I could pick one, make a decision that would smash open the planet, make a path and lead me through.

★★★

Chances are few for teenagers and young adults growing up in the isolation of merely getting by. Choices can be slim, if they exist at all. There is no clear answer when it comes to ways to slip the hindering skin of poverty and lack of opportunity, but if you're lucky you sometimes find resilience and tenacity where you least expect it: within.

I have always been dogged in my search for the better. No matter the situation I always strive for the positive: my mum's resilience handed down, worn proudly as my own.

My thirst for discovery had me dismantle myself into tiny pieces so I could see what went with what, the things I needed to survive and what was dead weight, the things I could do without. I built my bones back better, stitched my skin on tight and put my head on straight, bled the best bits of myself back in so I could walk strong, stand up straight and have a good go at life.

Sometimes it's not just a case of better this, that, the other. It's about teaching young people the skills to survive, how to kick the doors and keep on kicking until one opens, to concentrate on those small shafts of light, not the ones that are dim or locked. It's about not giving up. You can't teach resilience, but you can talk it through until you reach an understanding of what it might look like, given the chance. What does it take to make a difference to your life? What are the tools you need to build yourself a couple of steps so you can look up, see over the hedge, the treeline, the fields and the river, look forward across far-reaching towns, cities, continents? Jobs and universities: think about the possibility of maybe. Time moves at a different speed when you run the route towards recovery, that moment when the absence of ticking numbers shifts slowly over to another vision of life beyond what is known. That swing towards salvaging some semblance of self is so incredibly powerful when you realise not only the dimness of what you have lost, but those brief sparks that remind you of what you have got.

23

Lighthouse

I spent the rest of the day in bed, recovering physically, all the while trying to pull my old skin self back on. I knew I had a seed of a plan, and I knew the place to plant it. I knew the location of my first happy memory: down on the beach, home turf.

At some point in the afternoon Mum appeared in the door and I must have lied and told her I had a cold coming, or flu, and I remember her bringing me tomato soup and homemade bread, but still I kept the secret of my collapse to myself. I continued to sleep until darkness filled my bedroom window and I imagined it fallen fully into my home bay, filling the rock-pools and caves with silver-searching fog, and like an animal of the night I knew I had to go to it, and I quietly got dressed, swung my saddle-bag over my shoulder, made a flask of coffee and went to it.

The ocean has always had a way of pulling me, turning me towards reset. Its meandering grey shape is a slate wiped clean; it is the home of my travelling, trembling hand, telling me to be silent, to write my mind back to the right kind of wild. The ocean spoke to me that night, its deep pushing and pulling of breath no longer threatening but calling. If I could return to some aspect of innocence I might have a shot at clearing my mind until I found the opening to my own peace. Like a cave it must have existed inside, somewhere I could curl into, feel nature's damp wet room engulf me like a womb. I knew I had to go back to the beginning in order to find myself, the start of things going wrong, my childhood.

As children we find it easiest to blame ourselves for the things that didn't go right, the things that didn't make sense. For some reason we think the grown-ups know how things should go, expect them to show us the best route to happiness because they want it too. As adults we know this isn't true. None of us have answers. We don't know what we do or don't do, or what we want or don't want until we stumble upon it or lose it. The summer of my seventeenth birthday I wasn't sure what I wanted, not quite, but I did know what I didn't want, and that was the last four years. I wanted more than the runaround, more than the hedonistic lifestyle. I was intelligent. I was talented. My poetry was finally being published in reputable magazines across the country. I knew I was so much more than I had become, the drunk, the idiot, all things to all people, my friends, my mum, my family, but not myself. I realised suddenly that my search wasn't about finding my true self – I knew me well enough – but it was about showing it, being brave enough to show me, so finally I could work on my freedom, my reality.

Down on my beach, the sand and cliffs and rocks were set in shadow. An opaque fog had lifted off the Channel and had settled into our bay, the everyday things I knew so well shifted out of place and the tiny slice of distant moonlight making the night dance. There was something else too: the beam from the Eddystone Lighthouse.

The Eddystone I have known since birth. A constant reminder of my place on the earth, it sticks out like a giant push-pin in a map that I have yet to fully navigate, but even at the age of six, looking out the flat window at the black-blue night, I knew it was my companion, and the one thing I could rely on.

Lighthouses are where history and legends meet. By their nature, they attract tales of shipwrecks, adventure, ghost ships. They stand for safety, but remind us of all that is wild, and they are untameable, dangerous, and attractive.

The Eddystone of my childhood was the fourth consecutive lighthouse to mark the same small, dangerous Eddystone Rocks, just thirteen miles south-west of Rame Head. It was built to save lives after so many ships, travelling one of the most important naval routes in Europe, hit those rocks and sank without trace. I often think of how many folk lost their lives out in our bay, how many souls were out there, searching for dry land, me included.

During the unfolding of that night the lighthouse out at sea opened up its many gilded arms and shone its beams towards me. It showed me the bay and every beautiful and stupid thing I had done: the walks stuffed with wild words and the silences I spent sitting, listening, being. It showed me the bad stuff too, the pathways that led nowhere but I took anyway, because earlier in my life, at the age of fourteen or fifteen, I didn't ask for guidance from my mum or stepdad. My baby-busy mum was always proud to tell me she trusted me, that I was her good girl, but I was just a kid, and the bad stuff happened because of it.

Trust has no place on the shoulders of children, not really. It's an excuse not to take care of those under age, a weight that me and my sister still find hard to shake. We are strong, but not because of the things that have gone right in our lives: we are strong because of the things that have gone wrong.

That night, the lighthouse bright and me full of sound sleep and sustenance, I stood out on my usual rocks, the rocks where I used to play for hours as a small girl, the rocks where I first learnt the power and the pity of self-harm, and I looked. I looked at the sea splashing white sparks on the ebb-flow turning tide and I looked at the thick fog, and inland towards the cliffs and it was then that I had to make a decision. I had to do something, different.

Because I'd been sending out my work and getting it published in poetry magazines since I was fifteen, those tiny rippling caustics of success made me think about what success might look like, what the future might be like if I set my sights on being a writer, not just writing. I wondered about all the words that were out there, the words that didn't just walk alongside me but the ones that ran and jumped and kicked up a fuss, the words I hadn't met yet, but that wanted me to comb the beach and collect them all up.

If I knew them all, if I understood their meanings, I'd be able to write better poetry, plays, songs, essays, stories. As I stood on the beach and stared into the flashing abyss, I realised that every creation I was ever likely to construct, all figure and form, was waiting inside of me. Every sentence was ready to be written, ready to be read, I just needed to gather up all the words, pick them like spuds from out of the ground and carry them home.

Beneath the mantle of night-time fog, the moon occasionally joining the lighthouse with its brilliance, I collected up a little driftwood and set about making a fire. I always carried a lighter and tinder in one of my stepdad's Royal Navy baccy tins, and it wasn't long before I had a small comfort fire to look at, think, drink coffee beside long into the night. Hours passed, or maybe they were just irregular minutes, ticking down the moments of youth until I could see me as an adult.

I had no friends, none that were any good. I knew without doubt that I had put an end to their destructive roundabout routines by filing them away in my head. I had no father, he was long gone, and my sister was in love and had moved permanently to Seaton. While my mum loved me, she had my brother to care for. Despite all this, that moment on the beach and for the first time in my life, I didn't feel alone. I had my writing, my first love, and I had a plan to get away. I had something else too: the lighthouse. As I walked home I felt the warm glow on my back, threads of gold passing either side of me and lighting my path forward.

***

The next day I returned to the beach and I wrote a play. I still don't know where it came from and I wasn't sure if it was a play at all but I edited it and typed it out the way *The Writers' and Artists' Yearbook* said you were supposed to and I sent it out to local theatre groups, and that in turn led to conversations with a director from the Orchard Theatre Company about the potential of 'my work'.

My work.

It was just a short, single-act play, mostly monologue, fourth-wall stuff, but I'd enjoyed writing it. That first foray into writing dialogue set me up for later in life, when I started to write fiction, and while the director didn't commission it, he told me I had talent, and at the age of seventeen that was enough for me to think about, hold onto tight.

While my hands were used to digging for potatoes, used to fishing and scrubbing floors, I realised this could be my work now. Suddenly I'd discovered a way of communicating that was way more fun than self-obsessive poetry, inadvertently I'd tripped upon the art of dialogue, a practice learnt from all the women on our council estate and it fell into my playwriting like rain upon the ocean.

Conversations came into my head and I dreamt of all the characters who had said them and the babysitting and house-cleaning money I no longer spent on drink but my once-a-week bus fare into Plymouth where I spent it in Ottakar's, the city's bookshop, on plays by authors whose names I could barely pronounce. I was a city fox now, sniffing out books like they were prey, vital for my survival.

It was there in that bookshop that I picked up a leaflet on college courses at Plymouth, and where my heart stopped dead: theatre studies. I stuffed the flyer into my pocket and sat in the bus station, the flyer and all its words burning a hole in my pocket, waiting until I was on the bus. The moment we set off towards Cornwall, I unfolded the piece of paper, read it over, and wondered about the thing called further education. It was beyond, out there, distant.

Throughout the ride home I wondered what the course might look like, how much it might cost, wondered if some-one like me was allowed to be a part of that world – if I was allowed to write, read, study what I wanted, what I realised I needed in order to survive.

An hour later as the bus rolled down the hill to Downderry, the hill where only six weeks earlier I was found unconscious by the side of the road, I pushed up to the window and looked down towards the passing-place in the hedge where I'd been discovered, saw the ghost of me lying in the dust-mud: insignificant, useless, stupid. How far I had come, how much further I was yet to go, but with that tiny bit of paper in my pocket, at least I finally had a plan.

★★★

I jumped off the bus and ran home, hoping Mum was there, that she would have time to ring the number. When I saw her I excitedly gave her the flyer.

'Of course I'll ring.' She smiled. 'You're my little writer.'

Mum immediately rang the college and asked to be put through to the drama department while I waited, my heart in my mouth. I wanted to do something more than imagine it and Mum must have seen this, because she wouldn't take no for an answer. It was October, and the course had started, it had been going a month and it was oversubscribed.

Mum and the course director got talking and it turned out he'd recently moved into the village. It also turned out that he liked her spirit, her tenacity, and somehow I got to audition for the course. I had two GCSEs, English and art. In theory it was no way near enough to get in, but the following week I took the bus into Plymouth, went to the college and sat in front of a theatre of strangers.

What the fuck.

Deep breath.

I felt the air in the room settle against the thick black rubber floor, the blackout curtains behind me pulling in close, too tight. Suddenly it felt like night-time. If ever there was a moment to feel the silent slash of imposter syndrome, this was it.

I cleared my throat.

Somebody clicked on a spotlight.

I suppose I said my name, the title of the piece I was about to read out, from memory, my words, my poetry and thoughts. I think the ten-minute monologue I had been working on had something to do with God - definitely it contained teenage angst - but I can't remember much more than that.

My head floated up and out into unrealistic clouds, my blood pumping, bells and whistles in my heart, too loud. People like me didn't do things like this. I was poor country working-class. I was meant for the farms and the fields, the mop-buckets and the wipe-around cloths. I thought about my mum, how she wished this for me, her words ringing in my ears, 'Be a writer, Tash.' I thought about the young girl out on the cliff-path, a notebook in the back pocket of her jeans and a stupid dream to be someone some day: Daphne du Maurier, eat this.

Deep breath.

Try not to pass out.

When I finished the group of students and the lecturer stood up and clapped, and from that moment on I knew I had finally stumbled onto the right track. Finally the imaginary world that I had seen in a beautiful piece of sea-glass had suddenly become a reality, no longer in my hand but in front of me. I had found my audience.

***

Education can end the vicious circle of poverty once and for all. Like a tree, poverty has many roots, but among the many causes, one factor stands out and that's education. Not every person without an education is living in extreme poverty, but most of those living in extreme poverty lack even a basic education. Without a doubt it is the great equaliser, and not just because it can lead to good jobs and better wages but, like in my case, it opens doors to other people, life skills, resources and opportunities to move forwards.

Many kids, me included, do not feel like they belong in school. Belonging is a powerful motivator of human behaviour. It's the difference between feeling accepted and appreciated, or feeling like an outcast. Children who feel included in their school communities are more likely to attend class, do their work and build lasting friendships with other students. It's well established that belonging is important, but sometimes the magnitude of this importance is overlooked.

Imposter syndrome, often described as a pseudo-medical name for a class problem, plays a great stomping part in the lives of us working class. Growing up, we are taught by society that our place is at the bottom. It is one of the greatest factors that determines not just what you can and can't do with your life, but what you think you can do. It is a tiny bitch voice that whispers the opposite of sweet nothings, like sour grapes, bitten, then spat; for some of us down here it is megaphone, loud, echoed, your own words shouting that you are too dumb to study, too thick to take on a good job, too uncultured, too low to the dirty-dregs ground. At a young age I found a way to ignore the voice, and when I got older I told it to piss off, leave me the fuck alone. That voice is the difference between engaging and deep shock, belief and stepping forward, or fear and stepping down, stepping back.

Engagement is a serious business: it involves commitment, intensity and optimism that there will be a favourable result at the end of it. While I didn't engage with secondary school in any clear sense, my curiosity for books and learning eventually pulled me through.

This was by no means luck, because luck doesn't belong to people like us. Luck is the phenomenon and belief that defies the experience of the working class. I was destined to be a writer, it was all I ever wanted to do, all I could do, and when I saw the connection between writing and learning, I suddenly felt the wraparound warmth of belonging, all stars and satellites and planets aligned, my destiny finally found.

24

Sunrise

Each day the sun pulled me outside and onto my new path, like a supervisory beam that promised to reveal all the things I was yet to learn about myself, my past, my future. In coming weeks and months I knew without a doubt that it would show me a clear route forward when all I'd ever known until then was mute light, long shadows, abrupt shade.

The beautiful sunrise that threaded golds and ambers between the blues of the horizon and washed into the ocean each morning no longer found me stuck in the sand. No longer did it find me yearning for a future I couldn't imagine. It found instead a young person moving forward, no longer drifting, motoring towards my original calling.

I was about to go to college, about to study books other than the ones I could scavenge from jumble sales and the mobile library, and what was more, I was going to do it in Plymouth, a city just around the corner from Whitsand Bay, but a city none the less. Engaging in education for the first time was my rising sun, meant for me and me alone.

People talk about first-generation education, those from a working-class family who are the first to go to university, but this wasn't even that: I was the first in my family to do A levels, only two because of my minimal GCSEs, but it was something. I was the first to do a lot of things as it turned out.

Growing up I was always the outsider, the renegade, and in truth I'm proud of that. I never wanted to opt for second best. A highly competitive child, I won everything, mostly sports, the thing that my immediate and extended family laughed at. No matter how good I was at something, how I wanted them to praise me, I was mostly laughed at, and that made me all the more determined to succeed, it didn't matter at what. Going to college was all about knowing more, properly, reading books I didn't want to read and having to, because I recognised that the push to success was learning what you didn't know, not rolling around in what you did.

Most of my family are afraid of formal education. For some reason it offends them. It's seen as something to fight, rebel against, even. They are all highly intelligent, but there's something that twists and twitches within them, which means they don't like being told something they didn't know by a stranger. This is not unusual for working-class families: it's a defence mechanism to warn against danger, false information, 'the other'. Education is akin to witchcraft, especially here in Cornwall where we Celts are naturally suspicious.

Trust goes a long way but it has to be learnt, like anything, and I have always been open to everything that trusting someone or something brings. My heart is an open book and I will always be proud of that, despite everything it is full of words and stories and ideas that I have gathered up and I have always been ready to put it into other people's hands, the palms of strangers, the undercurrent of my childhood washing up, the fields and the sea, and I say here, read.

Like many people who grew up in poverty, knowledge was the key to opening doors that I'd always assumed would need a boot to break down, the key I needed to discover a world full of rooms that were occupied by people like me, people who were creative, curious, different.

The day I started college, six weeks behind everyone else, was the day my life changed for good. That first moment I stood outside the nineteenth-century Arts Municipal building in Devonport, looking up at the clock tower, I felt my own inventive clock start to rewind and start again. No longer was I one of none but one of many. As I walked towards the front steps I was joined by others, strangers, but with the commonality of going somewhere, doing something. The entire time a voice in my head was telling me I was a fraud, I didn't belong there. My instinct was to run, head down to the river and get the ferry over to Millpool, find Sian, find drink, find the easy-fitting fleece I was used to wearing. The drive to escape the spiral of poverty and my desire for a better life kept me walking, moving forward until I found the door with 'THEATRE STUDIES' written on it and a sea of smiling faces, my heart in my mouth, then slowly, eventually shared out.

Those initial days and weeks and that first year were hard. I'd cadge lifts with people Mum had got talking to in her new job, serving in the fancy village tea room that used to be Tom's Store, and sometimes when those lifts fell through I'd stand at the bottom of our lane and stick out my thumb, no longer a rucksack full of drink on my back, but books, pens and a shiny new notepad. Never more had I wanted to be somewhere, no longer for the short-fix escape but the long-haul pull of serendipity, my rightful place in the here, there, now. The beach and the bay with all its madness and clutter and violence firmly behind me, a city full of pace and plays and people lit up like a beacon in front of me, lightning bright.

Hope is the difference between doing something and giving up. It is the balance between success and failure. Without hope we fall backwards, downwards, for me it is that small girl looking through blue windows at the storm outside while another climbs the stairs, one crashes out to sea and another lays the raging foundation inside of me.

Hope is not something given or taken away: it is what I have stored in my head and my heart, not what I lack. It is the optimism and courage to plan for a better life, every day and always.

The day I crossed the river Tamar to start college was the start of the best bits of the rest of my life. Every day I spent reading scripts, discussing dialogue, acts, structure, things I didn't even know I knew, and every day I got in early by cadging lifts and hitchhiking. I was the only one on our course to come from Cornwall, the only one with the worry of getting to college on time, the only one who couldn't join the local youth theatre because the Downderry bus left the city depot at 5 p.m.

At the age of nineteen I met my first proper girlfriend and we moved into a basement flat together in Plymouth. I was out of my beloved council house that no longer felt like home and out of Downderry, the village where I'd always found myself mostly alone.

When most folk dream of Cornwall they dream of dwelling, but for those of us brought up in poverty, all most of us can think about, dream about, is leaving. Sometimes you have to escape, leave the only place you know to dig and divide up, make sense of it, decide if you want to go back.

This is probably the hardest decision any of us living in the country has to make: chase down your dream or watch it go down the toilet as you scrub about with a posh person's scented bog-brush. The secret is, you've got to leave with some purpose in mind. It's no good moving out and away only to settle for less than best. I had a plan to succeed, and I mostly kept to that plan.

Once I had left home I knew there would be no turning back. My brother, now aged seven, moved into me and my sister's bedroom, and me and everything I owned – clothes, books and nature finds, which included chunks of driftwood, rocks, pebbles, feathers and shells – moved out.

I knew, too, that I would never move back to Downderry, would never, no matter how hard I studied or wrote or hoped (I didn't), be able to afford a house in those twin villages of Downderry and Seaton that my forefathers had built from the shoreside up.

At nineteen, I was more than happy to leave.

That second year of college I worked early mornings and late evenings as an office cleaner around the city for a less than minimum wage so that I could afford the rent, and no matter how I missed the country, I loved every aspect of this new adventure. I still dipped in and out of a hedonistic lifestyle and had started to shoplift food daily to survive, but I kept my studying on track, and my work started to appear regularly in poetry magazines. A play I wrote called *AMEN* was performed at the Plymouth Barbican Theatre.

I felt like I was Laurie Lee all over again, setting off on this new path, my destination a beautiful dive no longer into unknown oceans, but rising up into the air, the element of movement. I was determined to keep alive my dream of being a writer, my mum's hard-work ethic, which she taught me as a child, burning flame-deep inside. Occasionally I returned home to Downderry on the weekend with my new girlfriend, and we'd walk the coast path together, me telling her about how things used to be, how they could be now, telling her how bad things were when she already knew. The new perspective of home, the ocean and the cracked paths and roads I walked alone, was no longer so daunting, my home village merely a painting I had stepped out from. I knew then, a year on from when I first moved away from home, and at the age of twenty, that I would never climb back fully into it. It was beautiful, incredible, but better hung on a wall and looked at from across the river.

The bigger debate here is that of transition and opportunity for young people. Sometimes we have to make a leap of faith and jump physically into the unknown to make sense of ourselves and the world around us. This run and jump towards what might well be an object of oblivion is what many rural poor people have to do to survive. It is a way of saving ourselves from what we know, and for me that was what I was doing when I jumped at the chance to live with others, my first proper girlfriend, and embrace a life of experience, adventure and books.

Not once did I look back, not for one minute did I pine for that lonely village of Downderry. I had a new ocean, Plymouth Sound, the next bay along from Whitsand, but a world away from my lonely childhood, and I still had my lighthouse to look out for me, just in case.

★★★

I am Cornish proud, but for every strand of the childhood and teen trauma I endured, that single village will never be a friend to me. When I think about it I feel overwhelming pain. When I visit it I feel a deep desire to escape all over again. Suddenly I am thrown back into the sinking sand. I am the lonely girl playing out in the rock-pools, the have-not girl with nothing to her but flight and fight, trips and falls. I am the crying kid, staring into the abyss of a complicated childhood, grey future, blue windows, violent dad.

That college course was my one solitary light. I was a writer, and I was determined to make good on that promise to myself. No matter what, I would write and study and learn all the brilliant words, the words that would help lift me above the undercurrent and set a course out towards my own lighthouse and a future beyond the waves.

Epilogue: Flow

All wild water and rivers at some point return to the sea. No matter where we go or where we think we're going, it's inevitable that we end up where we're meant to be. As part of my watercourse I, too, was meant to return to the ocean.

I returned to Cornwall in my mid-twenties, an age when many decide to leave home, but I was done with hunting. I had finally dug up a little something inside myself, had fallen in love while living in London with the woman I've been lucky enough to call my partner for twenty-six years, had my first collection of poetry published there, and I brought these two best parts of my life home with me to Cornwall. Another village, but the county and place I came from.

Something inside me knew my return would dredge up the best and the worst of times, the moments when, as a kid and teenager, I spent either at war, or mixed in the muddle of reconciliation, the peace-pieces that my young life occasionally offered up, like thrown meat. I knew this was going to be trench stuff. Cornwall was my home. It was the blood and bone of me but, still, it was also my one solitary enemy. I had to dig into it to pull stuff up, cut it up so that I might understand it better, in bite-size chunks: my father's violence, my deep-rooted loneliness and my struggle to define my gender and sexuality when I had no watermark, no peers to define myself by.

Love and poetry and new opportunity brought me back, but there was something else too, something that only those born beside the coast can truly understand: it is the pull of the ocean. As a Cancerian I am by default the deep sea at its most calm and chaotic, and I am the tidal moon reflection that swells and rolls upon the ocean. I go seabed deep and I know this. I knew it on that first day of my return, but still I came.

In the end it comes back to the pull of the tide and the way wet grit and earth smell at the tail-end of a surging storm, the crash of waves in the bay as you sleep and the soft intake of breath as it retreats. It is my favourite and least favourite sound; it is comforting, confusing, but, still, it is the sound of here, the sound of home. The overwhelming ocean will always be in constant motion, no matter who or where I am. It exists in each and every one of us Cornish: whether we live here or are in exile, our identity is a living, breathing thing. That is why it's hard for so many of us to reconcile that sometimes we have to leave because we can no longer afford the high rents or a ridiculous mortgage for a modest cottage in our childhood village.

We Cornish are an ethnic minority, yet the poorest of us are being washed from our native land, pushed out of our villages and towns by the out-of-county wealthy. The heart of our communities is being ripped out and the soul of what that word means is starting to be replaced with ghosts, the memory of a place and a heritage that soon will be simply known as 'once was'.

Sometimes there are no solutions except empathetic thinking. The rural poor might be without much but if we continue to be neglected, pushed out and off our land, then soon it will be too late. The past will exist as a distant memory, a mess of mistakes that will never catch up to a just future, a fairer, even-handed society.

The village of my childhood is a keeper of secrets. If you take a minute to stop, turn an ear to the tide or the earth, close your eyes, and listen.

Notes

p. 11   'The dictionary definition . . .' According to the Oxford English Dictionary.

p. 13   'Before the pandemic . . .' Joseph Rowntree Foundation, 'UK Poverty 2020/21', 13 January 2021, https://www.jrf.org.uk/report/uk-poverty-2020-21.

p. 53   'The National Rural Crime Network states . . .' National Rural Crime Network, 'Captive & Controlled: Domestic Abuse in Rural Areas', 2019, https://www.northyorkshire-pfcc.gov.uk/content/uploads/2019/07/Domestic-Abuse-in-Rural-Areas-National-Rural-Crime-Network.pdf.

p. 61   'According to the Trussell Trust . . .' The Trussell Trust, 'Mid-Year Stats', 2021, https://www.trusselltrust.org/news-and-blog/latest-stats/mid-year-stats/.

p. 99   'The UK House Price Index shows that Cornwall's . . .' UK House Price Index, July 2022, https://www.ons.gov.uk/economy/inflationandpriceindices/bulletins/housepriceindex/july2022.

p. 138   'In 2022 the Bank of England warned . . .' Richard Partington, 'UK households face biggest fall in living standards since 1950s, say experts', *Guardian*, 26 February 2022.

p. 139 'The *British Medical Journal* reports...' Margaret Whitehead, David Taylor-Robinson and Ben Barr, 'Fuel poverty is intimately linked to poor health', *BMJ* 2022 (376), 10 March 2022; Ofgem Annual Report and Accounts, 2021–22, https://www.ofgem.gov.uk/sites/default/files/2022-07/OFG2169%20Ofgem%20ARA%202022_Web.pdf.

p. 160 'Research by the Royal College of Nursing...' National Youth Agency, 'Overlooked: Young people and rural youth services' (report), August 2021, https://static.nya.org.uk/static/d15ff8e9b33bd4cff-7b138043e50a358/Overlooked-Report-NYA-Final.pdf.

p. 194 'A new Samaritans survey...' Samaritans, 'Men in rural communities least likely to seek support when struggling to cope', 1 March 2022, https://www.samaritans.org/news/men-in-rural-communities-least-likely-to-seek-support-when-struggling-to-cope/.

p. 196 'Using primary-care data...' University of Birmingham, 'Cannabis users at "much higher" risk of developing poor mental health', 1 October 2021, https://www.birmingham.ac.uk/news/2021/cannabis-users-at-much-higher-risk-of-developing-poor-mental-health.

p. 226 'The Countryside Charity has highlighted...' The Countryside Charity, 'CPRE research: Explosion in holiday lets is strangling rural communities', 13 January 2022, https://www.cpre.org.uk/about-us/cpre-media/cpre-research-explosion-in-holiday-lets-is-strangling-rural-communities/.

p. 226 'As well as this, the Campaign to Protect . . .' The

Countryside Charity, 'New research: a huge rise in holiday lets is strangling rural communities', 13 January 2022, https://www.cpre.org.uk/news/new-research-a-huge-rise-in-holiday-lets-is-strangling-rural-communities/.

p. 233   'In its report *Gender and Poverty* . . .' National Education Union, 'Women are more likely to experience persistent poverty', 17 January 2019, https://neu.org.uk/advice/women-and-poverty.